"I don't give a fig where you think I should go!" she exclaimed.

"Don't you see the danger? Don't you know what the mere sight of you does to a man?"

She opened her mouth to ask what he meant, but it was too late. His left arm went around her to hold her captive while his right hand cupped the back of her head, preventing her from turning away.

His mouth came down on hers with desperation she could feel in every line of his body. His lips were challenging, not punishing. They were firm, warm and tinged with sweet wine. She had never felt anything as exciting as this before and she was dizzy with the heady sensation.

Surer now, more confident, he softened his assault to coax an answering moan from her. She scarcely recognized her own voice in that sigh. Encouraged, he deepened the kiss and Gina knew she was being branded, claimed, owned entirely by this man. Only James Hunter could have robbed her of the will to resist.

Heavenly and wicked at the same time.

* * *

A Rake by Midnight
Harlequin® Historical #1013—October 2010

Author's Note

As I near the end of the Hunter brothers' stories, I have been asked by readers what I have planned for the future. That's a difficult question to answer. By the time I finish one book, the next character is usually whispering in my ear, telling me a story that I just have to write. So when I finished *A Rake by Midnight,* Charles Hunter was telling me about this woman he knew, who… Well, you get the idea. And now that I'm nearing the end of that story, a new voice is calling my name. He inhabits the same world of Regency Noir, but he is reluctant to make a comment so early on. Very hush-hush, you know. Clandestine operations, and all that. Please check in for updates!

Meantime, I hope you enjoy *A Rake by Midnight.*

With affection and gratitude to my readers, who have embraced my characters and the world they inhabit.

A RAKE BY MIDNIGHT

GAIL RANSTROM

TORONTO • NEW YORK • LONDON
AMSTERDAM • PARIS • SYDNEY • HAMBURG
STOCKHOLM • ATHENS • TOKYO • MILAN • MADRID
PRAGUE • WARSAW • BUDAPEST • AUCKLAND

Recycling programs
for this product may
not exist in your area.

ISBN-13: 978-0-373-29613-2

A RAKE BY MIDNIGHT

www.eHarlequin.com

Printed in U.S.A.

Prologue

London, England
July 13, 1821

Her first awareness was of bone-chilling cold at her back, then the incessant cadence of muted voices. She blinked in the flickering red-hued darkness, but pungent smoke stung her eyes so she closed them again, waiting for the air to clear. Incense? No. Something acrid that clogged and burned the back of her throat. Something more intoxicating?

She tried to focus, to gain her bearings, but found the task impossible. Searching her mind for her last lucid memory, she had a vague notion of drinking a glass of wine—bitter wine—given to her by a handsome blondish man. Mr. Henley? Her stomach roiled and she feared she would vomit.

She ached. Every muscle, every part of her, screamed in outrage, but she did not know why. Time was shifting, blurring. She couldn't remember. Why couldn't she remember?

The chanting stopped and a single voice rose above her. Someone standing at her head. The shadows closed in, then leaned over her, becoming vague faces and outlines. Yes. She was elevated, lying on a stone slab. The man above her stopped talking and reached over her to open whatever was covering her.

Bare! She was being exposed to all those faces surrounding her. She tried to move, to cover herself, but her limbs did not respond. Why couldn't she move?

Nameless terror squeezed her chest, cutting off her breath. She tried to scream, but she could only utter a tiny squeak barely audible above the chanting of dozens of voices. Everything had gone dreadfully wrong, but she could not make sense of it.

Another man appeared, kneeling between her legs. Lifting his robes. She knew. Oh, now she knew. She was to suffer Cora's fate.

Now terror had a name. *The Brotherhood.*

"No!" a distant voice screamed. Her sister's voice? Dear Lord! All was lost if they had Bella, too.

But suddenly the night was chaos and nothing made sense to her muddled mind. The clash of blades, shouts, shrill whistles and, suddenly, a blade at her throat. Searing pain. The warm ooze of blood as it seeped from her wound. She turned her head and closed her eyes, waiting for the inevitable, praying it would be quick.

But death did not come. Instead she registered the sound of running feet and distant shouts. A warm cloak covered her nakedness as she was lifted from the stone altar and cradled in strong arms. The cloying smell of incense still heavy in the air permeated his robe, but there was an underlying scent of clean masculinity. Something heated and strong. She clung to him, her fingers digging into his shoulder and arm, terrified he'd let her go. Terrified, too, that he might not have come to save her. She opened her eyes, knowing it was too late to fight anyway.

James Hunter. Oh, why did it have to be *him?*

Chapter One

September 12, 1821

Night again. Darkened streets, shifting movements in the shadows, muffled sounds, whispers on the wind, the damp chill of a suffocating fog. And always, the impending threat of disaster at her back. Gina O'Rourke hated the night, though she had begun to live her life in the hours between dusk and dawn—as if nothing evil could happen to her if she kept watch.

She brimmed with relief as she watched the lamplighter touch his torch to the lamppost outside the sitting room window. She could have sworn there were shadows in the park across the way.

Turning away from the window, she picked up her embroidery and sat by the fire where the light was best. As she pushed the needle through the fine linen she tried to direct her thoughts to the future, something she had not been able to do since *that* night.

Tomorrow, perhaps, she would speak to her brother-in-law

about finding her and Mama a place of their own. Andrew and Bella should have a chance to be alone, and to nurture their marriage without Mama's interference. Nothing so far away as St. Albans, but perhaps a cottage in St. John's Woods would do nicely. There, Mama could complain and fuss to her heart's content with no one inconvenienced. Except Gina. But there was something...*safe* in that sort of life. Safe and comforting, as only the familiar could be.

Yes, a quiet life without drama or danger was just the thing. No one would ever have to know about her past—about *that* night. She could stop racking her brain, trying to remember the horrid bits and pieces that came before finding herself carried away from the altar, cradled in James Hunter's arms. Just his scent, woodsy and heated, had calmed her then. Now the memory of it unsettled her in a most troubling way.

The front bell rang, followed by the sound of boots and a muted voice speaking with Andrew's butler in the foyer. She glanced at the clock. Nearly midnight. Andrew's meeting had run quite late, and he was still closeted in the library with Lord Wycliffe, but who would call at midnight? She stood, ready to make a quick retreat, but she was not quick enough. James Hunter appeared in the doorway and removed his hat.

"I beg your pardon, Miss O'Rourke. I came to see my brother and Edwards asked me to wait while he informs Drew that I am here. He must not have known you were using the room."

Gina struggled to think of something to say but found herself tongue-tied. She sank back on the settee, her heart racing, and wondered if her mere thoughts had been enough to summon him. Stranger things than that had happened to her lately.

Leaving now would be obvious and rude. And revealing. She retrieved her needlework again and rested it on her lap, praying her fingers would not tremble when she took up her needle.

"I believe he is in some sort of late meeting, Mr. Hunter," she told him. "I doubt you will have long to wait."

"With such charming company, I shall pray he delays."

She met his gaze and realized he was just being mannerly, and only because her sister was married to his brother. All the Hunter brothers were polite to a fault. Still, she could never encounter him without reading the memory of that wretched night in the depths of his violet-blue eyes. She saw pity there, too, and abhorred the thought that she was pitied. She could not help but wonder if he still saw her as she'd been that night—naked until he had covered her with his cloak. Heat shot through her and she swallowed her tiny moan at the mere thought.

He dropped his hat on a chair and went to a console table to avail himself of the sherry bottle there. He glanced at her over his shoulder and raised an eyebrow by way of invitation.

"No, thank you," she murmured, looking toward the sitting room door. Where was Edwards? And why did James, of all people, have to find her alone?

"How have you been, Miss O'Rourke?"

"Well, thank you." She glanced down at her embroidery but her right hand went to a spot near the hollow of her throat and the livid gash of scar tissue there. She met his gaze, swallowed hard and dropped her hand quickly. Why did he have to be so devilishly handsome? She might be able to bear it if only he were old or ugly or boorish instead of tall and uncommonly good-looking!

"I am glad to hear it," he murmured.

She stood, gripping her embroidery hoop in her left hand. "I…I am a bit fatigued. If you will excuse me?" She took several steps toward the door.

His eyes narrowed and he moved to block her way. "No."

Surely she had not heard him correctly. "What?"

"No, I will not excuse you. I've had just enough to drink to not give a damn for social niceties. 'Tis past time we had a talk, Miss O'Rourke. We cannot keep on as we have been."

A slow chill seeped through her. Surely he did not mean to discuss that night? "I do not know what you mean."

"Yes, you do. We must come to an understanding for the sake of our families."

"We are not at odds."

He took a swallow of his sherry and studied her with darkened eyes. "Being at odds would require a misunderstanding. Alas, that would require conversation. And we, Miss O'Rourke, have had precious little of that. Mere niceties exchanged in public is our forte. This is the first time we have been alone since…well, ever, and I intend to make use of it. God only knows when the opportunity may arise again."

"And my wishes?"

He shook his head. "I have tiptoed around your wishes, Miss O'Rourke, and could continue to do so for the next millennium if left to you."

He was right. She would never have chosen to have this conversation. Never have spoken it aloud. And this was, perhaps, the worst count against the infamous Blood Wyvern Brotherhood—they had robbed her of self-respect and dignity. The men at that ritual had been cloaked and hooded. She had not seen their faces, but they had seen her. *All* of her. And now, when a man looked at her and smiled, she wondered if he had been one of them—one of the villains who had meant to rape and kill her that night.

"I…I really think…"

"Your sister is married to my brother. For that reason alone, there will be countless times in the future when we are in each other's company. It would be easier if we could come to an understanding instead of this awkwardness we now engage in."

Gina looked down at her slippers, just peeking from beneath the hem of her yellow gown. "That night...you..."

A full minute passed before James finally filled the void. "I can think of nothing I did that night to provoke your ire. I did everything I could to shield your modesty and to stop the bleeding...."

She *was* grateful. Truly grateful. But why could he not understand that, in her weakest moment, with nothing to hide her modesty, he had witnessed her deepest humiliation. He would never forget it—she had seen that much in his eyes. Each time he looked at her or talked to her, he would recall her as she'd been that night.

Panic and now-familiar anger began to bubble upward. She needed to escape before she said or did something unforgivable.

He stood between her and the door, and she tried to skirt past him. He reached out to stop her with a hand on her arm. She gasped at the warmth of his touch and the queasy sensations it stirred in her middle.

He lowered his voice as he drew nearer, and the heat of his breath tickled her ear as he leaned toward her. "I thought you and Isabella were so brave that night, to hunt down your sister's killers. I felt nothing but admiration for you. And for that, you shun me?"

Not for that, but for the knowledge in his eyes and the hours before her rescue. Hours that were still a blank to her. She could not go forward until she knew what transpired during that time. Had she been assaulted? Was she still a maiden? She looked up into his questioning eyes and shivered, trying desperately to think of something to say.

"Despite any personal feelings, for the sake of our families, Miss O'Rourke, shall we declare a truce?"

Personal feelings? The notion that he might dread seeing her, too, had not occurred to her before. She managed a slight nod. She'd agree to anything if he'd just let her go.

"Mr. Hunter will see you now."

They spun to find Edwards standing in the doorway.

A muscle jumped along James's jaw. He released her arm without another word, stepped back and bowed. "Miss O'Rourke, a pleasure, as always."

Gina watched him depart, then went to the console table to pour sherry into a glass and nearly choked on it as she drank it in a single gulp. She had to find those answers. To fill in those lost hours. She could never really be herself again until she did. And she needed to know that those men would never hurt another woman.

She placed her empty glass beside Mr. Hunter's and squared her shoulders. No more cowering in the dark. She would reclaim her life if it was the last thing she did!

Jamie studied the fire through the deep red contents of his glass, finding it difficult to keep his mind on the conversation after his encounter with Miss Eugenia. The memory of her always lingered with him long after she did. Tonight, was it the bloodred color of his wine that triggered the memories? Was it frustration? Lust? Anger? Did it matter? From their first meeting in the park in early July to this very night, he could not shake the memory of her away. Waking, sleeping, in a crowded room or a solitary moment, the thought of her would rise in him like an unholy obsession, disquieting him, kindling a deep burn in his soul.

Her form, with its soft, lush curves, promised delight. Her hair, a deep brown, gleamed with multicolored strands of chocolate, chestnut, caramel and copper when the light touched it. Her eyes—a deep greenish-hazel reminiscent of summer forests—captivated him. Her mouth—ah, that mouth! Inviting, plump lips curved up at the corners as if a perpetual smile was lurking, waiting to bloom with the slightest provocation—and, by the heavens, how he wanted to provoke it. Kiss it. Explore the silken depths beyond those rosy petals. Lose himself in her.

But Miss Eugenia cared nothing for him. Or, at the very least, she was not comfortable in his presence. Worst of all was that she had singled him out for this dubious honor. Her manner with Drew and Charlie was quite cordial. Clearly it was James she disdained.

"So deep in thought, Jamie?"

He came back to the moment and looked at his older brother and Lord Marcus Wycliffe, his superior at the Home Office. "I've things aplenty to think about, not the least of which is why you sent for me tonight."

Drew settled back in his chair, a bland expression on his face, a sure sign he expected trouble in one form or another. Jamie took his glass to the fireplace, stood with his elbow propped on the mantel and glanced toward his younger brother, Charles, who was prowling the room with restless energy. "I think Charlie and Wycliffe's presence here gives you away. Something about the Brotherhood, is it not?"

The Blood Wyvern Brotherhood, they called themselves. As members of the ton, they had thought themselves above the laws of decency and God. Only a week or so had passed since the last attempt of the covert section of the Home Office had failed to round up the remaining members of the ritualistic cult. Well, partially failed. They'd brought in all but a few unimportant dabblers and the one man at the top—the most evil of them all—Cyril Henley.

Drew nodded his confirmation. "We wanted to wait until the women had retired for the evening."

Jamie thought of Miss Eugenia, ready to flee with her

embroidery in hand. But he would not expose her. If she could not sleep, at least they had that much in common.

"Wycliffe wants to send you both abroad," Drew told him.

"Abroad? Me and Charlie?" Jamie turned to his superior. Why would Wycliffe send them away in the middle of an investigation?

"There has been no sign of the Brotherhood," Wycliffe told them. "No whispers. No sightings. And no more women have gone missing. With his cohorts captured, the secretary suspects Henley has left the country. Or perhaps someone else has disposed of him for us."

In Jamie's experience, which was prodigious, the Home Office wouldn't be that lucky. Men like Cyril Henley were like cockroaches. They survived all attempts to eradicate them, then came back to infest the world with their own sort of filth.

Wycliffe interpreted Jamie's silence for skepticism and nodded. "I doubt it, too, Hunter. But the secretary is convinced he has left England. Gone to France, Germany, Italy or perhaps even the Americas. He is bound to find followers and victims enough wherever he goes, as long as he does not make the mistake of trifling with the ton again. But this mad dog is our responsibility." Wycliffe paused to take another drink from his glass. "And that is why I recommended you to the Foreign Office."

Jamie opened his mouth to speak, but Wycliffe held up one hand to halt him. "You want these curs caught as badly as I do, Jamie. You, Charlie and Andrew know more than anyone else about this case. Andrew is married and does not work for the Home Office. You and Charlie are all we have left of the men who have been on this case from the beginning. If Henley is gone and the Brotherhood crushed, who better to send after him?"

Charlie stopped his pacing. "Transfer to the Foreign Office? Now there's an intriguing notion. Another day, I might be tempted by the proposition. But not at the moment. There are too many loose ends here. And I've fallen behind on my paperwork."

Jamie almost laughed. When had Charlie ever cared about paperwork?

"What do you say, Jamie?" Wycliffe asked.

"I think it is highly unlikely that Henley has gone anywhere." No, he would be thinking himself impervious to the Home Office. It was far more likely he was biding his time, waiting for the Home Office to put the case aside in favor of more urgent matters. He met Wycliffe's dark gaze. "I think I'll pass."

Wycliffe sighed. "I believe the secretary is expecting your acceptance. He has made arrangements."

"Tell him to arrange someone else."

"I thought you wanted to advance."

"Not at the expense of this case. Henley has not gone anywhere." Jamie noted Drew's distress and the look on Wycliffe's face and realized there was more to this than they were telling. "Why are you so anxious to get us out of the country?"

Drew sighed and sat back in his chair. "There is a price on your head."

"Henley?"

Wycliffe finished his brandy and stood. "Him, or any of the other cases you've brought to justice recently. I thought you'd be better off out of reach for a while. Take time to think about it, Jamie. Make yourself scarce. I will stall the secretary while you reconsider."

Jamie was no coward, but the thought that someone wanted him dead badly enough to pay for it was sobering. Henley would be looking for any way to stop Jamie from coming after him. "Give me another week, Wycliffe. I'll make my decision then."

His superior nodded. "Take care in the meantime."

Charlie gave a low whistle as they watched Wycliffe take his leave. "I wonder just how many people want you dead, Jamie," he ventured.

Jamie chuckled. "I can envision a queue from parliament to St. Paul's. But I have no intention of leaving the country. The bastard is here. In London. I feel it in my bones. Henley would never abandon his hunting grounds. I'd wager everything I own that someone is hiding him. His family, perhaps, or friends. Each time we get a lead, or think we're closing in, he disappears in a puff of smoke."

Drew looked doubtful. "How *do* you propose to find him?"

"Draw him out. There's a bounty on my head? Good. I shall make myself visible. And when he comes after me…"

"Setting yourself up as a target is a rotten idea, Jamie. He won't come for you himself. He'll hire cutthroats. And I don't want you dead."

Charlie began to pace, his head down. "Can we talk you out of this?"

Jamie pointed to his ears. "Deaf."

"Talk to Lockwood about this, Jamie. He still has connections at the Home and Foreign Offices, and he may have insights or be privy to information—"

Jamie took a deep breath. He did not want to involve their eldest brother, Lord Lockwood, in this quagmire. He had a wife and new child to think about, not to mention the duties attached to his title. "Not unless we are desperate. But this has to end now. Two months ago we thought it was over but they rose again. Last week we got the rest, but not Henley. I swear, the man is as slippery as an eel. As sure as I'm sitting here, Henley will find other hearts as dark as his own and rebuild his cult. He has a taste for killing now." And pray God he did not come after Eugenia to finish the job.

Drew combed his fingers through his hair and sighed. "There is a bounty on your head. Go, Jamie. Transfer to the Foreign Office. Make it a holiday. Let someone else handle this."

Jamie looked down into his glass again. Good sense and reason told him Drew was right. However. "I've been on this case from the beginning, Drew. I intend to see it through to the end."

"'Pears to me it's more personal than that."

Jamie tossed the remainder of his wine down and stood. Damn Drew's perception! "I want that blasted scum dangling from a rope for what he's done, and justice for—" he stopped himself from saying *Eugenia* and substituted "—for all their victims. And I bloody well want an end to all the secrets and lies."

"It always comes down to that with you, does it not— needing to know every last detail, every last truth? Why, Jamie? What drives you to that?"

"Truth never fails. There is no argument against it. It is the only rampart that remains when all else is crumbling. Truth tames chaos. It is just, honest and right. You can stand by it unashamed, depend upon it. If I did not stand for truth, what else would matter?"

"I pity when you finally learn that some questions are better left unanswered, and that the truth does not always serve you best." Andrew pushed his glass away and shook his head. "The world is not as black and white as you think, brother, and the truth is a double-edged sword. If you chase after it, be damned sure you are prepared to get cut."

"Living with lies could never be better," he said with unshakable certainty. "C'mon, Charlie. It appears I am going to need you to watch my back."

Chapter Two

Gina had expected shock, perhaps even outraged protests, but not stunned silence. Apart from the heavy rain outside the windows and the decisive tick of the tall case clock on the wall opposite the fireplace, the library was silent. Not even the clink of a teacup being replaced in its saucer broke the spell.

She glanced around the circle at the faces of her friends. Her sister, Isabella, looked as if she were sitting atop a coiled spring, ready to catapult off the settee and restrain her. Lady Annica, a darkly beautiful woman, wore a puzzled frown; Lady Sarah's expression was curious with a tinge of sympathy in her violet eyes—eyes so like her brother's that it always caught Gina by surprise. Grace Hawthorne, whom she had just met today, was more difficult to read, but Gina thought there might be a small crack in her serene countenance.

Gina cleared her throat and prayed she could keep her voice steady. "I was given to believe this group might be of some help in the matter. If not, then I apologize for broaching the subject."

A collective sigh was expelled and Isabella rose. "Gina! Are you mad?" She hurried to the library door, tested the lock, and returned to her chair.

"Nearly so," Gina admitted. Indeed, there was very little difference between true madness and what she'd been feeling for the past two months. "But I have come to believe that finding Mr. Henley is the only way I can change that."

"How do you propose to do that, dear?" Grace Hawthorne asked as she set her teacup down and smoothed her sky-blue skirts.

"I do not know how much you may have heard about my family's recent problems, Mrs. Hawthorne, but they have been extraordinary. The dust has settled a bit, what with Isabella and Lilly marrying, but I am still…" Gina stopped to clear her throat again, which was frequently raw since Lord Daschel had nicked it with a knife. "Still at odds."

Grace, who had been out of the country with her husband, gave a little smile of encouragement and Isabella hastened to finish Gina's explanation. "Almost as soon as our family arrived in London in May, our oldest sister, Cora, was kidnapped and murdered. Gina and I undertook to find the killer when the authorities had given up. Cora lived long enough to tell us that her killer was a member of the ton. With that as our only clue, we sought out men who fit that description and who had an interest in…in dark rituals and self-indulgence. Gina came close enough to be kidnapped by Mr. Henley as the next ritual sacrifice. But there were complications."

Gina looked down at her hands, clenched tightly in her lap. "Most of the men were arrested, and Lord Daschel, the man who murdered Cora, was killed. Then a fortnight ago, all the others were found and arrested but for their leader, Cyril Henley. I have been feeling so…unsettled. So vulnerable. And worse—increasingly angry. When I leave the house, I cannot stop looking over my shoulder or settle the nausea in my stomach. I cannot bear the thought of going through the rest of my life like this. I *must* do something to bring an end to it. And I fear nothing will end it until the villain is caught." Through the thoughtful silence that followed her declaration, Gina heard Lady Annica sigh.

"We understand more than you might think, Eugenia. You have come to the right place. The Wednesday League is prepared to assist women in your circumstances. We have certain resources and can work in ways that the Home Office cannot. But tell us, as precisely as possible, what you want to accomplish."

"Immediately after that night, I recalled nothing. Within a few days, memories began to return, but some of it still eludes me. I doubt it will ever come back entirely, and perhaps that is a blessing. But I want…" She could not tell them that she wanted the answers to what had happened to her. That she wanted the truth—all of it—good or bad. They would tell her to leave well enough alone. But there was something else she wanted, too. "I want…justice."

Lady Annica smiled. "We shall see that you get it, Eugenia, one way or another."

"I must be a part of it," Gina told them quickly. "I cannot sit idly by, waiting for someone else to free me from this poisonous feeling. Twice, the authorities have failed to capture him. How can you help me succeed when others have not?"

Lady Sarah stood and came to rest her hand on Gina's shoulder. "Give us a chance, Gina. We've succeeded in equally difficult circumstances. And what would you do? Haunt the Whitechapel streets alone? Prowl the rookeries after dark? That would be far too dangerous. Of course you will be involved in every aspect of the investigation, but surely you see the sense in allowing someone else to go about in your place."

"Please, Gina," Bella entreated. "What if something happened to you, too?"

If something happened? A sharp pain pierced Gina's brain. *If?* Oh, why couldn't she remember? Small bits and pieces, fleeting fragments, were all she had. She took a deep breath and pushed the uncertainty of the past two months away. "I do not want to waste another moment feeling like this."

"Give us a reasonable length of time, Gina," Grace appealed. "If we are not successful within a month, we shall find some way to involve you further."

That was more than Gina had expected, though not as much as she intended to take. No, she intended to confront those men, and she intended to have her answers. She took a deep breath and nodded. At least she would be moving forward.

Lady Annica stood. "Excellent! Shall we adjourn to *La Meilleure Robe?* I shall send ahead to Madame Marie requesting that she ask Mr. Renquist to be there."

"We are going to a dressmaker?" Gina asked in disbelief.

Grace leaned over and patted her clenched hands. "Madame Marie's husband is a Bow Street runner, dear. Quite the best of the lot. If he cannot help us, no one can."

Madame Marie, the French émigré owner of *La Meilleure Robe,* had been known to turn down clients on a whim. One was considered very fortunate to have a gown fashioned by the modiste to the aristocracy. The O'Rourke girls had been privileged to have had a number of their gowns made by her when they'd first arrived in London—gowns that had been meant to launch them in society but remained unworn in their wardrobes.

Gina was treated to a vastly different experience on this visit. She and Bella were ushered into a comfortable back dressing room which almost resembled a parlor where the other ladies were waiting. There were side tables and comfortable chairs arranged in a semicircle facing a small dressmaker's platform with mirrors behind.

When they were seated, Madame Marie entered from a side door and spread her arms wide. "La! 'Ow long 'as it been, ladies? Many months, yes? I pray you 'ave not gotten into more trouble."

Lady Annica removed her gloves and bonnet. "Not us, Madame. A friend of ours needs help."

Marie's glance skipped across the gathered faces—Lady Sarah, Grace Hawthorne, Charity MacGregor, Lady Annica, Bella and Gina, herself. Madame's gaze settled on Gina, and she felt a blush rise to her cheeks. Was it so obvious?

"François will be 'ere in a moment. 'E will want to 'ave the story from the beginning, eh? Be comfortable, and I shall tell the girls to bring tea. We must chat afterwards, yes?" And with that, the handsome Frenchwoman disappeared through the side door again.

Gina sank into a chair beside Lady Sarah. She was having misgivings about recounting her story—or at least what she could remember of it—to a man. The tale was difficult enough to share with another woman.

Bella came to her and took her hand. "You are very brave to be doing this, Gina. Do not let that courage fail you now."

Brave? Thank heavens they did not know the fear she lived with daily. The fear that Henley would come after her again. But she would conquer that fear for her rough justice. "Mama mustn't suspect."

Bella laughed. "Oh, you may be certain of that. I cannot even imagine what she might do—after she recovered from her swoon, of course."

"You may trust us all," Lady Sarah told her, slipping one arm around Bella's waist as she leaned close. "Everything that transpires in this room is utterly confidential."

Lady Sarah was the sister of Lord Lockwood, Andrew, James and Charles, and she was reassured to know that none of what was revealed here would be repeated to any of them. Relief brought a smile to her lips.

"Furthermore," Lady Sarah continued, "since you have said that you wish to be involved, you will have to enter society, Gina. It is the only way to gain access to the information we seek. We shall arrange for you to attend all the best functions, the more extravagant balls and crushes, and whatever other events that seem appropriate."

"Oh, I…"

"You met the Thayer twins at my oldest brother's house before…well, before. They have just arrived back in town after their summer holiday. Hortense and Harriet are quite lively and they know simply everyone and everything that goes on. In their company, you would have entrée to anywhere you wish to go."

Gina also recalled that the Thayer twins were singularly beautiful with their combination of copper hair and startling green eyes. But were they discreet?

The thought of entering society left her short of breath, but she had no time to protest when the side door opened and a maid carrying a tea tray entered, followed by a pleasant-looking man of average height. This would be Francis Renquist, Madame Marie's husband. His hair was sandy brown and his blue eyes had crinkle lines at the corners. Instinctively, Gina knew she could trust him.

"Ladies," he greeted them with a small bow, and when he straightened he rubbed his hands together. "I understand you have something for me?"

The maid left the tray on a side table and closed the door behind her, after which Lady Annica spoke. "We need to find some men, Mr. Renquist. Some particularly elusive men."

His bushy eyebrows rose. "What have they done, my lady?"

"Have you heard of the Blood Wyvern Brotherhood, sir?"

The color drained from his face. "How are you involved with these men?"

"We are not involved," Lady Sarah soothed. "Nor do we wish to be. We merely wish to locate the last of them, after which we shall inform the authorities where to find him."

"Even so…"

Lady Annica busied herself pouring out cups of tea and bringing them to the ladies, speaking as she did so. "Miss O'Rourke—" she indicated Gina with an inclination of her head "—and her sister, Mrs. Hunter, had some dealings with them a few months back. They are aware of the dangers and do not intend to encounter or confront the man involved. They simply have an interest in seeing that the perpetrators are safely locked away."

Gina blinked and squelched a pang of guilt. She fully intended to confront Mr. Henley. How else would she get her answers? But she feared the ladies would withdraw their support if she told them as much.

Mr. Renquist looked doubtful. "What, exactly, do you hope to accomplish?"

"Location, Mr. Renquist. That is all that we shall require of you," Grace Hawthorne said. "We do not want you to apprehend him or even speak to him. Just find him."

"As you are aware, these matters are rarely so simple."

"This will be, Mr. Renquist," Lady Sarah assured him.

"The Home Office is expending every resource at their disposal to bring this man to justice. Why must you risk involving yourselves—"

Lady Annica lowered her voice. "It is a personal matter," she said with a note of finality.

Mr. Renquist turned to look at Gina for one long moment. She held her breath, seeing that he wanted to refuse and was measuring her resolve. He must have read the determination in her heart because he let out a long sigh and nodded. "I will look into it, ladies, but I cannot make any promises. I will meet you here to report my findings twice a week unless there is need for more urgency. If you will let my wife know the days and times most convenient for you, I shall arrange to be here."

"Excellent!" Lady Sarah smiled and touched Mr. Renquist's arm as he turned to go. "Would you please send Madame Marie to us? Miss O'Rourke will need to commission a gown to account for her frequent visits here."

A moment later, Madame Marie appeared in the doorway, one finger tapping her cheek thoughtfully as she studied Gina's form. "Hmm. Something low and provocative, eh? Guaranteed to bring a man to 'is knees, yes? They will be so distracted that when you ask the questions, *chéri,* they will be compelled to give you the truth."

Gina suspected she would wear sackcloth if it would get to the truth.

By the time she and Bella arrived home, Gina barely had time to freshen up for afternoon tea. She hurried down the stairs on her way to the parlor, but the sound of muffled voices from the library stopped her. *Brotherhood,* she heard, and *Henley.* Not given to eavesdropping, she nevertheless hesitated outside the door. The sound of Andrew's voice, and those of James and Charles, was more than she could resist. Was this the business that closeted the brothers together in the library so often? *Her* business?

"But the leads are drying up," Charles's voice carried to her.

"…looking in the wrong places," Andrew replied.

"Where would *you* look?" James asked. "Parlors and sitting rooms?"

A laugh, cut off in the middle, answered that question. "Go back to the hells and Whitefriar taverns. Farrell will help. He's family now."

Gina shivered. Her sister Lilly's new husband was a bit frightening to everyone but Lilly. Even though he was family now, she suspected it would not be a good thing to be in Devlin Farrell's debt. But James's next words disavowed her of that notion.

"He has offered to help, and I will likely find a use for his particular talents. With him covering that end of the inquiries, Charlie and I will look to other avenues. But, as Charlie said, the leads are drying up."

"I can see you have your own suspicions," Andrew said.

There was a long pause before James spoke again, almost as if he were weighing his words carefully. "The one source we haven't explored in depth is his family and close acquaintances. They've been reluctant to speak with us and have denied any knowledge of the affair. But, damn it all, Drew, they've got to be involved in some way. Henley is canny enough, but he could not elude us so nimbly without help from someone in society, and who more likely to help him than his family or friends? God knows, his family would want to keep the secret of his involvement as long as possible. Their own reputations are at stake. And a man like Henley would not hesitate to prevail upon friends."

Gina frowned. If Henley's family was wary of James and the Home Office, she wondered if Mr. Renquist would be able to get past their defenses. Oh! She recalled there had been a woman at one of the two tableaus to which Cyril Henley had taken her before that last fateful night who had been almost as horrified as she. The woman had been familiar with everyone there, but her sensibilities had been more kindred to Gina's. Both had blushed and studied the floor when one tableau featured a nude woman reclining on a backless couch with nothing but a light shawl draped across one hip and her nether regions. Was that woman Henley's family? Or a friend? Could she know Henley's whereabouts? Or was she somehow connected with one of the other men?

Oh, if only she could remember the woman's name!

The rattle of teacups and saucers warned Gina that someone was bringing the tea service, and she dashed toward the sitting room. It would never do to be caught lurking outside the library door.

Bella looked up from her reading and patted the settee beside her when Gina rushed in. "Mama took Nancy and went shopping. Come sit, Gina. We rarely have time alone together these days."

Gina retrieved her embroidery from a side table and sat beside her sister. "We shall have to hoard all the moments we can."

"I know. Mama has been sighing and fretting over letters from her friends until just recently. I worried that she might want to go home, but it seems she is over the worst of her homesickness."

"I pray we will find a place of our own nearby. I would adore to be close to you and Lilly."

"Even when Mama finally goes back to Ireland, you should stay with me. Or Lilly. There is a dearth of eligible men in Belfast."

Gina poked the needle through the fine linen. "You know how it will be, Bella. The die is cast. Cora is gone. You and Lilly are wed. I am the last of us, so it falls to me to become Mama's companion in her old age."

Bella put her book aside and studied Gina's face. "I always thought we would all marry and shuttle Mama between us. In another few years, she will not want to live alone, and between us all, we could take turns."

"Heaven forbid!" Gina managed a laugh. "Would Andrew have married you, or would Mr. Farrell have married Lilly, if they had known Mama came in the bargain?"

"Andrew has managed quite well," Bella chuckled. "He did not think you and Mama should be without protection. And I am certain Lilly's husband feels the same."

Gina bit her tongue to keep from reminding Bella that her husband, and Lilly's, were the sort they'd needed protection *from*. Instead, she shrugged and guided the needle and silk floss through the linen again.

The sitting room door opened and Edwards brought in the tea service, followed by Andrew and his brothers. She and Bella stood to greet them.

"May we join you? Seems like forever since we've done anything quite so domestic as having tea with the ladies."

"Please," Bella said, her gaze holding her husband's and a soft color suffusing her cheeks. The room had shrunk to the two of them.

Was that what love looked like? Gina looked away, feeling as if she were intruding and she noted that James, too, was watching them. His gaze shifted to her and she blinked. He gave her a lopsided grin, as if they shared some secret that had eluded the others. She returned his smile, feeling schoolgirl shy.

"I hope you do not mind our interruption, ladies," Charles said. "We ran into Edwards in the corridor and he advised that it was just the two of you."

"Not at all," Bella said. She gestured at a console table that held several carafes and glasses. "May I offer you stronger refreshment?"

Charles grinned and went to the table. "Don't mind if I do."

Gina sank back to the settee. She wondered if her guilt at eavesdropping could be read on her face. She retrieved her needlework and rested it on her lap in a pretended study of her work while Bella took charge of the teapot.

"Where is the lovely Mrs. O'Rourke?" James asked as he took a teacup from Bella.

"She is out shopping," Bella said. "I think she is up to something. She's been quite giddy the past few days."

Andrew raised one eyebrow and Gina stifled a giggle. Bella was right—he'd been very good-natured about the O'Rourke invasion, and he was, no doubt, trying to imagine Mama giddy. Shrill, perhaps, feigning helplessness or demanding. But giddy?

The conversation floated around her and she felt herself withdrawing again, as she had so often since that night. Though her eyes remained on her needlework, her right hand went to the scar near the hollow of her throat as she thought of how James had bandaged the gash. He had seen her at her worst. Had he not, perhaps she wouldn't mind being around him quite so much.

Bella's voice cut through her thoughts. "Gina!"

She started and glanced up again, the question in her eyes.

"James asked if you are well," Bella told her.

When she realized she was trying to cover the fading scar, she dropped her hand quickly and nodded. She met his gaze and swallowed hard. Remembering his offer of a truce, she gave him a weak smile. "Quite well, thank you."

The stiff set of his shoulders relaxed slightly. "Good," he murmured, as if he had expected her to give a different answer.

An awkward silence stretched out as Bella and Charles glanced between them. Was her discomfort so terribly obvious?

She was relieved when everyone turned toward the sitting room door at a clatter in the foyer accompanied by raised feminine voices. A moment later, Mama burst through the sitting room door with nary an acknowledgement, apology or explanation.

"Oh!" she exclaimed, removing her straw bonnet edged in black silk ribbon and fanning herself with the brim. "Public coachmen are so rude! Why, this one did not even want to help me with my packages! Nancy and I had to fetch them all."

Gina tried to imagine their poor maid, now carrying the entire lot up the stairs to Mama's room. "What did you purchase, Mama?"

"Quite a few things, dear. Several bolts of cloth, for when I am out of mourning—" she gestured at her black bombazine gown "—and some very nice Belgian lace, trims and notions. Then I went to Fortnum and Mason to purchase tins of dried fruits, exotic teas and preserves."

Bella frowned. "I am certain Cook has enough—"

"They are not for cook, silly girl." Mama sighed as she sank into a comfortable chair. "They are for us to take home. So difficult to find the finer things in Belfast, you know. Why, Belgian lace costs twice as much in the shops there! I confess, I delight in knowing I shall be the envy of all my friends."

Gina smiled. These were the sure signs that Mama was beginning to heal from Cora's death. "Surely there will be time enough to find everything you want."

"Time enough? Why, there's scarcely any time left at all! We shall be returning to Ireland within the fortnight."

Gina could only stare at her mother in disbelief. She'd said nothing about returning to Ireland so soon! Not even a hint!

Bella intervened. "I thought you'd stay longer. With Lilly just wed, she may need you."

Mama gave her a jaded look. "I believe the Farrells have no need for me at all. Mr. Farrell seems to have Lilly well in hand." She turned to spare Andrew a glimpse. "As does Mr. Hunter seem to suit you well. No, you and Lilly have no need of me. Eugenia and I shall leave within a fortnight."

Fortnight? She could not possibly be ready so soon! Mr. Renquist had indicated it could take *months* to find Mr. Henley. She stood in her agitation, acutely aware that James Hunter was watching her with marked curiosity. "Could we not stay until Christmas?"

"Christmas? Good heavens, Eugenia!" Mama put her hat aside and accepted a teacup from Bella. "Why, we cannot leave our house in Belfast unattended so long. Was it not always our intent to give you girls a season and leave for home afterward? You will recall I originally let the house in St. James until September. Just because we removed here and have been in mourning does not mean I changed our plans."

"Mrs. O'Rourke, you are welcome here as long as you wish to stay," Andrew told her. Gina wondered how much that offer had cost him.

"Kind of you, I am sure," Mama said. "But I've already made arrangements. I decided that traveling overland is far too tedious and booked our berths yesterday, and today I ordered crates to be delivered for our goods." She spread her arms wide as if she dared anyone to argue. "'Tis a *fait accompli*."

"Excuse me." Gina prayed she could keep her composure until she exited the sitting room.

Chapter Three

Gina breathed deeply of the fresh air, her mind whirling with the news. So this is what Mama had been "giddy" about—the prospect of returning to Ireland! She needed to think. To plan. This new development changed everything.

If she was to have any chance of learning what happened in those lost hours, of finally being free of the past, she would have to act quickly. Indeed, she would not be able to wait for Mr. Renquist to make progress. As much as she dreaded mixing in society, she would have to enter the search herself, just as Lady Sarah had suggested.

She found a quiet spot in the garden and sat on a bench balanced between two stone lions. The late afternoon breeze made her shiver, a reminder of oncoming autumn, and she hugged herself as she focused on the toes of her slippers, trying to unravel the problem at hand.

Lady Sarah had already made arrangements to call for her tomorrow evening and accompany her to the Auberville Ball. The Thayer twins would be in attendance and, if all went well, Lady Sarah would arrange for more invitations, and Gina would join their circle.

She would not ask Mr. Renquist to investigate what she'd overheard in the library. She'd leave him to his sources and *she* would seek out Mr. Henley's family and friends in society. The only thing she could not do was return to Belfast with this matter unresolved. To never know the truth. Never feel safe again so long as Mr. Henley roamed the earth.

The toes of two highly polished Wellingtons appeared before her. "Chilly, Miss O'Rourke?"

She looked up to find James Hunter standing before her. The familiar uneasy heat rose in her but she controlled it with a deep breath before she spoke. "A bit, Mr. Hunter. I should not have come out without my shawl."

"Shall I fetch it?"

She shook her head. She did not intend to stay a moment longer than necessary.

He sat beside her, close enough for her to feel his heat, but not close enough to touch. "I gather your mother's announcement was a surprise to you?"

"Completely. I had no idea she wanted to leave so soon."

"And you do not?"

"Yes. No! I mean, I want to go home, but this is so sudden, and there were things that I still wanted to do."

"*Things,* Miss O'Rourke? For instance?"

"I…I have not been much out in society due to…well, circumstances. I would like to experience a bit of the excitement of London."

He gave a chortle that made her shiver. "I would think you'd have had enough excitement to last for one season."

She looked sideways at him. There was nothing sarcastic in his countenance, and nothing chiding. Just a simple statement of fact. "A different sort of excitement than being abducted, Mr. Hunter."

His eyes caught hers and held them. "I understand. I shall be sorry to see you go. I would have liked to waltz just once with you. Have you been to Vauxhall, or the museums?"

She shook her head. "Cora was killed not long after we arrived. And everything since then has conspired to keep us otherwise occupied."

He laughed outright this time. "That would be a bit of an understatement, Miss O'Rourke. Your family has been the talk of the town. I must say, the O'Rourkes have collided with London in a most forceful manner."

"And yet your sister has offered to sponsor me. At great risk to her reputation, I surmise."

"Has she?" He looked surprised, and Gina realized he was thinking such a sponsorship was risky. "Well, Sarah knows best. She is an excellent judge of character. With her as your sponsor, your success is assured."

She didn't care a whit for social success. She only wanted to meet the people who could lead her to Mr. Henley, but given the conversation she'd overheard earlier in the library, she imagined all the brothers would forbid such a thing. Thank heavens they would be too busy with their own business to meddle in hers.

She shivered again and Mr. Hunter shrugged out of his jacket to drape it over her shoulders. Still warm from his body, it smelled of lime shaving soap and something clean. Starch? Very comforting, yet provocative. And once again, it conjured memories of that night. "Thank you," she managed, suspecting she should have refused and gone inside.

"My pleasure, Miss O'Rourke." He stretched his legs out and crossed his ankles. "One never knows how to dress for the weather this time of year."

"Is…is there a reason you followed me, Mr. Hunter?"

"I wanted to thank you for not running the moment you

saw me, as is your custom. Indeed, I think our truce will work admirably well."

"My dislike of you has been nothing personal, Mr. Hunter."

"You dislike me?"

Mortified by her gaucherie, Gina winced. "Oh, forgive me. I did not mean that the way it sounded. What I meant to say is that you make me uncomfortable...I mean—"

"Please do not explain further, Miss O'Rourke. I do not think my tender ego is up to it." He grinned and her stomach did an odd little flip-flop.

The sound of laughter preceded the arrival of others, and Gina slipped James's jacket off her shoulders and shivered in the sudden chill. She gave it back and watched as he stood and shrugged it on moments before Bella and Charles appeared around the hedge. Why did she feel as if they had done something wrong?

Charles bowed to Gina before he turned to his brother. "Here you are, Jamie. We're late for our appointment, and we ought to leave these good people to their evening."

Bella shook her head in feigned disbelief. "I tried to persuade him that they were welcome to stay for dinner, but Charles would not hear of it."

"Quite right. We are expected elsewhere," James confirmed as he stepped away from the bench.

The men bowed, but before they departed, James looked at her, something unreadable in his eyes before he turned and disappeared along the garden path. A vague feeling of disappointment filled Gina at their departure.

Bella led her through the library doors and went to the console table to pour sherry into a glass and bring it to her. "I had no idea!"

Gina accepted the glass and took a healthy gulp. "Of what?"

"That you were in love with James."

She choked, the sherry burning her throat. Love? Oh, to the contrary. She could barely endure his company. "You are mistaken, Bella. I am not in love with Mr. Hunter. If I am awkward in his presence, it is because I do not like to keep his company. He…he…*saw* me." Indeed, he was a reminder of all she had endured. Of all she had lost. And that was what she'd been at a loss to explain to him mere moments ago.

Bella gave her a wise older-sister smile. "Perhaps that is why he is so drawn to you. 'Tis almost painful to watch him when you are in the same room. He cannot tear his eyes from you."

"Because he imagines me naked! It…it is lasciviousness, Bella, and nothing more."

"Truly?" But Bella looked doubtful. "He looked genuinely distraught when Mama announced she was taking you home to Ireland."

Because he would have liked to waltz with her? She caught her breath at the sudden pain in her chest at the realization that, had things been different, had that night never occurred, she would have liked to waltz with him, too.

That night at the Crown and Bear tavern, Jamie Hunter rolled his eyes in disgust. "Good Lord, Charlie, you haven't had that much to drink. Focus, man!"

Charlie grinned, a canny look on his face. "I'm not far gone, Jamie. I'm thinking of something else."

"Some*one* else, more likely. Who is it this time?"

"The sweet little thing you just cast off. Suzette."

"That was two months ago." Jamie leaned back in his chair and folded his arms over his chest. "But Suzette can make the blood boil, can she not? Alas, what will she do when you move on to another demirep? She's damned near made a career of the Hunter brothers. You're the lone holdout, Charlie."

"Well, I am not holding out any longer. Suzette was saving the best for last. She is fond of the tall, dark and handsome sort." He waggled his eyebrows at Jamie and chuckled. "I've seen the *congé* she has acquired from Lockwood, Drew and you. I'd be willing to wager she could retire if she sold those jewels."

"Why would she retire when she has yet another Hunter brother to fleece?"

"I daresay you all got your money's worth. I know I shall."

Jamie shrugged. He couldn't say why he'd tired of Suzette Lamont, only that he had. Though, when he thought about it, he'd reached that decision very soon after his family had become involved with the O'Rourkes.

He suppressed a shiver and came back to the conversation. "Just be a gentleman when you leave, Charlie. Suzette deserves that much."

"Aye, she was so devastated when *you* left that she took up with a German not a week later. Ah, but she's done with him now, and 'tis my turn."

"Made a pauper of him, more likely. Watch your purse strings, brother."

"Jealous?"

Was he? Perhaps just a touch. Suzette was skilled and had taught him much about pleasing a woman. And he was beginning to feel the effects of prolonged celibacy. The fleeting thought that perhaps he needed a woman to take the edge off his lust for Eugenia made him shake his head in disgust. He downed his whiskey in a single gulp.

This eschewing of mistresses was what came of being around his older brothers. They'd become domesticated so quickly that he could scarce believe it. Lockwood had taken to marriage like a duck to water. Andrew, a libertine to rival the worst, was now a happy house cat, curling by his fire with his favorite new toy—Bella.

Ah, yes, and here came the latest in a long line of newly domesticated tomcats. Devlin Farrell. A man whose slightest twitch had roused terror in seasoned criminals was now a well-contented newlywed who literally worshipped his wife.

"Gents," he greeted them. "I see you started without me."

Charlie laughed. "I have no doubt you'll catch up, Farrell."

Devlin signaled the barkeeper and a tankard of ale magically appeared. "I have no intention of catching up. Lilly is waiting at home. Wouldn't want to disappoint her."

Jamie snorted. He very much doubted Lilly would be disappointed tonight, or any other night if he was any judge at all. If there was no saint like a reformed sinner, Devlin Farrell would soon have his own niche at St. Paul's.

After a long drink, Devlin answered their unasked question. "No sign of them, but I've confirmed they are still in the vicinity. Tell the secretary his information is wrong."

"We suspected as much." Charlie sat a bit straighter, as if he had suddenly shaken off the effects of the whiskey. "And is there, indeed, a price on Jamie's head?"

"A rather large one."

Jamie grinned. "How much am I worth?"

"Ten thousand pounds."

Charlie whistled and rolled his eyes. "There should be at least a dozen takers at that price."

"At least," Devlin agreed. "But common cutthroats do not have the finesse to take our Jamie by surprise."

Ten thousand pounds was, nevertheless, a daunting sum. Jamie shifted uneasily in his chair, taking the threat seriously for the first time. Who would come after him first? He held Devlin's gaze. "Will it be the Gibbons brothers?"

The corners of Devlin's mouth quirked. "They're mean as snakes and will turn on you in a trice, but blast if they aren't sometimes useful. They'll do anything for money, though I don't know what they do with it once it's in their hands."

"Wish they'd get a bath," Charlie muttered. "Or buy some manners."

"It's a mystery." Devlin shrugged. "They live in a hovel, never invest in a bar of soap, pick their clothes out of rag piles, eat garbage and even share their whores so they only have to pay for one. They must have a fortune amassed somewhere."

"Two more pathetic creatures I've never seen."

"Oh, I don't know...." Devlin's right eyebrow shot up as he glanced between Jamie and Charlie.

Jamie and Charlie burst out laughing and toasted each other as if to confirm Devlin's analysis.

Devlin sat back in his chair and his expression sobered. "In view of the risk to you, Jamie, I'd like you to accept a bodyguard or two. I know just the men, and—"

"They'd get in the way. Make me conspicuous. And do not think to set them on me without my knowledge. I'd mistake them for bounty hunters and have to kill them."

Devlin did not look happy. "I might have a lead for you. If you handle it with your usual skill, you could end this thing quickly."

Jamie sat forward and lowered his voice. "What do you have up your sleeve, Devlin?"

"That night, at the ritual, when the charleys arrived and the brotherhood scattered down the tunnels, I recognized a few men. Some, you already know about. But I haven't mentioned that I saw Stanley Metcalfe and Adam Booth. They looked confused and frightened and, unless I miss my guess, that was their first time at a ritual, and is the reason I did not pursue them. They've kept their noses clean since, though."

How like Devlin to keep that information to himself until it was needed. Until Metcalfe or Booth could prove useful. "And?"

"As the last men on the periphery of the brotherhood still free, they might be useful to you. Might have some information. One of them could be in touch with Henley. They might know his family and have knowledge of… Well, you can imagine how helpful they might be."

If they could be trusted. And if they were still alive.

Jamie dropped some coins on the table and stood. "Get home to Lilly. And thanks for the tip. I'll be looking for them tomorrow."

Massive crystal chandeliers glittered multicolored shards of light across the room, laughter was shrill and the wine was free-flowing. The evening promised to be a huge success. Alas, Lord Auberville hadn't been able to tell him who, precisely, had been invited to the ball, so Jamie concluded he'd just have to see for himself. Charlie left him at the door to find the card room and a game of whist, leaving Jamie free to wander the perimeter of the dance floor. With a nod here and a smile there, he acknowledged a few friends and acquaintances, but nary a sign of Stanley Metcalfe or Adam Booth. Had someone tipped them off?

He was thinking he'd take any Metcalfe at this point, and there, in answer to his prayer, was Stanley Metcalfe's sister, Missy. Dressed in deceptive white, she was holding court in a circle of men. He wondered if she realized her popularity was attributable to the poorly kept secret that she granted certain…liberties, if one could get her alone in a garden.

He advanced on the group, knowing that most of the men would depart when the music stopped. The rest…well, he would just have to be quicker. He greeted the men, took Missy's hand and bowed over it.

"Miss Metcalfe, you are looking especially lovely tonight."

She twinkled at him and giggled. "How kind of you to say, Mr. Hunter."

"Just giving you your due, Miss Metcalfe."

The orchestra finished the set and one young man stepped forward. "I say, Miss Metcalfe, would you do me the honor—"

Jamie smiled apologetically at the young man. "Taken. I shall return her to you directly after." He took Missy's hand and led her away as she muffled yet another giggle.

"How naughty of you, Mr. Hunter," she said as the next dance, a sedate reel, began. "I have no recollection of granting you a dance."

"Then I must thank you for not giving me away." There would be an unavoidable risk in carrying on their conversation as they met between steps, so he led her into the dance, waited until they met for a turn, and then tugged her toward the terrace doors.

"Oh!" She pressed one dainty hand against her chest when they were outside and the terrace door closed behind them. Her eyes widened in feigned innocence. "We really shouldn't…"

He really wouldn't. But Missy needn't know that. "You break a man's heart, my dear."

She gave him a pretty pout. "What else am I to do? You dance with a girl now and then, and ignore her the rest of the time. Is that fair?"

"Fair? Oh, my dear, more fair than you can know. If I were to subject myself to your charms too often, why there is no telling what I might do. Perhaps I ought to take my pleas to your brother."

"No need for that, Mr. Hunter. He would likely just refuse you."

"Or he could give me his blessing to call upon you. Is he here?"

"No. He…he is keeping to himself these days."

"Do you know where I might find him? His club, perhaps?"

"You'd do better to petition my father, sir, but he is ill at the moment, and not receiving."

How coincidental that all the males in her family were currently unavailable. And suspicious. Something was being covered up, of that he was sure. "Is there no recourse for me at all?"

She moved closer until her breasts were pressed against his chest, and looked up at him with a sloe-eyed heat. "You could take what you want. I like men who take what they want."

He groaned. What was the harm in taking what was freely offered? He spanned her waist with his hands and held her still as he tilted his head down to hers. "You are too tempting, Miss Metcalfe," he said against her lips. When he deepened the contact and she moaned, he waited for the excitement, the rush of pleasure and anticipation. In vain. All he could think was that the rosewater she had splashed on was rather overpowering, and not at all like the stirring scent of Miss O'Rourke's skin.

Fortunately, he already had what he needed from Missy— she did not know where her brother was. And she was not what he wanted.

He stepped back from her. "We must get you back inside before anyone notices you're gone. I would dislike people talking about you."

She stamped her foot in frustration and was about to protest when the terrace doors opened and her erstwhile

swain appeared. Thank God they'd broken contact or Jamie
suspected he'd be fighting a duel at dawn.

"Miss Metcalfe became overheated," he explained. "Do
keep her company whilst she cools down."

He edged past the young man and into the ballroom. When
he glanced back, Missy Metcalfe was watching him with
consternation. He gave her a wink, thinking she could prove
useful in the future.

Inside, he scanned the room before leaving, but stopped
dead when he met deep hazel eyes at a distance. Could it be?
Yes. Miss O'Rourke was standing between Hortense and Harriett Thayer, looking a bit bemused as one of the twins—he
could not tell them apart—told a story. Eugenia was dressed
in a pink confection that complemented her complexion
perfectly. Her lustrous golden-brown hair was done up in a
perfect cluster from which ringlets fell to dance below her
shoulders. He tried to imagine how those ringlets would feel
tangled between his fingers.

What the bloody hell was Miss O'Rourke doing here? Did
she not realize she was at risk for as long as a single member
of the brotherhood was on the loose? She was one of the few
people left alive who could recognize them.

The sound of conversation was nearly deafening but Gina
could barely hear it over the thundering of her own heartbeat.
Even supported by the Thayer twins, she wondered what had
ever made her think she was prepared for this.

Standing in the ballroom, she could not banish the thought
that one of the men present may have been at the chapel that
night. Someone who might have been a part of her abduction,
had hoped to be a part of her ultimate shame and death.

She shuddered and forced the thoughts from her mind. She
had known entering society would not be easy. She could not

let that stop her. She was running out of time if she meant to have her justice.

Just as she squared her shoulders and lifted her chin, her fears materialized. She glimpsed James Hunter in a group of revelers. James, who *had* been there. Who had seen her as nature had made her. But he, at least, had not meant her ill.

"Oh, look! There's Missy Metcalfe." Hortense nudged Gina in the ribs as she leaned closer to her ear. "Quite the little flirt, that one."

Gina shook off her vague misgiving and chuckled as she thought of the pot and the kettle. Missy Metcalfe, whoever she was, would surely fall far short of Hortense's skills.

Harriett, though, was a bit more sedate. Only a bit. "She prefers the company of men, Hortense. That does not make her a flirt."

"No, Harri. It makes her a—"

"Hush! Do you want someone to hear?" Harriett pasted a smile on her pretty face and waved to the young lady in question.

"She is quite lovely," Gina allowed.

Hortense turned and swept Gina's form head to toe in an assessing gaze. "You needn't worry, Eugenia. She cannot hold a candle to you."

"Oh, but she is fair and lively while I am—"

"Dark and mysterious," Harriett finished. "I can well picture young men hanging on your every word. And that gown! Pink becomes you. You must make it your signature color."

Gina smoothed the pale pink watered silk over her hips. The gown had been made for her not long after her arrival in London, and she had lost weight since then. It did not hang on her, but it gapped slightly at the scooped décolletage and Nancy had pinned a posy of violets there to fill the gap and save her modesty.

Hortense pinched her arm. "Upon my word! There is Mr.

Hunter heading our way. Mr. *James* Hunter. Are you not somehow related, Eugenia?"

"His brother is married to my sister," she confessed, searching the crowd for a sign of him as she experienced a pang of panic.

"How divine," Hortense declared with a wink. "What I wouldn't give to have such a man going in and out of my house. Do you often manage to encounter him?"

"Rarely." As rarely as she could manage.

"Pity," Harriett ventured. "He has a reputation to be envied amongst the ladies of the ton. There is scarce one who has not contrived to elicit a walk in the gardens with him."

"Why?" she asked.

The twins giggled and Hortense answered. "You cannot have missed how handsome he is. Oh, those eyes make my knees weak! And I have heard it whispered—no, I will not tell you by whom—that he kisses like a fallen angel. Heavenly and naughty at the same time. How I would love to know how that feels."

Gina closed her eyes, remembering how she had felt when he had carried her from the altar. Comforted. Safe. Mortified. But what would it have been like to let him kiss her?

She raised her hand to her throat where her scar was hidden beneath a wide pink ribbon to which a cameo had been fastened. Heat flowed through her, warming her blood and firing her imagination.

"Ah, well," Harriett continued, "I would make the most of your connection. If you are seen on his arm, your reputation as a 'desirable' is made."

Gina shook her head, not wanting to disappoint the twins. "Mr. Hunter has far more important things to do than 'make' my reputation." Her stomach fluttered when a crooked smile quirked his mouth as he met her eyes.

He arrived before them, bowed to Hortense and Harriett,

then turned his attention to her as the music began. "Our first waltz, Miss O'Rourke," he murmured in a deep, intimate voice as he took her hand.

She was amazed that her knees did not give out as he led her onto the dance floor.

Chapter Four

She detected an angry undercurrent in the way James Hunter took her hand and led her onto the dance floor. Was it not she who should be indignant at the way he'd claimed her and given her no room to demur? With the slightest tug, he spun her around and pulled her against his chest just as the music began.

"Fancy meeting you here, Miss O'Rourke," he said as he led her into the first steps of the waltz.

Gina raised her eyebrows at his clipped tone. "I do not recall consenting to a dance, Mr. Hunter."

He looked at her through those violet-blue eyes, rather wintery now instead of holding their usual warmth. His entire demeanor had changed since leading her away from the twins. "I wasn't actually asking."

Disappointment washed through her. She had wondered, if they waltzed, how it would feel to be in his arms, but not like this. Now she only wanted to escape. What had she done to provoke him? As she moved to draw away, his hand tightened at her waist.

"Careful, Miss O'Rourke, or everyone will know our business."

She fought to keep her face impassive and her manner as cold as his, but his demeanor bothered her more than she dared let him know. "We have business? If so, I am unaware of it, sir. Indeed, I thought we had called a truce."

"We have. Correct me if I am wrong, but I do not recall recklessness being a part of it."

She collected her wits as he swung her in a wide circle. "I…reckless? I haven't the faintest notion what you mean."

"Have you not?" Their progress around the dance floor had brought them close to an open terrace door and he waltzed her outside without missing a step. "Then allow me to enlighten you."

He stopped suddenly and released her in the dim glow of a hanging lantern, leaving her to catch her own balance. She had never seen him like this before—angry and challenging—and she did not like it. She lifted her chin and glared at him, daring him to berate her for anything.

But that did not stop him. "There are people around who… who could wish you harm. And here you are, flaunting yourself for all the world to see. Are you daring Henley to come after you, Miss O'Rourke?"

She blinked. He was right, of course, but she could hardly tell him that finding Henley had, in fact, been her goal. In his present mood, he was likely to throw her over his shoulder and carry her home. She lifted her chin a bit higher. "I fail to see how that is any concern of yours, Mr. Hunter."

The expression on his face was stiff and brittle, as if it might crack at any moment and reveal his true feelings. "You don't? Then allow me to count the ways. One—" he held up one finger "—you are my brother's sister-in-law. Two—" another finger went up "—I have already pulled you from Henley's reach once. Three, I am currently working to see that Henley is punished, and four…" His voice trailed off, as if he had thought better of continuing.

"Four?" she challenged.

He laughed, but there was not the slightest hint of humor in it. "You would not want to hear that one, Miss O'Rourke, believe me. Shall we say that my reasons are legion, and that your presence is a distraction and a deterrent?"

What could be so dreadful she could not hear it? She took a deep breath and let it out slowly, regaining a small measure of composure. "Very well. But your reasons are not my concern. I am tired of being a prisoner in my home. I am tired of being punished for something that is not my fault. I have had enough of allowing fear to dictate my life. No more, Mr. Hunter. Do you hear me? No more."

He gripped her upper arms and leaned toward her. His scent weakened her knees and for a moment the possibility of a kiss hovered in the air between them. She was breathless, torn by hope and fear. Then, in a very low voice, he said, "I hear you clearly, Miss O'Rourke, and as much as I admire your courage and determination, I abhor your foolhardiness in taunting a dangerous man."

She finally inhaled, trying to find her voice. How could she tell him that she had doubts, too. At least a dozen times a day, and twice already tonight. "Nevertheless."

He looked completely flummoxed by her refusal to see the matter his way. And her promise of utter confidentiality prevented her from mentioning that she had gained courage and support from his own sister and several of the most important ladies in the ton, so she merely held her ground.

He released her and stepped back. "Very well, Miss O'Rourke. Have it your way, then. But you cannot stop me from shadowing your footsteps."

"You shall soon become very bored," she warned. "Unless you have a secret *tendresse* for one of the Thayer twins."

The hint of a smile twitched his lips. "Redheaded hoydens. Trouble, if ever there was any, and certainly incapable of keeping you out of it. That would be like setting the fox to guard the henhouse."

"I do not need anyone to keep me out of trouble. I am quite capable of that, myself."

His gaze swept her from head to toe. "Really?"

A flash of heat washed through her. Was he thinking of that night in the catacombs beneath the chapel? He was right—she had gotten herself in trouble before.

She drew herself up and spun on her heel to go back to the ballroom. *He will not humiliate me into doing as he wants, and he will not intimidate me, either!*

Jamie watched her go, half wanting to go after her, and half wanting to lock her away in some safe place until this business with Henley was finished. Why had he never noticed that stubborn streak?

He plucked a rose from a bush climbing the arbor he passed on his way to the stables and held it to his nose. Sweet and blossoming, like Miss Eugenia, herself. His body stirred with the thought of her soft heated flesh beneath him, her dark hair spread upon his pillow and those lush lips parted with a sigh as he entered her. He groaned and shook his head. He had no right to be thinking of her in that way. She'd made it plain that she disliked him.

Happily, there were many who did, and he was not adverse to settling when his first choice was not available. He'd find Devlin, see if there was any news, and then go look for female companionship. Perhaps that would take the edge off his adolescent yearning for Miss O'Rourke. And Charlie? Well, Charlie would catch up when he could. Aye, Charlie always knew where to find him—some sort of brotherly instinct.

He tossed a coin to the stable boy who brought his horse,

then mounted, turning southeast toward Whitefriars and the Crown and Bear. If Devlin was not there, Jamie would have a drink or two and go find ease at Alice's. Her girls were known for their enthusiasm and accommodating nature. God knows he could use a bit of that.

Clouds had gathered, obscuring the moon and bringing a chill. This was a night made for chicanery and it was early yet in Whitefriars. Anyone who made an honest living was home abed, and the others…well, the others never slept. As he arrived at the Crown and Bear, the place was alive with noise and laughter. Somewhere down an alley, voices raised in a quarrel carried to him as he left his horse in the stable yard behind the tavern and tossed another coin to Cox, the toothless and bald man who tended the stock.

A few faces turned to look when he entered, then went back to their tankards. A quick scan of the room told him that Farrell wasn't there. He crossed to the bar and waited while Mick Haddon, the barkeeper, poured a measure of his favorite rye whiskey and brought it to him. Haddon was a good man fallen on hard times, and a cut above the usual trade in the Crown and Bear.

"Farrell in back?" he asked.

"Home. Rarely see him these days," Haddon answered.

Jamie raised his glass. "To domestic bliss," he said before he swallowed the contents.

Mick snorted in reply. "Anything I can do for you?"

"What has Farrell told you?"

"To keep an eye out for Henley, and an ear to the ground."

"And?"

"Nothing, though this is the sort of place Henley would come if he were in a drinking mood. And had he not already crossed Farrell."

Silently, Jamie agreed. Henley wouldn't go to his club or

to any reputable tavern or gambling hell. He'd frequent only the dregs of London. Places where he'd be unlikely to run into any of his old friends or new enemies. But someone, somewhere, knew where he was and was helping him. Sooner or later, Jamie would find him. He was a very patient man.

"Any unusual activity? Rumors?" he asked.

"Just the usual sort," Haddon said as he poured another measure for Jamie. "A woman turned up dead in an alley not far from here last night. The charleys were asking around, but it seems she and her husband had a row, and you can guess the rest. I believe the husband has been taken away."

"Domestic bliss," Jamie repeated as he finished his drink.

Haddon laughed this time and nodded.

Jamie left his glass on the bar and returned to the stable yard. Old Cox handed him the reins and ducked his head, as if avoiding Jamie's eyes. His horse danced sideways, skittish about something. Rather than mount, he led his horse out of the yard to the cobblestones, an uneasy feeling raising the fine hairs on the back of his neck. Something wasn't right.

He bent down to slip the dagger from his boot just as the report of a gunshot sounded close at hand. Brick and mortar scattered in a wide pattern behind him and his horse reared, frightened by the noise. He released the reins, knowing the well-trained animal would not bolt. He rolled to the side, coming up on his feet again near a doorway, his dagger in hand.

Suddenly the price on his head was not quite so amusing. He'd left his pocket pistol at home, not anticipating that he'd be visiting the rookeries tonight. The sound of running footsteps down an adjacent alley told him that the assassin had taken his best shot and was now making his escape.

He was in full pursuit down the alley, gaining on the culprit, when it occurred to him that this had all gone off too smoothly. He knew these streets well enough to know the assassin was leading him toward a blind alley. An ambush? But who would be waiting for him? Henley? The Gibbons brothers? He was alone. Should he take the chance?

"Oh! I nearly swooned when I saw him waltz you out the terrace door!"

Gina gave Hortense a bland smile. "Nothing happened. He was merely inquiring as to my mother's health."

"Was he, indeed?" Harriett teased. "And why should your mother's health be a concern of his?"

Gina laughed. "My mother's health is everyone's concern. She makes it so at every encounter."

"Then you cannot confirm or deny the rumors concerning Mr. Hunter's…skills?"

"Alas." *Indeed.* The memory of that brief moment of promise brought a little smile to her lips.

"Ah! I see you are gaining confidence, Gina." Harriett squeezed her hand and winked at her sister. "Our little protégé is blooming."

Yes, she was gaining confidence but she was far from being at ease. She was acutely aware that there could be men present who had heard of her ordeal. Perhaps even a few who had been there, who had seen her. Though they were unlikely to mention it, she had felt the weight of clandestine eyes upon her.

She glanced around the ballroom as they strolled toward the punch bowl, wondering if James Hunter was still there, watching her. When her eye caught Miss Metcalfe dancing a lively reel with an eager young man, she was suddenly struck with a memory. Metcalfe! Was that not a name she'd heard before? A man who had been a friend of Mr. Henley and who had been at that scandalous tableau?

"Harriett, what can you tell me about Miss Metcalfe?" she asked. "Does she have family?"

"Goodness, yes! A handsome brother by the name of Stanley."

"Is he here tonight?"

Hortense craned her neck to look about in one direction while Harriett scanned the other. "I do not see him. Come to think of it, Harri, have we seen him at all in the last few weeks?"

Harriett chortled. "No, but it does not matter. I do not think he would suit you, Gina."

"Oh?"

"He is engaged to a dear friend of ours. Miss Christina Race. Have you met her?"

Gina shook her head. In truth, she'd met very few people since arriving in London.

"She and Missy have been almost inseparable since the engagement, have they not, Hortense?"

Hortense nodded. "Like peas in a pod. Would you like to meet them? The reel is almost over and I believe I saw Christina near the fireplace."

Her heart beating harder, Gina donned an airy smile. "That would be lovely. The more people I meet, the less you will have to coddle me."

"Pshaw!" Harriett laughed. "We adore coddling you, Gina. Why, introducing a pretty newcomer lends us a certain mystery and importance we do not possess on our own."

Gina laughed. She had noted how many heads the twins had turned, and not just because they were identical. They certainly did not need an unknown newcomer to gain attention.

The twins flanked her as they headed toward the fireplace at one end of the ballroom, nodding at acquaintances as they passed. Their progress was slow and perfectly timed to coincide with the end of the reel.

Gina had been watching the dancers and when they stopped she turned her attention back to the group at the fireplace. Surprise coupled with a twist of her stomach shot through her. There stood a lovely woman of average height with glossy black hair and eyes nearly as dark. Her fair complexion deepened with the pink of a blush as she recognized Gina's face. The woman from the tableau—and she was engaged to Mr. Metcalfe!

Hortense performed the introduction. "Miss Eugenia O'Rourke, I am pleased to present our dearest friend, Miss Christina Race. Miss Race, please meet Miss O'Rourke."

Gina noted the tiny plea in those eyes. Clearly the woman did not want to acknowledge their previous acquaintance. How could they ever explain that away? She took a deep breath. "Miss Race, how nice to make your acquaintance. I pray you will not hold these two against me," she said with a nod toward the twins.

The woman smiled and squeezed Gina's hand in gratitude. "If you will do the same, Miss O'Rourke."

Harriett arched one elegant eyebrow. "Come now. Our reputations are not quite that bad."

Laughing and jesting with a young man over her shoulder, Miss Metcalfe returned from the dance floor and was quickly introduced. "O'Rourke? Is your sister the one who finally tamed Lord Libertine?"

Gina frowned, unfamiliar with the title.

Hortense laughed. "She means Andrew Hunter, Gina. That was our pet name for him until your sister domesticated him."

She smiled. "Yes, then. Isabella married Mr. Hunter and they seem quite content."

Miss Metcalfe sighed as she fanned herself. "That gives the rest of us hope, then. If he succumbed to the parson's mousetrap, there can be hope that one of us might yet snare James or Charles Hunter."

"I…I wouldn't know, Miss Metcalfe."

"Yet I saw you dance with James," she said, almost like an accusation. "That is, until he sneaked you out to the garden."

Gina was taken aback by the woman's bluntness. "He was doing his duty to me, Miss Metcalfe. And reminding me to mind my manners."

Miss Metcalfe fell silent after Gina's rejoinder and Hortense introduced her companion. "Miss O'Rourke, may I present Mr. Adam Booth? Mr. Booth, please meet Miss O'Rourke."

The man bent over her hand and a flicker of something passed through his eyes as he straightened and met her gaze. "Have we met, Miss O'Rourke? I could swear I've seen those remarkable eyes before."

He'd been at the tableau. Had he been at the ritual? She slowly withdrew her hand from his and forced a smile. "You are too kind, Mr. Booth. I doubt we have met since I have not been much in society. In any case, I am certain I'd have remembered a gentleman as handsome as you."

He grinned and the tension went out of his posture. "Well, I shan't forget you again, Miss O'Rourke. Alas, I must be off to meet friends but I pray you will save me a dance 'til the next time we meet." He bowed over her hand.

She gave him a stiff smile. Had there been something familiar in his request, or was she being overly sensitive? "I shall look forward to it, Mr. Booth."

Alone now, the ladies proceeded to discuss Mr. Booth and his various attributes—the width of his shoulders, the color of his gray-blue eyes, the size of his…bank account. Gina relaxed, the conversation so similar to those she'd had with her sisters long before any of them married.

"And you, Miss O'Rourke? Who do you prefer?" Miss Race asked.

"I am far too new to the scene to have a preference," she said, though Jamie Hunter's face came to mind.

"My dear," Harriett said, "I know just what you mean. Why, if Miss Race hadn't already taken Mr. Metcalfe, I might cast my cap in that direction."

Gina seized that opportunity. "When am I to meet Mr. Metcalfe?"

Missy Metcalfe rolled her eyes heavenward. "I can't imagine where he's been keeping himself. Between his friends and his club, we scarcely see him at home anymore. Why, Christina sees him more than we."

They all turned to Miss Race for confirmation.

"I, uh, did see him earlier tonight. I believe he said he was gambling with a few of his friends."

"Men," Hortense said, as if that explained everything.

Miss Race drew herself up as if she'd made a sudden decision. "Accompany me to the ladies' retiring room, Miss O'Rourke? I'd love to hear about your native land. I've never been to Ireland, though Stanley and I have discussed taking our wedding trip there." She linked arms with Gina, leading her away from the group.

When they were out of hearing, Miss Race pulled Gina into a private corner. "I must thank you for not giving me away. I saw that you recognized me, too, and I prayed you would not mention it to the others."

Gina gave a self-deprecating laugh. "I'd have had to give myself away, Miss Race, and I was not about to do that."

"Call me Christina," she said before rushing on. "And I want to assure you that I do not frequent such places as the one where we first met. Stanley had been invited by some of his friends and did not understand the sort of…affair it was to be, or he swears he never would have taken me. And I…

well, I could see that you were not accustomed to such things either."

"I had never seen a complete stranger unclothed before. But to do so in such a public manner, and in such a pose, was a great surprise to me."

"Wicked London," Christina murmured. "There is quite a different world here than the one we inhabit, Miss O'Rourke."

She weighed the risk of mentioning Mr. Henley so soon, but she hadn't much time herself. "You must call me Gina, then. Meeting you has been quite fortuitous. You see, I am actually looking for some of the people in our group that night."

The woman shuddered. "Why?"

"I lost something that night, and I believe one of them might have it, or know where it is."

"I cannot recall anyone finding something that night. But I wish you luck of it, Gina, and I must say I admire your courage. For myself, I hope never to see any of them again."

"Oh. I understand." Gina turned away.

"I did not mean you!" Christina stayed her with a hand on her arm. "Is there anything I can do to help?"

"Did you know them all—the people in our group?"

She shook her head and looked down at the floor as if searching her mind. "That was the first time I stole away to go anywhere privately with Stanley. I did not know many of his friends, then, and I have not seen those particular ones since. Most were like you, complete strangers."

"Would you ask Mr. Metcalfe if he remembers that night, and who was there? If he would be willing to meet with me, perhaps I could persuade him to help."

Christina looked doubtful. "I shall ask him, of course, but I think he'd rather leave that night in the distant past."

"Tell him that I urgently and desperately need his help. Tell him that my entire future depends upon it."

Christina searched her face and then nodded. "My goodness! What did you lose?"

"Something irreplaceable. Something I must recover."

"But of course I shall tell him, my dear. The very next time I see him."

"Tomorrow?" she urged.

"I… Yes. Are you going to the Albermarle crush Tuesday next?"

She recalled seeing that name in the calendar and stack of invitations Lady Sarah had given her and nodded.

"I shall ask him to accompany me there."

"Thank you." Gina squeezed her arm in gratitude.

Chapter Five

Jamie seized the reins again and swung up into his saddle. He hadn't wanted to disturb Devlin Farrell tonight, but now it couldn't be helped. The brazen attack on his life had raised too many questions that only Farrell could answer.

The butler left Jamie to cool his heels in Farrell's study, so he helped himself to a small glass of sherry and took the liberty of pouring one for Devlin. His nerves needed steadying. The warmth from the alcohol had just begun to untwist the knots in his stomach when Devlin entered the study, barefooted, his hair tousled, and still securing his dressing robe.

Jamie was amused to note the lack of a nightshirt where the robe gaped. From the expression on Devlin's flushed face, he gathered he hadn't exactly been sleeping. "Sorry," he said as Devlin downed the contents of the waiting glass and glowered at him.

"I gather this is more important than what I was doing?"

Jamie grinned. "That would depend upon your priorities, I suppose. My life?"

Devlin looked him up and down. "You seem none the worse for wear."

"I was fortunate. Even so, I barely ducked in time."

"Ducked? A pistol?"

"One very good shot."

"Not good enough," Devlin said, filling Jamie's glass.

"Oh, it was good enough. But there was something not quite right that put me on my guard just in time."

"Thank God for your instincts," Devlin murmured.

"So, it seems your intelligence was right. There actually is a price on my head. Though I think we both know the answer, I'd like confirmation of who is behind it. And, if possible, who was foolhardy enough to attempt it."

"The Gibbons brothers?"

Jamie shook his head. "I didn't smell them." But he'd been uncertain enough not to follow the shooter down the alley where an accomplice might be waiting. Somewhere in the back of his mind, he must have suspected something of the sort.

Devlin was silent for a few moments, an expression of concentration on his face. "I can think of a few more who might take that chance, Hunter. But I doubt they'd own it. I know your principles, and I know you'd need proof before you'd take action, and proof will not exist for such a deed. If the man had a partner, we could…convince his partner to talk. But if he is acting alone…"

"Given the circumstances, I doubt anyone would act alone," Jamie growled. "Have a word with old Cox, will you? Someone has gotten to him. I don't know if it was a bribe or a threat, but I'd stake my life that he knew what was afoot."

"Cox?" Devlin had stiffened and Jamie knew he was angry. Cox was Devlin's employee, and he'd be furious that the man would compromise his position. "What makes you think so?"

"When I went for my horse, he was behaving strangely. Wouldn't meet my eyes. 'Twas one of the things that warned me that things were not what they should be."

Devlin gave a grim nod. "Rest assured, Cox and I will have a chat first thing in the morning. I am certain he will be pleased to share whatever information he has."

Jamie could guess how "pleased" Cox would be by the time Devlin was through with him. "And you, Dev? Have you heard anything?"

"Nothing helpful. One of the lads reported seeing Henley in the rookeries. Said he appeared to have money and was dressed like the fop he is. The lad lost him before he could find out where his quarters are."

"Not helpful? To the contrary. That information confirms my suspicions. Henley has not left the country, and he has someone helping him if he has access to money and is well groomed. That means he has decent accommodations somewhere. And if he can lose your 'lads,' he hasn't let his guard down." He hesitated on his way to the door. The next bit of business was delicate, to say the least. "Dev, if you had a sister…"

"For God's sake! Have you got some poor girl in trouble?"

Jamie laughed. "Never. But your wife has sisters, eh? And if you had reason to think one of them might be in danger, what would you do?"

He studied Jamie for one long moment. "Miss Eugenia?"

"Perhaps."

"Who else? Your only sister is married to a man more than capable of taking good care of her. Drew would slice the hands off anyone who'd touch Isabella, and I'd do much worse, believe me, to anyone who would raise a voice to Lilly. The only sister left is Eugenia."

"After months as a recluse, she has decided all of a sudden that it is time for her to enter society."

"Miss Eugenia? Timid little mouse?"

Jamie sighed. "You do not know her if that is what you think, Devlin. Before that night at the chapel, she was full of fire and sparkle. I gave thought to…well, never mind. Any chance of that is past. But now she is venturing out into the same society that Henley and the rest belonged. You mentioned Metcalfe and Booth. I pray you are right about them— that they were not a part of the Brotherhood, but had only been invited to the ritual that night. But I worry that someone else, someone we don't know, could recognize her."

"I see the problem. They'd want to put her out of the way so she couldn't identify them. Have you talked to her?"

"She is determined. She will not listen to reason. You've seen her, Dev. You know what a beauty she is. She cannot help but draw attention. There is, quite literally, no way to keep her contained."

"One way. But it falls to you or Charlie."

Jamie nodded, already knowing what he was going to say. He'd hoped Devlin would know of another way, a safer way.

"Dog her footsteps. Wherever she goes, be there, too. It should not delay you long. Lilly told me that her mother is going back to Belfast in a fortnight and Miss Eugenia with her."

"How can I keep her safe when someone is shooting at me?"

Devlin chortled. "I doubt you will be following her to the parts of London you were in tonight. And once she is safely abed, you'll be free to follow your leads. A few hours a night for a fortnight. That cannot be too much a chore."

"Perhaps I could trade off with Charlie to keep her from

getting suspicious. I do not like to think what she would do if she suspected we were watching her."

"Charlie?" Devlin laughed. "If you turn a woman like Miss Eugenia over to your brother, you're not the man I thought you were."

The next night, Jamie blessed his sister and her penchant for writing things down. Taking Devlin's suggestion to heart, all he'd had to do was call on her this afternoon, ask her for a cough tonic, and then take a quick look through the papers on her little desk while she was in the kitchen concocting the brew. His hunch had been right. Sarah was easing Eugenia's way into society, using the Thayer twins as her companions for meeting the "right" people.

Now, there in the midst of the Albermarle ballroom, shining brighter than any crystal chandelier, and right where his sister's notes said she would be, was Miss Eugenia. Despite the crush of people, he had spotted her within seconds of entering.

Yes, he had Eugenia's complete schedule for the next fortnight. Convenient. And it barely troubled his conscience at all. Sarah would never know. And it wasn't as if he wanted the information for nefarious purposes. Quite the opposite. He could not keep her at home, nor could he let her wander into disaster, so following her was the only way to safeguard her. And there was no sense in hiding it since she would soon suspect something of the sort. He might as well throw down the gauntlet.

As he approached her group, peopled by the crème de la crème of the ton, he noted that she was even more stunning tonight than last night. Her gown was of a deep violet watered silk. A row of tiny leaves had been embroidered at the hem and décolletage. A matching neck band displaying a perfect oval amethyst hid her scar, and she looked as untouched and

serene as a Madonna. How was it possible that she grew love-
lier each time he saw her?

As if she could feel the weight of his eyes, she turned to
him. A fleeting smile curved her lips, then died as if she had
remembered something unpleasant. He hid his disappointment
as he approached the group.

Harriett Thayer was the first to acknowledge him. "Mr.
Hunter! How delightful. We so rarely see you, and here, two
nights in a row, we are fortunate enough to encounter you. To
what do we owe this rare pleasure?" Her smile was coy and
her eyes slid toward Miss Eugenia. Harriett, at least, suspected
the real reason for his being there.

He smiled as a few of the young men bowed and wandered
away, unsure which of his varied reputations was responsible.
"Why, to your charming company, ladies. What else could
lure a gentleman out on a cold night?"

"Then we shall require you to warm yourself by dancing
with all of us," Hortense teased. "There is a scandalous lack
of eligible men here tonight."

"Then you first, Miss…Hortense?"

She took his offered hand. "How very clever of you, Mr.
Hunter. Most people cannot tell us apart."

"I am observant, m'dear. Under ordinary circumstances, I
cannot tell you apart, but I know, for instance, that you have
a charming little quirk of raising your right eyebrow. When
Miss Harriett attempts it, her left eyebrow raises."

"The mirror effect," she said with a little laugh. "Drat! We
have been found out, Harri."

He led her to the dance floor where a lively reel was in
progress. Both Misses Thayer were excellent partners, quick,
supple and skilled. The pace kept them apart quite a bit and
spared him the necessity of making mundane conversation.
When he returned her to her friends, he claimed Miss Harriett
for a stately march.

"I conceive you have an interest in our Miss O'Rourke, do you not?" she asked when they met for a bow.

"I own it. She is family now, you know."

"I mean beyond that, Mr. Hunter. You do not look at her as a brother would."

Denial was useless, but perhaps he could manage her suspicions of his reasons. "Your perception astounds me, Miss Harriett. Will you expose me?"

"Tout au contraire!" She gave him a saucy wink. "I shall do all I can to encourage her. Not for your sake, Mr. Hunter, but for the good of all womankind."

"How would such a suit serve the good of all womankind?"

"Cupid's arrow has already brought your brothers Lockwood and Andrew down. Should you follow, I vow that women of the ton would be vastly encouraged. Yes, women everywhere would take heart that *any* man can be caught."

He laughed at her outrageous analysis of the situation, though he realized there was a grain of truth in it. He and his brothers had all been single far too long, and he was apt to remain so for a good deal longer than Miss Harriett suspected.

When he returned Miss Harriett to her companions, there was another young lady he had not met. Miss Hortense performed the introduction to Miss Christina Race. She was a darkly ethereal woman, as quiet and composed as the deep green gown she wore. When he bowed over her hand, she returned his smile.

He watched Miss Eugenia from the corner of his eye, noting that she looked anxious. Was she concerned that he would not mind his manners? No. She knew him well enough by now to know he would not embarrass Miss Race.

He led her onto the dance floor for a quadrille and attempted polite conversation as they met, parted and met again. "I believe we have been previously introduced, Miss Race?"

"I do not think so, Mr. Hunter. I am certain I would have remembered."

"Then how is your face familiar?"

"'Twould not be so odd, sir, as we frequent the same events. Perhaps you have seen me across a room? Perhaps at the punch bowl? Or perhaps we have passed in the street?"

He conceded the point, though he still suspected they knew each other in some manner or another. "How have you fallen into such bad company as the Thayers and Miss O'Rourke?"

She laughed softly and he was enchanted by the sound. "I have known Hortense and Harriett for quite some time. Our families are connected. I have only just met Miss O'Rourke."

"Tell me what you think of her."

He sensed a slight stiffening in her frame as he passed her beneath his arm. "She is quite agreeable. In fact, she has requested that I join their group tonight. I think we shall get along famously."

Miss Eugenia requested? An innocent enough way to meet and become acquainted with new people, though he could not help but think she was up to something. Miss Eugenia was not random in her actions.

The dance ended and Jamie's anger rose when he returned Miss Race only to find that Miss Eugenia had disappeared. She'd known she was next and had tried to subvert him. How little she knew of his determination! It would take more than she was capable of to keep him from his purpose.

"Miss O'Rourke offers her apologies, but she was…ah, fatigued and has gone to the ladies' retiring room," Miss Harriett explained.

Harriett Thayer was not a good liar. He smiled, offered a

bow, and excused himself to take up station at the corridor leading to the ladies' retiring room.

Before long, and thinking she was now safe, Miss Eugenia rounded the corner on her way back to her friends. He fell into step beside her and took her arm, guiding her back toward the ballroom. "Ah, my patience has rewarded me. How could I possibly leave without our dance?"

Gina covered her astonishment as best she could. She'd been so sure she'd evaded him. He was more patient than she had thought. "I confess to a certain curiosity, Mr. Hunter. Have you always been quite this…social? Or is this a new habit?"

He laughed. "You have me there, although I do tend to be more social than my brothers. And, when there is something to interest me, I am positively unshakable."

"Hmm. So then am I to gather that you are testing the boundaries of our truce? Or are you sweet on someone here?"

"Both, if I am to be honest. And, since it is my fate to dote upon someone who hates me, if you refuse me I shall be quite inconsolable."

He led her into the strains of a waltz and Gina sighed. She was glad he had saved their dance for last. Oh, she had dreaded it, and had even tried to avoid it, but now that the inevitable had happened, she found her excitement rising. James Hunter always made her feel as if she were about to embark on an exciting adventure.

"So thoughtful, Miss O'Rourke? Or are you anxious to return to your friends?"

"They are quite diverting," she allowed, but she was more concerned with keeping him away from Miss Race. If he made the connection between the girl and the Brotherhood, he would instantly know what she was doing. And yet, she could not help but ask, "Had you not met Miss Race before?"

A brief look of uncertainty passed over his features. "I had not had that pleasure. I must say she is quite lovely. I find it difficult to believe I managed to miss her before."

"Connoisseur of lovely women that you are?"

He laughed and swung her in a wide circle. "Are you calling me conceited, Miss O'Rourke?"

"Heaven forbid! Fickle, perhaps…"

"For what it is worth, I rank you among the loveliest to grace the ton, Miss O'Rourke. And by my reckoning, you are generating a good deal of interest."

The hair raised on the back of Gina's neck. She had felt the stares, but she suspected they were for a different reason, and likely from men who had seen her naked on a stone altar. And interest was not what she wanted to generate. She'd rather blend into the background—the better to overhear snippets of conversation that could be of help to her.

"There is that look again," Mr. Hunter said. "The one that tells me I've said something wrong."

"Not wrong, Mr. Hunter. It is just that…well, I do not want to generate interest."

"Then why have you come out in society?"

"I…I thought I should experience London before returning to Ireland."

His eyes narrowed and he drew her off the dance floor. "That is a bare-faced lie, Miss O'Rourke. It was a lie the first time you told it, and it is now. I would hazard you have experienced more than enough of London."

She gasped at his sudden fierceness. "The wrong London. I wanted to take a happier memory home with me."

He took her hand and led her into the famed Albermarle gardens among dozens of strolling couples. Still, it was more private than the ballroom. He found them a bench surrounded by sculpted evergreens and gestured for her to sit. As much as she would have liked to return to the ballroom, she followed his direction.

"Now, Miss O'Rourke," he began as he stood in front of her, one foot propped on the bench next to her hip, as if to keep her from bolting. "I know you are up to something. Do not bother to deny it."

"Really, sir. I needn't explain myself to you."

"You are going to explain to someone. Me or Andrew. Or better yet, your mother."

Gina shuddered. Her mother would have hysterics followed by locking Gina in her room until their return to Ireland. "I've told you the truth before. I am tired of hiding in fear. I will not live the rest of my life locked away or shunning society. I've done nothing wrong."

"Apart from sneaking out and joining in fast company to go places no decently brought-up young woman should ever go? Apart from keeping company with the likes of Henley? Apart, even, from nearly getting yourself killed?"

She had underestimated his anger. And he had misjudged hers. He had backed her into a corner, and he was going to pay the consequences of that. "Are you saying that I am to blame for what happened to me?"

"Only in that you made a series of wrong decisions for all the right reasons. But you cannot ignore the fact that you are a female, with all the vulnerabilities of that sex."

"I am not ignoring it, but I will not allow it to prevent me from doing what I must."

"And what is that, Miss O'Rourke?"

"Talk to people, discover if anyone knows what has become of Mr. Henley. See to it that he is captured and punished."

"Even if that means exposing your…"

Gina's stomach turned. Exposing her shame? The fact that she had been splayed on a stone altar? That she was to have been raped and killed for the titillation of dissolute men? No! Dear Lord, no. She did not want any of it made public. But if she was not willing to risk that, Henley was sure to get away with what he'd done to her and countless others. "Even then," she confirmed, keeping her voice steady and determined.

He looked into her eyes, measuring her determination. "Miss O'Rourke, the Home Office is doing all it can. How can you think you will succeed where they have not?"

"For precisely that reason. They have *not* succeeded. How can I possibly do worse? And how can I return to Ireland knowing that vile man is still free? Free to come after me. Free to debauch other innocent women."

"You think we failed you." Anger coupled with something darker crossed his handsome features. "Then surely you can see the folly in putting yourself in harm's way."

"Mr. Henley is in hiding. He is no threat to me as long as I am in society because he will not risk being seen. I only want to discover if anyone knows where he can be found. I promise you, Mr. Hunter, I will give you that information the moment I have it."

"You will..." He looked at her in disbelief and raked his fingers through his dark hair. "Damn it, the only thing you should do is go home to Ireland!"

She stood and turned toward the terrace doors and the ballroom. She hadn't taken more than a single step when he seized her arm and spun her around as he stepped forward. The momentum landed her squarely against his chest and she was forced to look up to see his expression—fury and frustration. "I don't give a fig where you think I should go!" she exclaimed.

"Don't you see the danger? Don't you know what the mere sight of you does to a man?"

She opened her mouth to ask what he meant, but it was too late. His left arm went around her to hold her captive while his right hand cupped the back of her head, preventing her from turning away.

His mouth came down on hers with desperation she could feel in every line of his body. His lips were challenging, not punishing. They were firm, warm and tinged with sweet wine. His tongue slipped along the seam of her lips, urging hers to open. Not knowing why, she did, and his moan was the answer. She brought her fists up, intending to push him away, but her hands opened and slipped around his neck. She had never felt anything as exciting as this before and she was dizzy with the heady sensation.

Surer now, more confident, he softened his assault to coax an answering moan from her. She scarcely recognized her own voice in that sigh. He pulled her closer, pressing her along the length of him until she could feel something as firm and unyielding as his chest pressing against her lower abdomen. Oh, how she wanted more of that feeling! Encouraged, he deepened the kiss and Gina knew she was being branded, claimed, owned entirely by this man. Only James Hunter could have robbed her of the will to resist.

Heavenly and wicked at the same time. Now she understood. She couldn't move, couldn't break the spell of his arms, and she didn't want to. No, she never wanted this kiss to end. She was breathless at the way her breasts tingled as they pressed against his chest and at the way a needful ache bloomed where his erection burned into her. She wanted him. She needed him.

He released her with a choked groan and stepped back, leaving her to stagger without his support. "You…you have my apologies, Miss O'Rourke."

She spun around and ran for the terrace door. He must never know what that kiss had done to her. Never see it in her eyes or read it on her face. She'd been ready to surrender everything to him when he'd only kissed her to shut her up or teach her a lesson. Well, he'd never have that opportunity again!

Chapter Six

Gina was certain there was some trace of that kiss visible to the guests in the ballroom. She was changed somehow, and there would have to be a sign of that. She glanced toward Hortense and Harriett, who were laughing and fanning themselves flirtatiously while engaged in conversation with at least five young men. How could she join them when her heart was still racing so?

She glanced around for a familiar face, someone she could talk to. Where had Miss Race gone? She'd promised to bring Mr. Metcalfe. A quick glance around the ballroom revealed that the girl was not dancing. In fact, she could find no trace of her. Surely she wouldn't have left without a word?

A flash of green caught her attention and she watched as Miss Race entered the ballroom from a terrace door. She paused to pat her hair into place and sweep a gaze about the room. When she saw Gina, she gave a small smile and a nod as she came toward her.

She was flushed when she took Gina's hand and led her

into the corridor. "I looked for you, Gina, but you disappeared. Stanley was here, but he could not stay."

She tried to hide her dismay. "I...I have missed him?"

"He said he knew who you were and was willing to help you, but he does not like to stay too long in any place."

"Has he always been like that, Christina?"

The girl frowned. "Only since...the middle of summer. It is as if he is afraid something will happen if he stays too long."

Could Mr. Metcalfe be trying to avoid Mr. Henley, too? But Mr. Henley would never attend a ball—too brazen, and too many people knew him. Or did Mr. Metcalfe fear the authorities were after him? What a hopeless muddle.

Gina squeezed Christina's hands. "Did he say how he could help me?"

"Oh, yes." She rummaged in her little beaded reticule, pulled a small object out and pressed it into Gina's hand. "I was to give you this, and tell you that he will find you at a more opportune time. I took the liberty of telling him I have been invited to attend the Morris masquerade three days hence, and that you will be there with Hortense and Harriett. He said we should look for a leper."

Leper? That would mean a black hooded robe and bell about his neck. He should be easy enough to find. "Three days? Could I not speak to him sooner?"

"I am afraid not. He said he had much to do. Now, you must excuse me. I should return to my party."

Gina tried to hide her impatience as Christina hurried away to join a group of young people who were preparing to leave. Almost forgotten in her disappointment, she looked down and opened her hand. A key? Pray, what did it open?

Throw down the gauntlet? What a bloody good idea that turned out to be! Instead of basking in triumph with little

Miss Eugenia packing for home, Jamie was the one who'd been defeated with a kiss and at the mercy of a sweet-smelling nymph who gave as good as she got. Gave better, actually. And the accusation that the Home Office—*he*—had failed her ripped through his heart. It was bad enough to fear it himself, but to hear her say it was a confirmation of all his worst fears.

He riffled through the papers on his desk at the Home Office looking for his notes, certain there would be something to either bolster his case or tell him where Henley was hiding. Fast. He had to end this before Henley came after Eugenia. There had to be something he had overlooked. Something so subtle that it had escaped him.

"Good Lord! You take to abandoning me at balls and I find you working into the wee hours! What has happened to you, Jamie? All work and no play is not like you."

He glanced up to see Charlie leaning against the doorjamb, his arms folded over his chest and looking for all the world as if he'd just slept twelve hours. "Not like *you*," Jamie corrected. "What are *you* are doing here—and do not tell me you were trying to find me."

Charlie shrugged and came to sit in the chair across the desk from him. "My mind wanders. You know how easily bored I am. And I'm looking for company. I hate to carouse alone."

Jamie finally pushed his papers aside and gave his brother his attention. "You haven't been carousing, Charlie. You're far too fresh for that. Come clean."

He grinned. "Not precisely carousing. But I've certainly been in that part of town. I met Devlin at the Crown and Bear."

"Lilly will not thank you for leading him astray."

"Me? Perish the thought. I am merely learning from the master."

"Master of what? Are you taking up a life of crime?"

His grin faded as he sat forward in his chair. "I am trying to decipher Devlin's sources, his network of informants. Alas, I lack his reputation to give strength to my requests, but I am gaining ground there."

"I wonder if I should ask what is required to become credible to that lot of scoundrels."

"I wouldn't. Not for the squeamish." Charlie quirked an eyebrow.

"I should also warn you to be prepared for rumors concerning Miss O'Rourke and me."

Charlie blinked, then shook his head. "You had me there for a minute. I almost thought you, of all people, had found the 'one.' Well, never mind. So you want society to *think* you're courting? Is Miss O'Rourke going along with this?"

"She will likely be quite distressed when she learns of it. But my requests that she stay at home and be protected have fallen on deaf ears. She intends to ask her own questions and meddle in Home Office business. Henley will be looking for a way to get at her. She is one of the last who could testify against him—that he drugged and kidnapped her."

"So you intend to hang on her every word? Discourage any other suitors? Make it impossible for her to locate Henley?"

"Precisely."

"And if she sends you away?"

"I shall stand fast."

"You know what society will say about this affair, do you not? That you are beyond smitten, and that the O'Rourke girl has made a jackanapes of you."

Jamie laughed. "Not to my face, they won't."

"Ah," Charlie said, "and this will work well into your usual scheme, will it not? In seasons to come, it will be whispered that your heart is broken and no marriage-minded chit should set her cap for you. Damn clever."

"My usual scheme?"

"Your reputation in the ton, Jamie. Nary an ingenue nor a courtesan has held your attention long. 'Tis just a matter of time before you move along to the next entertainment."

He forced a grin and a shrug. "You will not give me away?"

"Never! Furthermore, I shall join you in your game. I do not intend to let you go about alone at night again. Whoever wants you dead will not have an easy time of it."

"Or Henley will get two Hunters for the price of one."

"I am so pleased that you let the gentlemen go off to their club after church," Mama announced as they sat down to the table and shook her napkin out to lay it across her lap. "Now it is just me and all my girls. Well, the ones I have left." She sniffled and touched her handkerchief to the corners of her eyes.

Gina shot a quick glance at her sisters and noted that both Bella and Lilly did the same. By their tense expressions, she realized they all feared that Mama was winding up for a bout of hysteria.

"But enough of that," Mama continued, laying their fears to rest. "We all miss Cora dreadfully, but we must accept God's will. I am simply grateful for the opportunity to have my little family all to myself. There are things we must discuss. Plans to form and decisions to be made."

"There is time for that, Mama," Bella said as a maid served a platter of cold sliced meat.

"Not much time at all, dear. Less than a fortnight. 'Twould be sooner if I could arrange it."

Ten days, by Gina's reckoning, counting this one. Yes, she was painfully aware of the ticking of the clock. Ten days to find Henley. Ten days to avenge Cora and reclaim her own future.

"And we must look to the future. I will scarce be settled at home when I will have to come back here. March, will it not be, Bella?"

"M-March?" Her sister colored a most interesting shade of fuchsia.

"Oh, do not deny it," their mother smirked. "I know my daughters. Your husband did not waste much time getting an heir on you. You shall have an early spring babe. And I know a girl wants her mother at such a time. Never fear, Bella. I shall be here for you."

Bella looked at Gina and Lilly for help, but as Bella did not deny their mother's conclusion, there was nothing they could say.

"And Lilly, you shall not be far behind, I think. From the look of that strapping husband of yours, I would not be surprised to welcome twins by summer."

"Mother, we have been married little more than a week!"

"Aye, it does not take long. My girls will be no less fertile than I. And your husband looks no less virile than Bella's. Boys, I'd warrant. A great pity your father will not be here to see it. He always wanted sons."

"Then perhaps you should stay rather than go and have to return so soon," Bella offered. "Andrew has often said you are welcome to stay as long as you please."

"Aye, but we cannot leave our home in Belfast vacant so long. The servants will be stealing us blind. No, we must return as soon as may be, and Gina will have to stay there when I return in the spring. Someone must watch over the house."

Lilly raised her eyebrows and leaned forward as she spoke. "But you cannot leave Gina alone, Mama. A single woman…"

"Faugh! Gina is a spinster now. Both older and younger

sisters are married. No one is like to offer for her now. She may as well make herself useful."

Gina was astonished. It had never occurred to her that her own mother would consider her little better than an unpaid companion.

"And she is scarred, besides," Mama continued. She turned to look at Gina with a frown. "You were never clumsy before, child. Falling on the stairs and cutting yourself with a broken glass—why, I never heard of such a thing happening before to any of my girls. And now you must cover it whenever you go about in public. I am certain you would much rather not leave the house. Yes, you will be more comfortable at home. In Belfast."

Gina's hand went to her throat as it always did at any mention of her scar. The story they'd told their mother about how it had happened was a bit flimsy, but she had believed it, nonetheless.

"Mama!" Lilly protested. "Gina is in her prime, and the physician said the scar will fade with time."

Bella nodded. "Lady Sarah has said that Gina is a great success in society. Why, a few young men have asked after her. If you must return to Belfast, you should leave Gina here with us."

She was warmed by her sisters' defense, though she doubted Bella's veracity. Who would have asked after her? She'd only danced with a handful of young men.

Mama shrugged. "What? Leave her with *you*? And no one to guide her? Why, Mr. Hunter and Mr. Farrell are hardly the sort to look after a young girl."

A young girl? Moments ago she'd been a spinster. Gina sighed as the simple truth dawned on her. Mama did not want to be alone. She did not want the last of her daughters to be out of reach. And Mama was likely to do anything she could to keep Gina by her side and at her beck and call.

"Mama—" Lilly began.

"Gina is coming home with me, and that is an end to it." Mama waved one hand in dismissal of the subject.

The remainder of lunch was punctuated with sighs and awkward spurts of bland conversation while Gina felt as if she might jump out of her skin. The future her mother had mapped out for her was never one she would have chosen. One, in fact, she found abhorrent and, in its own way, terrifying. But given her circumstances, and if she could not find the answers she sought, it would be the only course open to her.

She wouldn't give up yet, though. She still had ten days and she would make the most of them. Regardless of Mr. Renquist and the Home Office, she would just have to take matters into her own hands.

Her mother excused herself, declaring that she was quite fatigued and needed a nap. The table fell silent until they heard a door close somewhere above them.

"Gina, did you know what she planned?" Lilly asked.

She shook her head, still a bit stunned.

"We must find some way to divert her," Bella mumbled.

"It is hopeless, and you know it. When Mama has made up her mind, nothing can change it. Nothing will do but that she have her way."

"But you have not…"

"Escaped?" Gina smiled and looked down at her plate, largely untouched. "Perhaps I could learn to bear that, but I cannot resign myself to the thought that Mr. Henley will not pay for what he has done. That is the one task I cannot leave undone."

Bella's eyes darkened as she sat forward. "I've seen that look before. What are you planning, Gina?"

"I hardly know. I have made some headway amongst the ton, but progress is slow. I am to meet with Mr. Renquist tomorrow for his report. And…" she hesitated, reluctant to tell them about the little key "…and there has to be more I can do. Other ways to learn what I need."

Lilly dropped her napkin on her plate and glanced over her shoulder before lowering her voice to a whisper. "If you are game, Gina, I may have an idea. There were some street urchins—lads, Devlin called them—who helped find the evidence against the Brotherhood. They are quite engaging little pickpockets and, for a few coins, they could discover anything."

"I vow I am not going to turn any source away."

Lilly nodded and stood, determination in her voice. "I know just where to find them on a Sunday afternoon. Bella, you stay here and if the men return, tell them Gina and I have gone for a stroll through the park and shall be back presently. Gina, fetch your bonnet and shawl."

Gina glanced around the square at Covent Garden, almost as busy as Hyde Park on a summer afternoon, unable to shake the feeling that she was being watched. "How will we ever find them?" she asked Lilly.

"Just dangle your reticule from your wrist and they will come along. Walk slowly and smile as if you have nothing more on your mind than meeting friends. Ned will find us."

"What will your husband say?"

Lilly laughed. "He would likely ask how much we paid them, and then tell me it was too much."

"He will not be angry?"

"Not in the least. But I do not intend to tell him."

"Why?"

"Because I do not know if I can trust him not to tell Andrew or Jamie. Am I correct in thinking you would not want them to know?"

Gina grinned. "Oh, yes. Andrew would take his duty as

my closest male relative to heart and forbid me to do more than drink tea and embroider. I thought Devlin might be the same."

Lilly's eyes twinkled. "Devlin is far too protective, but he admires women who can think for themselves. Still, he would not want you to endanger yourself. Ah, but how can hiring a few lads endanger you? No, I think we are safe in this."

Gina was not nearly as worried about what Andrew or Devlin would do as she was about another man. "M-most importantly, I do not want James Hunter to know. He told me last night that, if he had his way, I would return to Belfast at once."

Lilly's eyebrows shot up. "No! He would not be so ungentlemanly."

"He was not in a gentlemanly mood. I am afraid he knows I am looking for Mr. Henley. And I might have suggested that I could hardly do worse than the Home Office."

"Oh, my!" Lilly did her best to contain her laughter. "I can imagine how he took that. Whatever possessed you to make that charge?"

"I cannot recall. Our conversations tend to deteriorate after a moment or two. It would be best if we simply avoided one another as much as possible, but he has decided to take my safety upon himself. Quite aggravating."

"I wish you luck, Gina. Knowing the Hunter men, you will need it."

Gina felt a tug on her arm and turned in time to see a ragged child trying to cut her purse strings. "Here now!"

Lilly peered around her. "Let loose, Ned."

"Mrs. Lilly! This a friend of yers?"

"My sister."

The lad released his hold on Gina's reticule, removed his cap and swept an exaggerated bow. "At yer service, Miss Sister."

"Miss Eugenia," Lilly corrected. "And we were looking for you, Ned, and some of your mates."

"Got a job fer us, Mrs. Lilly?"

"Indeed we have. But I shall let my sister tell you what she needs. Whatever she pays you, Ned, I shall double it if you deliver."

The boy grinned ear to ear. "You know I will, missus." He turned to Gina. "What do y' need, Miss Eugenia?"

"The location of a man named Cyril Henley."

"Gor! 'E's the one we looked fer before, missus."

"He escaped the net we cast, Ned. But his mates were brought in. He's the last of them."

Ned nodded. "I already knowed he got away, missus. I spotted 'im a couple days ago and told Mr. Farrell. 'E's lookin' for the gent, but I didn't know anyone else was lookin' fer him, too."

Gina held her breath. "Do you know where he is?"

"'E lost me, Miss Eugenia. Never knowed a gent so slippery. I recognized 'im from last time, but 'e got away before I could follow 'im back to 'is 'ole. Can I work fer both of ye?"

"I do not object to Mr. Farrell having the information, Ned, but he must not know I have hired you, too."

Ned seemed to consider this for a moment. "Well, since ye ain't askin' me to keep information from 'im, I s'pose there's no 'arm. Mum's the word, miss."

Ignorant of what a pickpocket would charge for such a service, she withdrew a crown from her reticule and pressed it into the grubby hand. "And another when you bring me the information."

The lad looked down at his palm and grinned. "Aye, miss. An' where'll I find ye?"

"You mustn't come to my home. I shall meet you daily at St. Mary's."

Ned glanced at the church on one side of the square and nodded. "Noon too early fer ye?"

"Not in the least."

He tipped his worn cap and gave an awkward bow. "Don't ye worry, miss. We know the warrens like nobody else. We'll 'ave yer gent soon enough. Oh, an' did ye know ye was bein' followed?"

A deep cold invaded her vitals. She scanned the crowd, looking for some sign of someone watching, but nothing appeared amiss. No one betrayed the least interest in her or her sister. Could Ned be wrong?

Chapter Seven

Jamie sipped his wine and allowed the conversation to drift over him as he watched the ladies across the drawing room. Earlier at the dinner table, sitting opposite Miss Eugenia had been a sweet agony of yearning. Each time she brought a spoon to those luscious lips, he remembered how they'd tasted, how they'd felted crushed beneath his own. Though it pained him to admit his own lack of self-control, he knew he'd do it again, given half a chance. And knew, too, that kiss had been the biggest mistake he'd ever made. He'd have been better to imagine it than experience it and yearn for it the rest of his life.

The ladies laughed at something Bella said, and then Miss Eugenia glanced in his direction. Their eyes met for a moment and he held back a groan. He wanted her in a way he'd never wanted any other woman, and with an intensity that left him breathless.

Upon reflection, he realized it was true—what Charlie had said. He had spent his adult life avoiding serious entanglements. He had gone so far as to shun the company of women who would expect more of him. But Miss Eugenia…no, she would be no different. Even as he watched her now, her hand went to her throat, and he knew she was remembering that night. He was a reminder of all she had suffered, of her pain and humiliation. There could never be a future with her.

Ah, but there was the next week or so, until she was whisked back to Ireland. And, torture though it would be, he would avail himself of every opportunity to be near her until then.

"…Cox."

Jamie returned his attention to his own conversation at the mention of that name. "Cox?"

Charlie grinned, as if he knew where Jamie's mind had been. "Were you not paying attention, Jamie? Devlin just told us that his stableman, old Cox, is dead."

"Dead?" Jamie frowned. "Accident?"

"Murder. We found him in a stall. He'd been covered over with hay, but the smell gave him away."

Jamie studied Devlin's face. Had Devlin avenged the attempt on Jamie's life? As usual, Devlin was inscrutable. "Coincidence? Or do you think it had something to do with the other night?"

Devlin's lips twitched, as if he might smile. "It wasn't me, if that's what you're thinking, Hunter. Were I a betting man, I'd wager he was silenced for whatever role he played in that debacle. If he had been paid to help an assassin, it wasn't by me. He'd been carved up like a Christmas goose. It wasn't pretty."

Knife, not a pistol? A pistol was more likely to be a hired killer, but a knife was more…personal. More familiar. Henley was quite proficient with a dagger. But then so were the Gibbons brothers.

He glanced back at Miss Eugenia and a vision of her suffering Cox's fate chilled him to the bone. She could identify

Henley. She could testify against him. Would she be next? Or would he?

Damnation! She had refused to stay safe at home, and he could not let her wander through society indifferent to the danger to her. No simple mooning after her would do. He would have to dog her every footstep. He would have to play the role of her most ardent suitor to keep her close. He would not let her die as Cox had.

It was time to pay the Gibbons brothers a visit. Gina would be safe enough tonight, since Mrs. O'Rourke forbade her girls from entertainments on Sunday nights.

The Gibbons brothers did not have a known address. When Devlin wanted to see them, he merely put the word out and, sooner or later, the brothers turned up at the Crown and Bear. Considering what Jamie suspected, they were not likely to respond this time.

Luckily, he had learned they were known to frequent a flea-infested gin house off Petticoat Lane by the name of the Cat's Paw. He elbowed the door open and eased in, giving his eyes a moment to adjust to the gloom. The odor of unwashed bodies and years of spilled ale and gin was noxious. Behind him, Charlie coughed to cover his disgust and they moved to a section of the bar nearest the door.

"What the bloody hell are we going to order?" Charlie muttered under his breath.

Jamie shook his head. The gin would strike them blind and the ale was likely the poorest to be had and diluted with filthy rain water. The tavern keeper, a man with one good eye and another that wandered, asked, "What'll it be, gents?"

"Bottle of whiskey," Jamie said. "Bring it unopened."

He noted they were drawing attention and was undecided if that was good or bad. The Cat's Paw did not attract men of Hunter's ilk, but most of the bully boys in the place would think twice before assaulting a gent in public. Once he and Charlie departed and entered a darkened street, however...

When the tavern keeper brought the whiskey, Jamie held it to the light. It was sealed and looked clear, not cloudy with the foul water hereabouts. He nodded at the tavern keeper, who opened the bottle and handed it to him. Jamie raised an eyebrow, took a swig and winced as the cheap rotgut burned a path down his throat. He passed the bottle to Charlie, who did the same.

Jamie tossed the tavern keeper a few coins and waved the unwashed tin cups away.

Charlie grinned as the tavern keeper turned to attend other customers. "I wondered what we could possibly order in here that wouldn't poison us."

"We'll see how big our heads are in the morning."

A tall figure emerged from the shadows at the back of the room. A shorter figure followed on his heels. They approached Jamie cautiously.

"I knows you," the taller man said. "One o' Farrell's friends, ain't ye?"

"Hunter's the name." Jamie inclined his head toward Charlie. "And this is my brother, Charlie."

"You th' gents askin' fer us?"

"Aye." He grabbed the whiskey bottle around the neck. "We want a private talk."

Richard "Dick" Gibbons, the taller and older of the brothers, led the way to a table in a far corner. He and his silent brother, Artie, sat against the wall, leaving Jamie and Charlie to sit with their backs to the room—a dangerous position in this sort of place. Jamie tilted his chair to one side, facing the room, and Charlie did the same, forming a rough semicircle. Artie grinned at their ploy.

Dick Gibbons held out his tin cup and Jamie obliged by

pouring a measure of whiskey into it, then did the same with Artie's cup.

"You remember what we wanted last time?" Jamie asked.

Dick nodded.

"I want it again."

The eldest Gibbons's grin made Jamie wary, and he suspected that Henley might have escaped the authorities a few weeks ago because the Gibbons brothers had warned him off. Selling that information to two parties, both Devlin Farrell and Henley, made for double profit. The Gibbonses were treacherous enough for such a move and greedy enough to risk Devlin's anger.

"Thought ye got 'em all."

"You know we didn't," Jamie countered, running his own bluff. "And you know who I want."

Dick seemed to contemplate denial and decide against it. "Henley, is it?"

Charlie took a swig from the bottle and eyed the Gibbons brothers warily. His glance at Jamie warned of caution, but Jamie was beyond that. There was only one way to deal with men like these—plainly. "Henley," he confirmed.

"'E's a dangerous one," Dick said. "'E offered a bounty fer ye, didn't 'e?"

"You know he did," Jamie confirmed. "Was it you who took a shot at me two nights ago?"

Artie's shoulders shook, but his laugh sounded more like a wheeze. His grin split to reveal two rows of rotten teeth. Dick shrugged, but did not answer Jamie's question.

"I thought a knife was more to your liking," Charlie said. "Was it you who carved up old Cox?"

"A smart man'd use whatever'd get the job done. We hears th' Hunters is dangerous, too. Wouldn't pay ta get too close."

"I didn't know that mattered to you and your brother."

"Don't." Dick sat back in his chair and took Jamie's measure. "If there's enough money in it."

Here was the confirmation that the Gibbons brothers would play a double game without the least compunction. "Name your price."

The Gibbons brothers put their heads together and communicated in whatever way they were able given Artie's reluctance or inability to speak. When Dick faced him again, he laughed, expelling a cloud of foul breath that nearly sickened Jamie.

"Considerin' the risk, hundred pounds," he said.

Jamie kept his expression neutral. The sum was enough to keep a small family for a year. The Home Office would never pay so much, but Jamie could muster that much from his personal accounts. And capturing Henley had become a very personal matter. "Done," he said. "On delivery."

"Ain't our usual way o' doin' business," Dick said, his dull eyes narrowing.

"If you know the Hunters' reputations, you know we honor our debts. And you know it would not be wise to cross us. You're already living on borrowed time as far as Devlin Farrell is concerned."

Both the Gibbons brothers looked nervous for the first time. Whether due to Devlin's wrath or the Hunters', it did not matter. All that mattered was that the Gibbons brothers would be unlikely to double-cross them again.

"How'll we find ye when we gots the information?"

"The Crown and Bear after midnight. If I am not there, leave a message with Mick Haddon and I'll find you."

"How lovely Vauxhall is this time of year," Lady Annica sighed, gesturing at the roses as the ladies strolled along one of the paths. She glanced over her shoulder and the vapid smile faded from her lips. "At last we are alone. Now, tell us what Mr. Renquist reported to you this afternoon, Eugenia."

The day had been warm and the sun was just dipping below the horizon as their group halted and gathered in a circle to hear the news. Gina took a deep breath before she began.

"He is not particularly hopeful. He says he has made inquiries in all the most likely places, all to no avail. He has not given up, however, and informs me there are still a number of sources he has not yet tapped."

Grace Hawthorne squeezed her hand. "You look discouraged, dear. But Mr. Renquist has proven his worth ten times over. We have a great deal of faith in him."

"Yes, but my mother has said she is looking into ways whereupon we can leave for Ireland sooner. I do not know how much more time I may have."

"Never fear." Lady Sarah's violet eyes narrowed, reminding Gina of her brother's eyes and causing a little tingle to race up her spine. "Should it be necessary for you to leave before we have found the scoundrel, we shall continue. Nary a man has eluded us for long."

The assurance was comforting, but Gina wanted to be present herself for Henley's capture. She wanted to witness *his* humiliation. "Thank you, Lady Sarah. I appreciate all the Wednesday League has done for me."

She hesitated and glanced at her sister, Lilly. Would the ladies be angry? Chastise her? Even so, they had been forthright with her, and she could be no less with them. "I have also employed some street urchins to keep watch for any sign of Mr. Henley. And to gather whatever information they can."

They fell silent for a moment as the lamplighters came by, illuminating the pathways for the evening. Lady Annica's husband, Lord Auberville, had arranged for their entire party to stay for supper and to see the fireworks, one of the last of the season.

Lady Sarah resumed the conversation as if it had never been interrupted. "Excellent. I employed two, myself, when it became necessary. I could give you their names and perhaps they could be pressed into service, as well."

Gina exhaled a long breath. "Thank you."

Lady Annica closed her parasol. "Ah, here come the gentlemen. I vow, Sarah, your brothers make a merry group. I would have thought they'd be carousing or scaring up a card game. What do you think could account for their devoted attention to us of late?"

Lady Sarah laughed and shot Gina a teasing wink. "I cannot imagine, though it has been suggested that one of my brothers might be smitten."

Gina stopped herself from turning around to see who was coming and Lilly gave her a nudge. "There, you see?" she whispered. "James or Charles Hunter is taken by you. Perhaps both. And either of them would do nicely for a husband."

Husband? Dear heavens! Lilly really had no idea of the nature of her relationship with James. Even if she were able and inclined to marry, he was the last man she would consider.

"Ladies," Lord Auberville greeted them. "You look as if you are hatching some scheme or surprise. Is it a game we can all play?"

Lady Annica smiled as she took his arm. "It is for ladies only, Auberville. I assure you, you would not want to be a part of this conversation."

He looked down at her and his smile was only slightly suspicious. "Ah, I see. Ladies' business, is it?" He turned to the others and quirked an eyebrow. "I have learned not to ask too many questions lest I become privy to information no man should know."

James Hunter was studying Gina rather too closely. A sardonic smile hovered at the corners of his mouth, telling her that he suspected what the conversation had really been about. She glanced away, afraid she might reveal too much.

Lord Auberville and Lady Annica led the way back toward the pavilion. "We have come to fetch you as our table is ready for us. I shall apologize in advance for the food, but the wine is tolerable."

Laughter dispelled the tension and they proceeded to the supper box. Dining for such a large party, more than a dozen, took several hours and the evening had grown chill by the time they were finished.

As they exited the dining area, Andrew glanced at his pocket watch. "It is still more than an hour before the fireworks. Shall we take in the musical performance?"

Agreement was quick, but before they'd gone far, Gina found James at her elbow. "Would you consent to stroll down to the river with me, Miss O'Rourke?"

"I…"

"The lights reflected off the water are quite lovely this time of evening."

"Go on, then," Lady Sarah said. "But be back for the fireworks. And mind your manners, Jamie."

He took her arm and turned her toward one of the promenades leading to the Thames. Gina looked up at him and sighed. "I would have thought your sister, of all people, would know that you haven't any."

"Manners?" He laughed. "Aye, you'd think she would. Alas, she thinks her brothers are perfect—a myth we tend to perpetuate. Will you give us away?"

"That would depend, Mr. Hunter."

"Upon what, Miss O'Rourke?"

"Upon how you choose to deal with me."

"I cannot foresee any changes in the near future."

"Then your reputation is in jeopardy."

"Are you still disgruntled about the kiss? I would say I

regret it and ask your pardon, but I don't regret it in the least. In fact, I count it among my most memorable moments."

She shivered, remembering the bittersweet yearning for something more, and glanced down at the pebbled path rather than betray herself. Unfortunately her little shiver had given her away and he chuckled knowingly as he leaned closer to her ear.

"I think you will not soon forget it either."

"Did you ask me to walk with you for the express purpose of taunting me, Mr. Hunter?"

He sighed deeply and turned her down a path that branched to their right. "We are a bit past formalities, Eugenia. When we are alone, at least, would you call me Jamie? Or James, if you'd like."

He had made her name sound like a caress or a sigh. She'd never really cared for her name until that moment. "If…if you'd prefer. But if you did not want to talk to me about what happened in the Albermarle gardens, why did you ask to walk with me? Now your sister thinks…"

"That I am courting you? Precisely. As will everyone else in our party. And, with luck, the news will spread like wildfire throughout the ton."

"You…you *want* people to think that? But why?"

"You have refused to stay at home and avoid places and situations where you might encounter trouble. Since I cannot stop you, this is my best chance of protecting you."

She halted beneath a lantern at a fork in the path and withdrew her hand from his arm. "I do not recall asking for your protection, Mr. Hunter. And, had you asked, I would have refused."

His voice carried a slight chill when he answered. "Not an option, Eugenia."

He had put himself directly in her path. Would people talk as freely to her now if they thought she was intimately connected to James Hunter? She rather thought not. This little charade of his would render her completely ineffective. "We must halt this ridiculous rumor at once!"

She turned back the way they'd come but had not gone more than a few steps when he caught her by the arm and pulled her down an unlighted path to the right. When they were quite alone and could not possibly be overheard, he halted and turned to face her.

"We will do no such thing, Eugenia. To the contrary, you will support the fable. There is no escape from it. I intend to dog your every footstep until you are gone back to Belfast."

"You have no right!"

His handsome face settled into hard lines. "Would you rather I take this matter to someone who does have the right? I believe my brother Andrew and perhaps Devlin Farrell are your nearest male relatives. Do you really think they would look more kindly on your activities than I do?"

"You wouldn't!"

"Care to make a wager on that, Eugenia?"

Good heavens—he would! From the look on his face, argument would be useless. She took a deep breath and calmed herself. A show of defiance would gain her nothing, but perhaps they could reach a compromise. "I shall do nothing to contradict you, then, but when you are not present—"

"You, Eugenia, will not contradict me. I will always be present."

"What are you saying?"

"That I intend to be at every function you attend. Furthermore, I shall escort you and your party home each night."

"Are you mad? People will be expecting a marriage. At the very least, an announcement. One of us will look a jilt when I return to Ireland."

"I shall take the blame. I have no intention of causing you or your reputation harm. But you must see that you have left me no other recourse to keep you safe from your own recklessness."

Trapped. She was trapped and she would be hard-pressed to make any progress finding Mr. Henley now. With James at her elbow every time she left the house, who would confide in her? Why, how would she even meet with Miss Race and Mr. Metcalfe at the Morris masquerade? This was intolerable.

She looked up at him in the moonlight, aware for the first time that they had ventured down one of the "dark walks." Somewhere in the distance, she could hear the strains of an orchestra playing a waltz. Nearer, the call of a bird disturbed from its nest startled her. If James had meant to find privacy, he'd succeeded.

He looked down at her and slipped his arm around her waist. "Eugenia, it will not be so bad. I promise."

How could she ever make him understand? Frustration surfaced as she looked into his eyes and her deepest fear slipped out unbidden. "Perhaps it is already too late to save me...."

"Not while you still breathe, Gina." His lips were soft and beseeching as they touched hers, as if making a request or waiting for permission to do more.

She responded in a way she hadn't known she could, and she realized just how badly she'd wanted this—this closeness, this intimacy, this deep and poignant longing. She surrendered to it, sinking against him with a little moan.

His arms tightened around her, one hand winding through her hair and making a fist, holding her immobile and unable to turn away. Unnecessary, since she'd lost the will for resistance long ago. She wanted to find what lay at the end of this.

Chapter Eight

God help him, Jamie knew better. Gina wanted nothing to do with him, she'd made that clear enough. But when she looked at him with those doe eyes, when he saw the spark—half question, half plea—in her eyes, he had responded without thinking. When she'd fit herself against his body, his own had hardened with his long-suppressed need.

Her lips parted with a sigh and he teased her tongue, relishing her boldness mingled with timidity in the way she tasted him and in the sweetness of her moan. He'd been afraid she would turn away so he held her tight, preventing her from slipping away from him. He needn't have worried.

From the moment he'd seen her tonight in her ivory gown with the daring décolletage, he'd been longing to do this very thing.

His fingers were tangled in her hair and he pulled her head back, the better to kiss her. The better to nuzzle his way from her earlobe to the hollow of her throat. He nudged the ivory ribbon around her neck aside and kissed the little line of thickened tissue where she'd been nicked by Daschel's dagger. He could not see that scar without remembering that horrible moment before he'd swept her from the altar when he'd feared she was dead.

He was afraid she would protest at his recognition of her wound, but the sweet vibration of her sigh against his lips nearly drove him wild with desire. Where? Where could he take her? He could not soil her gown on the grass and return her to the fireworks. Nor could he whisk her from the gardens and take her to a private inn, no matter how much he wanted to. But he couldn't let her go without tasting just a bit more because, when she came to her senses, she would never let anything like this happen again.

He edged his kisses lower, this time nudging the lace of her bodice out of his way and freeing one rose-peaked bud. She shivered, but he did not take pity on her yet. Instead he captured that little bud between his lips and circled it with his tongue. It hardened and formed a taut bead that tasted vaguely of sugared cream and made him hunger for more.

She made a whimpering sound and cupped the back of his head, pressing him closer and whispering something that sounded like his name. What wild music that made in his mind. He nipped gently in response and her hand tightened through his hair.

He relished her unpracticed responses, knowing she'd never done anything like this before. Whatever had been done to her the night of the ritual, whatever she had felt that night, could have been nothing like this. She was too surprised. Too caught up in the madness that possessed them both.

Her chest rose and fell rapidly and her heartbeat hammered against his lips. He knew the signs. She was his for the taking, and he was painfully capable of doing just that. Desperate to do it, in fact. But this was Eugenia. Stunning, brave and principled Eugenia. How could he disregard her wishes or sate himself at her expense? How could he risk loving her, *knowing* her, only to have her leave him?

A chill went through him and he slowly separated himself from her, straightening and steadying her until she could support herself again. "I...I apologize, Eugenia. I shouldn't have done that. I know I've said that before, but you have my oath it will not happen again."

She blinked, as if trying to recall where she was or what they'd done, blissfully unaware that the deepened pink of one areola still peeked above her décolletage—a temptation that nearly undid his good intentions. She winced as he sighed and reached out to tug the fabric upward.

Even through the deepened twilight he could see the stain of a blush rise to her cheeks as she turned away from him and struggled to put herself to rights. "You should not start something you do not intend to finish, Mr. Hunter."

Finish? Everything inside him begged to finish what he'd started. But her accusation...was it a rebuke for stopping? Or for beginning? He wanted to reassure her, and he touched her shoulder in what he hoped she would interpret as support. "Eugenia, my concern was for you. You cannot know what a man—"

She shrugged his hand away and turned to face him, her eyes burning like dark coals. "This is precisely the point, is it not? I cannot, but I should."

"What—"

"Never mind, Mr. Hunter. It is my problem and has nothing to do with you." She smoothed the hair he'd tangled and tucked it back into the ribbons.

He wanted to tell her that anything to do with her was his concern, but he knew that would only make her angrier. He was saved the necessity of a reply by a reverberating boom, the first of the fireworks.

She jumped, startled by the sound. "We should be getting back before your sister comes looking for us."

"Eugenia, about the matter we discussed…"

She took several steps back toward the path. "Our 'courtship,' Mr. Hunter?"

"Yes. Perhaps I should have asked you if you are husband hunting." He followed close on her heels, barely daring to breathe until he had the answer to that question.

She laughed. "That is the last thing on my mind at the minute."

He exhaled with relief. "Then I cannot see what objection you could have regarding our charade."

"*Your* charade," she corrected as she took the arm he offered.

"You can make this as difficult as you please, Eugenia, or you can cooperate. What you cannot do is stop me. My course is set. And you might want to consider the benefits."

"There are benefits? For whom?"

"If society thinks I am near to making an offer for you, my name may lend you some measure of protection."

She looked up at him through the deepening twilight. "Why are you so determined to carry out this scheme…James?"

"I am responsible for you. Had I succeeded in capturing Henley…"

She considered this as they entered the clearing and heeded a wave from Lady Sarah. "You most certainly are not responsible for me, but I…I suppose there can be no harm in pretending if you will try to use a bit of discretion. The less you flaunt it, the less there will be to explain when it ends."

"Agreed."

Gina glanced down at her décolletage to be certain everything had been put back in place. She was already humiliated enough and she did not want to rejoin their party betraying any sign of impropriety.

That kiss, more seductive than the last, warned her not to become entangled any further with James Hunter. Indeed, how would she manage to coax information from young men if James was always lurking? How could she trace the only clue she had?

She dropped her hand from his arm to smooth the fabric of her gown, trying to brush away any remaining trace of their indiscretion. Her fingers skimmed a small lump of metal dangling from the corset strings beneath her gown. The shape seemed to burn its impression into her skin. Thank heavens James had gone no further or he might have found the key Christina Race had given her. She *must* find the lock it fit.

Standing on the steps of St. Mary's Church as the bell rang the hour of twelve, Gina scanned the crowd for any sign of the street urchins Lilly had introduced to her. In the distance, she could see Nancy amongst the stalls of vegetable vendors. Soon she would rejoin Gina, and they would walk home.

She felt conspicuous and realized meeting so openly with a street child would be noted by any of the family's friends and acquaintances. She would have to think of a different place. Somewhere more private and less open.

A small head sporting a dirty blue cap bobbed through the crowd in a direct line for her. As he drew closer, he waved and finally joined her on the steps. "Mornin', Miss Eugenia."

"Good morning, Ned. Do you have anything for me?"

"Not yet, miss. I been lookin' though. I rounded up some o' the lads and told 'em to keep a look out. Promised a shilling to whoever brought the news."

Ned was a clever lad. The more eyes on the watch, the more likely Henley would be sighted. "Thank you, Ned. Is there some way you could send to me immediately when you have news?"

"Instead o' waiting until noon, y' mean? I dunno. Could knock on yer kitchen door, I suppose."

"No!" Gina could just imagine the questions she'd face if a street child turned up asking for her. "I…I could meet you twice a day."

The boy removed his cap and swiped his forehead with the back of his arm. "Naw. Shouldn't take us long to spot 'im, but that Henley is a wily one. If 'e catches us… An' we gots bigger problems than that, miss. If you wants him real quick-like, I'm gonna need 'elp. One of me mates thinks 'e saw the gent goin' into a gamblin' 'ell. I can't get in some o' the places 'e goes. I know 'e's one fer the ladies, an' I can't get in those places either."

Gina's mind whirled. She could not ask any of Henley's peers without alerting James. And he was likely pursuing that angle himself. Aside from that, she could not know if they'd been in league with Henley, which would only land her squarely in more trouble. And she dare not hire a woman for fear of the danger that might befall her.

No, apart from her own inquiries, her best chance of finding Henley lay with Mr. Renquist and this savvy urchin. But the threat of James watching her every minute would keep her from pursuing the matter. Unless she could find a way around him.

He'd declared his intention to escort her home every night. But what if she did not stay at home? What if she met with Ned, instead? She'd sneaked out at night before and managed quite well before she'd run afoul of Mr. Henley. And she'd learned her lesson there—never again would she go anywhere with someone she did not know very, very well.

"Ned, how late are you about at nights?"

"Don't usually sleep until dawn, miss. Some o' my best pickin's are in the wee hours when the gents are deep in their cups and not payin' attention."

"Then would you meet me after midnight? I could help you. Perhaps I could disguise myself and gain entry to the places you cannot. I will reimburse you for your losses and also pay anyone else you think may help. But we mustn't involve too many people. The more who know, the more likely our secret will get out."

He seemed to consider the matter for a moment, then brightened. "Aye. There's a few I know 'oo could 'elp. An' they won't tell, neither. When do y' wanna start, miss?"

The Morris masquerade was tonight. She was attending with the Thayer twins, but she could beg a headache just before midnight, allow James to escort her home, then sneak away as soon as his carriage disappeared around the corner. But tonight she had important business. If fortune favored her, once she spoke with Mr. Metcalfe, she would have no need of Ned's services. She would have all the answers she needed.

But Gina had learned nothing if not to be cautious. "Tomorrow night, Ned? Quarter past midnight?" Wherever she found herself tomorrow, she would be sure to be home by then.

"Aye, miss. I'll wait for ye down the street."

"Stay hidden, Ned. The neighbors are a bit nosy."

The atmosphere in the Morris ballroom—indeed, in all the rooms the masquerade spilled into—was lively and gay. More than half the attendees wore elaborate costumes. Others, like Gina, wore bright colors in lieu of a costume and merely sported a mask or a domino. Her mask was crafted from silk sewn with yellow feathers and sparkling jewels to complement her bright yellow gown and she dangled a yellow feathered fan from her left wrist. Hortense had dressed as a shepherdess while Harriett wore a nun's habit. And James, who had arrived to escort them true to his threat, wore a domino with his usual evening attire. When he had delivered them safely to the ballroom, he'd excused himself to greet some of his friends in the billiards room.

Under the protection of disguise, and relieved of the usual restraint of propriety, the gathering was rife with hilarity and spontaneity. And, unless Gina missed her guess, all were imbibing more than the usual amount of punch laced with alcohol, along with wine and ale.

She wondered how she might find Miss Race in the crush, but removed her mask often enough to make certain Christina could find her. But, so far, not a single trace of a leper. Surely Mr. Metcalfe would not fail to come. Christina had told her how anxious he was to speak with her. She felt the key hidden in her bodice and said a quick silent prayer that her long nightmare would end tonight.

"I do so love masques," Hortense said, shifting her hooked staff to her other hand. "Though I do wonder how I shall dance with this thing."

Mr. Booth, another guest who had deigned to wear a domino rather than full costume, approached them with a rakish smile. "I have always had fantasies about dancing with a nun. You must have pity on me, Miss Thayer, and fulfill my dreams at last."

Harriett laughed in a way no nun would ever laugh, both seductive and pleased. "Granted, Mr. Booth. But mind your manners, sir. I have friends in high places."

Hortense chuckled as Mr. Booth led her sister away. "And Harri has always had fantasies about Mr. Booth. Two wishes satisfied with one dance."

"Let us hope that everyone's wish comes true tonight."

"Whatever do you mean, Gina? What do you wish for?"

Answers. The truth. "Happy endings," she murmured.

"Amen," Hortense agreed. "And sooner would be better. But I think you need not worry over that. James Hunter has very obviously set his intentions on you. Any girl would be mad to refuse him. Charm, looks, wealth. What more could you ask?"

What more indeed? "He has not proposed yet, Hortense, and may not. And should he, I have not decided what my answer will be." There. That should cut short the wagging tongues of the ton and not raise any unrealistic expectations.

"Mark me, he will be back to claim a waltz. You will see him often before it is time to go and he calls for his carriage."

"I hope he will not hover," she said. She did not want Mr. Metcalfe to be hesitant to approach her.

She caught sight of Christina, in an elaborate peacock mask, just entering the ballroom. She was on the arm of a man Gina hadn't met and she wondered if this was the elusive Mr. Metcalfe. But where was his leper disguise? She waved and caught Christina's eye.

Hortense followed her glance and grinned widely. "Oh! 'Tis Christina and her cousin, Mr. Marley. He knows every dance ever and has the most devilish wit. Almost as devilish as Charles Hunter's. How lovely, they are coming our way."

The man in question bowed deeply to them as Christina made the introductions and then he promptly swept Hortense into the rollicking reel, leaving Gina to hold her staff. When they were alone, she asked, "Where is Mr. Metcalfe?"

"He said he would meet us here," Christina told her.

Mr. Metcalfe was clearly afraid of something. Even his costume had likely been chosen to veil his identity. She took a sip of punch, wondering what could cause him to be so cautious.

When the dance ended, Mr. Marley returned Hortense and claimed Christina with a promise that Gina would be next. A quick glance toward the punch bowl told her that Harriett was still occupied with Mr. Booth. When a figure dressed in a long black robe with a cowl pulled low over his face and a small bell around his neck approached her, her heartbeat sped. Mr. Metcalfe, at last!

He held his hand out to her without speaking and she returned Hortense's staff. Once on the dance floor, the leper turned and lifted his cowl just enough that she could see his face. Yes, this was the man who had been at the tableau with Christina. The dance was a waltz, which would allow them to talk without the interruptions of a reel. Very wise of Mr. Metcalfe.

"Miss O'Rourke, I implore you to drop this matter at once."

Whatever she'd expected to hear, it was not this earnest plea. "I cannot, sir. I am committed."

"You are ill prepared for what lies ahead. You cannot succeed."

"You do not even know what I plan, sir. How can you presume—"

"Because I know Henley. Far too well."

Gina almost panicked when she noted James on the sidelines, watching her. Had he come to dance with her? Or had someone alerted him?

"I cannot let him get away with what he's done to my family."

"And to you, Miss O'Rourke?"

Her cheeks burned. "You were there…that night?"

"To my shame."

She tried to pull away and caused him to stumble, but he held tight and resumed the step. "You must believe me, Miss O'Rourke. That was the first night I attended one of Daschel and Henley's 'passion plays.' I was appalled when I realized what was going to happen. But…there were so many there that I could not expose myself by going against them."

"Yet you were willing to allow them to defile and murder me?"

"Murder? I did not know about the murders until the

following day, when the news spread like wildfire through the clubs and hells of town."

Oh, how she dreaded the answer, but she could not stop herself from asking. "How many? How many 'postulants' knew who I was?"

"Perhaps a handful. Perhaps less. I was not certain until I saw you here tonight. Most of them were so far gone in their cups and with the hashish Daschel had burning in the incense bowls that they wouldn't have known their own mothers. Henley laced the wine with opium, you know."

Opium—enough of it—would explain her drugged state and her inability to remember what had happened to her in the hours before the ritual began. That, at least, could be the answer to one of her questions.

"Still, I cannot let him get away with it," she murmured more to herself than to Mr. Metcalfe.

"Believe me, I understand. But you must leave this for others. Others more ruthless."

"I can be as ruthless as I must, Mr. Metcalfe."

He shook his head in disbelief. "You are not a match for a man of Henley's ilk. You have no idea—"

"Then, pray, enlighten me so that I will not go into battle unprepared."

There was a long hesitation while Mr. Metcalfe evidently struggled with his conscience, then continued in a lowered voice. "Henley is a patient man. He has been waiting. Waiting for an opportunity to finish off his enemies. I am one of his loose ends. I know too much. I know who—" He stopped as if afraid he'd said too much. But when he continued, his words surprised her.

"And you, Miss O'Rourke, are top of his list. London is not safe for either of us unless, or until, Henley has been dealt with."

"By whom? Who is left to deal with him, Mr. Metcalfe?

The Home Office has failed twice. If not me, if not you, then who?"

He shook his head as if to deny her words. "I am merely trying to stay alive until he has been caught. I'd advise you to do the same."

She squeezed his arm to make her point. "I need your help, Mr. Metcalfe. Tell me what you know that makes you fear for your life. Tell me anything you know that could bring him down. Tell me what lock your little key fits and what I will find there."

"I've already said too much."

The dance ended and Mr. Metcalfe released her, glancing over his shoulder with a harried look. Before she could form a protest, he was gone, disappearing into the crowd almost instantly.

At least she finally had an answer to one of her questions. Now she knew *why* she couldn't remember the events of that night. But there was still so much more she needed to know. If she could not remember herself, surely there was someone, somewhere, who could fill in those lost hours.

Her head whirled with the implications of Mr. Metcalfe's warnings. She needed a moment to think, to gather her composure and plan what she should do next. As the next dance began, she crossed the dance floor to the wide terrace doors and slipped through, ignoring the couples gathered there and others strolling along the paths. She needed to find just a single moment in a quiet place.

She stopped at an ivy-covered arbor and gripped the lattice-work until her knuckles were white. Gradually she became aware that she'd punctured her thumb on a hidden thorn. She shook her hand. "Ouch!"

Mr. Metcalfe appeared out of the shadows and came to her side. Had he decided to tell her about the key?

He took her hand and lifted it to his mouth. He licked the

little droplet of blood. Shocked, she pulled her hand away. "Sir!"

He produced a handkerchief from the folds of his black robe and she accepted it reluctantly.

"Delicious," he said.

A chill spiraled up her spine. That was not Mr. Metcalfe's voice! Instinctively, she spun around to make a dash for the terrace doors, but the leper's hand clamped over her mouth and she was yanked back against a hard chest.

"How nice to see you again, my dear. You look just like a pretty little canary. I wonder if your neck will be as easy to break."

Henley! Dear God!

He began dragging her backward. "But you and I are like the phoenix, m'dear. We have both risen from the ashes, eh? Though I shall rise and soar whilst you shall burn again. Poor little bird."

A sound, half moan, half muted scream, rose from her throat and he clamped his hand tighter, mashing her lips against her teeth and closing her nostrils.

Henley's breath was hot and foul against her cheek. "Ah, and here comes your erstwhile savior. How fortunate for me. Now, if I only had a pistol. My, my. Yes, a knife will have to do again."

James was looking for her, turning in every direction, but he could not see them in the shadows of the arbor. Henley could slash him when he walked past! "Eugenia? Miss O'Rourke?"

Henley chortled. "So proper? Are you not his whore yet?" he asked in a raspy voice.

She brought her heel down sharply on his instep and pulled away at the same time. "Jamie!" she screamed.

He turned toward her voice and came running at full

speed. Henley uttered a foul curse and ran in the opposite direction.

Jamie reached her and gripped both her arms as he looked into her eyes. "Are you all right?"

She forced her tears back as she nodded and pointed in the opposite direction, her throat raw. *"Henley!"*

"Run to the house. Do not stop until you are there. Find Charlie and tell him what's happened." He took off in pursuit and she thought she heard him utter an equally foul curse.

Chapter Nine

The gardens were empty near the back mews. No sign of Henley, damn it all! The man could not have doubled back or Jamie would have seen him. He arrived at a scene of confusion at the stables.

"…just took his lordship's stallion and rode off," one groom was saying to another.

Jamie could still hear the hoofbeats in the distance. "Who?" he shouted.

The stable hands turned to him. "A leper, sir. Dressed like a leper. I was just saddling Lord Grenleigh's stallion when the man ran up, knocked me on my arse, took the reins and rode away. What'll I tell his lordship, sir?"

Jamie couldn't think of that now. Only that Henley had gotten away again and by the time his coach was made ready Henley would be enjoying a pint in whatever hole he hid in. "Have my driver ready my carriage and bring it around front. I'll give Grenleigh the news."

"Thank ye, sir." The stable master tipped his cap with a look of profound relief.

Damn Henley, that misbegotten son of Satan! Jamie strode back through the gardens, his head down, hoping to find some clue, some hint of Henley's presence or an indication of where he'd been. In the shadows of the arbor, the toe of his shoe skimmed something soft and pliable. He looked down, startled to see something that looked suspiciously like a hand.

He knelt and parted the shrubbery. A man's body, covered partially by the foliage, had been hidden beneath the branches. Dreading what he might find, he rolled the body over. *Bloody hell...*Stanley Metcalfe. The very man Jamie had been searching for this past week. Henley had gotten to him first.

Metcalfe's pale blue eyes were still open and his mouth gaped in a silent scream. A quick inspection of the still-warm body revealed that the crimson-stained vest had a clean cut through to the flesh. Metcalfe's death had not been easy. Had Eugenia seen the body?

"Holy Mother of God," Charlie whispered over Jamie's shoulder. "What happened?"

Icy cold pierced Jamie's heart. "Where is Eugenia?"

"Inside. I calmed her, told her to say nothing, and took her to the Thayers with instructions not to leave the ballroom. Then I came to find you."

"She told you Henley—"

Charlie nodded and knelt beside him. "Shall I assume he melted into the night as is his wont?"

He gave his brother a rueful smile. "Not quite. He stole Grenleigh's prize stallion."

"Not very sporting of him, was it?"

He ignored the attempt at levity. "He had her, Charlie. God only knows what would have happened...." He looked down at Metcalfe's body again, knowing that Henley had planned something of the same sort for her.

"But he doesn't have her now," Charlie said in a deadly calm voice. "And we shall see to it that he never has that chance again. Meantime, we will have to inform Wycliffe and our erstwhile host. 'Twould seem the party is over."

"Not yet." Jamie passed his hand over Metcalfe's face to close his eyes before he stood. "Let me take Eugenia and the Thayer girls away first. I need to talk to her before the Home Office interrogates her. And the Thayers do not need to be a part of this. My carriage should be waiting around front. Once I have them home, I will come back and we shall handle this as discreetly as possible. Oh, and tell Grenleigh he'll have to find other transportation tonight, will you?"

Charlie helped him arrange the branches again to shield Metcalfe's body from immediate discovery. "You know what this means, do you not?"

"That Henley is growing bolder. And that boldness must be a measure of his desperation."

"He will only escalate from here. He'll get careless and, sooner or later, we will catch him."

Jamie clenched his fists. "He'll come after Eugenia again."

"And you, Jamie. He has already tried to stop you, and he won't quit now."

Gina hid behind her vivid yellow mask, careful to betray no outward sign of distress, though she'd been seething with suppressed anxiety. Where was James? Had Henley used his knife? Was James dead in an alley somewhere? And how had Henley known where to find her?

Hortense and Harriett had been teeming with questions when they'd seen how shaken she was. She'd settled for a version of the truth, telling them only that she'd been accosted in the gardens by a man in a costume. They had steadfastly flanked her since that moment, refusing dances and making inconsequential conversation to cover Gina's lack of attention.

She could only watch the terrace doors and pray that James was safe.

She nearly collapsed with relief when she saw him come through the terrace doors and scan the ballroom until he caught sight of her. But the look on his face was not reassuring as he came directly to their little group. She managed a smile as he approached, certain he would not want her to give their business away.

Hortense sighed when he offered a slight bow. "Oh, here you are! Did you catch him?"

He glanced at Gina and she knew he was wondering how much she had told them. "I told Hortense and Harriett about the stranger who accosted me in the gardens before you arrived in time to rout him."

"To be accosted in such a manner by a complete stranger!" Harriett said with an indignant look on her pretty face. "I told Gina we should report the incident to Mr. Morris at once, but she would not hear of it until you came back."

He gave Gina a slight nod of approval, clearly relieved that she'd prevented the twins from spreading alarm though the gathering. "I will take care of that presently," he told them. "But first I think I should take you home. I would be remiss in my duty as your escort to allow you to be present if there should be any problems."

"Do you really think there will be problems? Could that dreadful man yet be lurking in the gardens?" Hortense asked.

"I believe I frightened him off." He cast a reassuring glance in Gina's direction. "But we should not take any chances. I've had my carriage brought round."

Harriett sighed, whether in relief or disappointment, she could not guess. "You are too kind, sir," she said.

They made a quiet exit and were safely on their way before any fuss could be made. The Thayer home was their first stop, and James handed the twins down from the carriage with a courtly flourish. Both girls thanked him graciously and quickly promised him dances the following night.

He settled himself beside Gina as the carriage started off again. Before she could ask, he posed a question of his own.

"Did he hurt you?"

She removed her mask and sighed. Where she had once been uncomfortable with James, she was now relieved to be alone with him. She hadn't realized the strain she'd been under to keep her composure until that very moment.

"He was going to break my neck. When he saw you, he said he had a knife. What happened when you went after him? I was so afraid you'd fought and that he…" She began to shiver, unwilling to even entertain the notion that James might not have returned to her. That Henley could have killed him.

He took her hand between his to stop her trembling. "He'd stolen a horse and gotten away before I got to the stables."

She frowned. "But you were gone so long."

"There's more, Eugenia. I have been searching for a man who could have helped us find Henley. Stanley Metcalfe. I found him dead beneath some bushes when I was returning to the house."

Dead? But she'd just danced with him. There must be some mistake. "Are you certain it was Mr. Metcalfe?"

"He'd been knifed. I wanted you safely away before anyone could question you. Should anyone ask, you know nothing about the entire affair."

Her eyes burned with unshed tears. "I danced with him. He warned me that Henley wanted to kill me."

"Metcalfe?" he asked, a note of disbelief in his voice. "Was this something to do with your search for Henley?"

"I…I was to meet him tonight. To persuade him to help

me. He'd been hiding from Mr. Henley, afraid to appear in public. Oh, I wish he'd never come to meet me."

"I didn't see you dance with him, Eugenia."

The tone of his voice should have warned her. "He was dressed as a leper. But he disappeared so quickly after our dance that I was unable to question him further."

"Leper? Was that not the costume Henley was wearing when he attacked you?"

She nodded. "I thought he was Mr. Metcalfe. I thought he'd come back to tell me…"

James groaned. "Blast it all! Henley killed Metcalfe and stole his costume to get close to you before you discovered who he was. But what did Metcalfe have to tell you?"

The hidden key burned its impression into the soft flesh of her bosom. If she told James about it, he would take it from her. He was so stubbornly determined to protect her from herself that she could not trust him. "Something more," she improvised. "Perhaps where to find Mr. Henley. Or where he is living."

"How did you draw him out of hiding?"

"Miss Race. His fiancée. She interceded for me. He was dreadfully afraid of Mr. Henley. He said he knew something that Mr. Henley would kill him for." Suddenly the horror of the situation struck her. "Oh! Miss Race! She will be devastated. I should go to her. Be with her when she hears the awful news."

"Did she come with him?"

"She came with friends. Mr. Metcalfe was in the habit of meeting her wherever she went."

"Then she would best hear it tomorrow in the privacy of her own home. But think carefully, Eugenia. Did Metcalfe say what he knew?"

"That is not the sort of thing I'd be likely to forget, sir. No. He did not tell me what it was."

He cupped her cheek and turned her face to his. "Now I've made you angry. That wasn't my intention."

She flinched at his touch. "I dislike being interrogated as if I've done something wrong."

"Wrong? No, Eugenia. But you've done something reckless and dangerous. You've put yourself at risk when you've promised you wouldn't. Ask questions. That's what you said you were going to do."

Gina's conscience tweaked her. That was all she'd done. So far. But she'd made plans to do more with Ned. She would have to meet him tomorrow night and beg off. The incident with Henley had shaken her more than she'd wanted to admit.

James ran his thumb over her lower lip, his voice deadly calm. "'Tis swollen, Eugenia. Did Henley steal a kiss?"

"He had his hand over my mouth. He was dragging me away from the arbor." To kill her and leave her body beside Mr. Metcalfe's, no doubt.

He leaned forward slowly, giving her time to turn away. But she couldn't. His mouth was soft and gentle as he cherished her lower lip before took her whole mouth in a kiss no less exciting than those that had come before, but somehow more comforting, reassuring.

The carriage stopped in front of Andrew's house, jolting her out of the hypnotic hold James had over her. Slowly, and with a heavy sigh, he released her scant moments before the driver opened the door. He got out and offered his hand to help her down.

"Are you returning to the masque?"

"Yes. Charlie is waiting and we will need to inform Mr. Morris that there is a dead body in his garden. He has likely sent for Wycliffe already."

"You will let me know what happens?"

"Tomorrow." He took her arm, walked her to the door and waited while she rummaged for her key in her reticule.

He took it from her and unlocked the door. "Good evening, Eugenia," he said as he opened the door.

She stepped into the foyer and stopped. At least eight crates were stacked floor to ceiling just inside the door. Suddenly she could not breathe. Had Mama found early passage?

"Eugenia? What…"

Alerted by her sudden halt, he followed her into the foyer. "You did not mention you were leaving," he said after a moment.

"I did not know." She turned and looked at him. "Mama must have found an earlier departure."

"When?"

She shook her head. "She did not say a word to me. Passage must have become available suddenly."

He looked at her and she knew there was something he wanted to say, but he merely bowed, turned on his heel, and closed the door behind him as he departed.

The thought of Mr. Henley escaping justice haunted her, but the realization that she might never see James again tore at her heart. How had she let things go so far? How had she let herself love James?

She could not change one, but she could do something about the other. There was no more time for fear or hesitation. Tomorrow she would meet Ned as planned, and she would do whatever she must to bring Henley's reign of terror to an end.

As he climbed back in his carriage and gave his driver instructions to return to the masquerade, cold fury gripped Jamie's viscera. Once again, Henley had damaged Eugenia. Once again, Jamie had failed to protect her. But any qualms he'd had about killing Henley to prevent a public trial had disappeared the instant he'd seen her swollen lip and the tiny bruise on one side of her throat. The knowledge that Eugenia had been so close to death horrified and angered him. Henley would pay for that.

Even more unsettling was the realization that his time with Eugenia was over. She would be gone from London and from his life. And the emptiness would return—the mindless, meaningless affairs, the endless days and nights, the soul-deep loneliness that no amount of friends or family could fill. Since he'd met her, the emptiness had receded and been filled with memories of her voice, her eyes, the warmth of her skin, the lushness of her mouth and the sweetness of her sighs.

No doubt it was for the best. He'd take that post with the Foreign Office. He'd lose himself in service to the king. Somewhere, he'd find a meaning for his hitherto wasted life.

On his arrival back at the masquerade, Lord Marcus Wycliffe was waiting for him in the foyer. "Charlie is with Mr. Morris in his private study. I said we'd join them as soon as you arrived."

Jamie nodded, noting that the orchestra still played and that guests were still strolling the rooms. "Has he told you what's afoot?"

Wycliffe rolled his eyes heavenward as he led Jamie down a corridor to Morris's study. "Just that there is a body in the garden."

Jamie nodded as Wycliffe knocked and opened the study door. Charlie and Mr. Morris turned to them, and Jamie noted the strained look on Morris's face. Without asking, Charlie went to a sideboard and a bottle of brandy to pour two more glasses.

"Now that we're all here, someone damn well better tell me what is going on here," Morris said.

Jamie took a glass from his brother. "I suppose Charlie told you there'd been an incident in the gardens?"

"And that's all he'd say until you and Wycliffe arrived. I thought I saw you earlier."

"I took the young woman in question home. I thought you'd want to keep this as quiet as possible."

"*What,* damn it all? What should I keep quiet?"

"One of your guests was assaulted."

"What? Who?"

"Miss O'Rourke. Rest assured, she is well and safely home. I cannot say the same for one of your other guests."

"Damn cryptic of you, Hunter."

"First, I wanted to see your guest list and ask if you spoke with Cyril Henley tonight?"

Morris reluctantly riffled through his desk drawer, brought forth a list of names three pages long. "Henley? I haven't seen him for months. I do not think he was invited tonight."

Since Morris did not seem willing to turn the guest list over, Jamie leaned forward and took it. He scanned the names until he found one he was looking for. Oddly, Henley had been invited, but so had Metcalfe. And that raised the question, why had Morris lied? He would have been the one to provide his wife with the specific names of friends he wanted invited.

"I encountered Henley in the garden," he said. "He was the man who assaulted Miss O'Rourke."

"Henley…" Morris flushed with a look half angry, half disbelieving. "Why would he assault Miss O'Rourke?"

Morris had to be aware of Henley's reputation with women. "His reasons aside, Miss O'Rourke recognized him. He wore a leper's costume to mask his identity. What of Stanley Metcalfe?"

"Er, yes. I believe Metcalfe was invited."

"He, too, wore a leper's costume. Miss O'Rourke danced with him. When Henley approached her in the garden, she thought it was Metcalfe."

"But what has that to do with anything?"

"I chased Henley to the stables where he stole Grenleigh's stallion and got away."

"Grenleigh? Hell and damnation! He'll have my hide."

Charlie gave a grim laugh. "He is not too pleased, but I lent him mine. I warrant the horse will turn up in a day or two. Henley will not keep anything that would give his identity or location away."

Morris drank the entire contents of his glass in a single gulp. "So this is it, then? Henley assaulted a girl who is safely home and took Grenleigh's prize stallion which will turn up in a day or two?"

"Alas, there's more to it than that. When I came back through the garden after chasing Henley, I stumbled across Mr. Metcalfe. He'd been stabbed in the chest and hidden in the bushes behind the arbor."

"Is he all right?"

"Afraid not, Morris. He's dead. The question is, how shall we handle this unfortunate event?"

Morris's mouth moved but did not form any intelligible words.

Wycliffe finished his brandy and slammed his glass down on the sideboard with a resounding thud. "Metcalfe. Damnation! Another lead silenced."

"So my question is this," Jamie continued, determined to get to the bottom of the matter. "Where did you send Henley's invitation, and when did you last talk to him?"

"I…I… He came to me. Here. He'd heard about the masquerade and wanted to attend. 'Twas he who asked me to put Stanley Metcalfe on the guest list. I did not see him tonight."

So Henley had devised this plan to get at Metcalfe. Poor bastard. He'd never had a chance. But there was still another question. "Why would you oblige a man like Henley? Surely you've heard the rumors."

If Morris had looked uncomfortable before, he now looked as if he were about to flee. "He was blackmailing me. I…I was present at Daschel's passion play. Or that's what I thought it was. It was actually a—"

"We know what it was," Wycliffe interrupted. "So he was threatening to expose you if you did not do as he asked?"

Morris acknowledged with a curt nod.

"There's more," Jamie guessed.

"I've been paying him. Large sums of money."

"How?"

"He waits outside my club. Demands cash."

Cash. Large sums of it. Why would Henley need large sums of money when he was living in Whitefriars? And was Morris the only one from whom he was extorting funds?

Morris was a member of Brooks's, an elegant establishment in St. James Street. Henley would have to lurk in the shadows to avoid being recognized, but it could be useful to set a watch on the place. A glance at Wycliffe and Charlie told him that they were thinking the same thing.

"Are you going to arrest me?" Morris asked Wycliffe.

"If you were no more involved with the Brotherhood than you say, Morris, you needn't worry. If you were…we'll be back. At the moment we need to deal with the damage done tonight.

"The guests are beginning to leave. We will keep this quiet until tomorrow. Charlie, go to the arbor and make certain no one stumbles across Metcalfe meanwhile. Morris, encourage the guests not to linger. Remove the punch bowl and cork the wine bottles."

"They will think I am penurious!" Morris blustered.

"Would you rather they panic when they learn there's a dead body in your garden or sneer when they learn that you've been paying blackmail, and why?"

The man sank heavily into his chair.

"We have use for you, Morris. Keep your mouth shut and your head down and you may yet get out of this untainted."

Chapter Ten

Gina stood still, rooted to the little stool while Madame Marie pinned the hem of her new gown. But it was not the hem with its little train that concerned her. It was the provocative décolletage. True to her word, Madame Marie had crafted a gown that was sure to draw attention. Styles were changing, but Gina had not yet worn a gown with a neckline that curved over her breasts and dipped to a point midway between them.

She traced the curve of the blue French silk with one finger, studying her reflection in the looking glass. "Are…are you certain I will not cause a scandal?"

"*Mais non!* The style is perfection for your figure, *chéri*. Smaller bosoms and there would be no point. Larger, and it would make you look like a demirep, eh? Ah, but this much will tease the senses and disarm your suitors. The men—they will appreciate the titillation, yes? They will tell you anything you ask."

"You…you're certain I will not be banished from polite society?"

Marie, a lovely woman, gave a full-throated laugh. "You must tell me when you plan to wear this gown, *chéri*. The ladies of the ton will be crowding at my door the next morning, demanding a gown of the same cut."

"If you are certain," she conceded, not at all certain herself. She was glad that Nancy, waiting in the outer room for her, could not see the gown. If the maid told Mama, that would be the end of it.

Madame Marie called entry at a soft knock on the private door and Mr. Renquist entered, then halted in his tracks, blinking several times. Madame had been correct. His eyes went directly to her décolletage. Oddly, after a moment of embarrassment, Gina felt empowered, as if she were in control of the situation.

"Have I interrupted?"

"*Mais non, m'amour.* What do you think of our little Gina now?"

"That it is a good thing she has the protection of the Hunter family."

"Ah, you appreciate the nuance?" Madame asked, tongue in cheek.

"Perhaps a bit too much nuance?" he ventured.

"Oh, la! You are such a proper one, François. Little Gina will 'ave the ton eating from 'er 'and."

Gina smiled, suspecting the modiste had been quite experienced before her marriage to Mr. Renquist.

"The male half," Mr. Renquist muttered as he sat on a small chair in one corner while Madame continued to pin her hem.

"Have you discovered anything, sir?" she asked.

"Progress is slow, Miss O'Rourke. I've learned that, until recently, Mr. Henley occupied rooms above a public house in Whitefriars. But for sleeping, he was rarely there. Following the raid two weeks ago, he disappeared, taking most of his belongings with him.

"Since then, he has been spotted from time to time at various establishments in Whitefriars, never staying one place very long. I gather that is the reason for his success in evading capture. Speculation has it that he has found quarters in more desirable environs but that he still frequents the pubs of Whitefriars.

"My sources were less forthcoming when I inquired as to Mr. Henley's companions. Apart from various prosti—soiled doves, he has occasionally been seen with the worst scum Whitefriars has to offer, the Gibbons brothers among them. On rare occasions, he has been seen with gents, and rarer still, genteel ladies.

"I am devising a plan whereby I may be able to cross his path, Miss O'Rourke. Should that be the case, I shall follow him and send to you of his location immediately, but you should know that I am bound to notify the Home Office, as well."

She nodded. She had no objection to the Home Office benefiting from Mr. Renquist's investigations. In fact, if they could manage it on their own, she would not have become involved. But, should she find him first…

Mr. Renquist cleared his throat and went on. "Mr. Henley departed his last accommodations rather quickly, and the proprietor has a small box of items he left behind. If you are inclined, I shall purchase it from him for the unpaid portion of the rent."

"Did you see what it contained?"

"The proprietor wished me to pay for that pleasure."

"Then yes, please. Acquire it by any means. If it contains even the smallest clue…"

"Aye, Miss O'Rourke. Consider it done."

* * *

Nancy tugged her sleeve, wanting to leave. "Oh, miss, should we really be here? Like as not, she isn't receiving."

Gina held her ground on the stoop of the Race home in Russell Square. "Then I shall leave my card. How can I not offer my condolences? Christina was very good to me when I had few friends in the ton."

"Yes, miss, but—"

The door opened and a maid in a starched white apron answered.

"Is Miss Race at home?" Gina asked.

"She is, but she is not receiving this afternoon, miss."

Gina took a card from her reticule and passed it to the maid. "Will you please tell her that Miss O'Rourke is here? I think she may wish to see me."

The maid nodded and hurried away, leaving the door open but no invitation to step in.

Nancy tugged her sleeve again and whispered, "T'ain't a good time, miss."

"She may only have been a fiancée, but she is nonetheless bereaved." James had not given her details of what had happened last night and Gina was desperate to assure herself of Christina's safety. Pray she had not been present for the awful deed, or that Henley had not gone after her when his attack on Gina failed.

The maid was back and opened the door wider to admit them. Nancy looked down at the floor and went to sit on a small chair in the foyer, where servants were accustomed to waiting, while Gina followed the maid up a flight of stairs and down a corridor.

After a soft knock, the maid opened the door to admit Gina and closed it after her. The draperies had been drawn and the room was cast in gloom. She blinked to adjust to the darkness. "Christina?"

A deep and melancholy sigh answered her. "Thank you for coming, Gina. I wondered if you would."

She followed the sound of the voice and found Cristina, still in her wrapper, curled up in a chair, at least a dozen handkerchiefs abandoned on the floor near her. She knelt beside the chair and took one of Christina's hands.

"I am so sorry, Christina. I blame myself. Had I not asked for his help…"

"It would have happened anyway." The girl looked down at her with infinite sadness in her hollow eyes. Her face was flushed and puffy from crying.

"But I forced him out of hiding. Had he stayed away—"

"Stanley has been hiding for weeks now, Gina. Mr. Henley was blackmailing him. It did not begin with you."

"Blackmail? But what could Mr. Henley have held over Mr. Metcalfe's head?"

"I cannot say. Other than his attendance at an event that went horribly wrong, Stanley was not the sort to engage in wrongdoing. I believe he felt complicit for something, though he swore he did not know the full measure of the consequences."

The Brotherhood. Of course. Mr. Metcalfe had said as much to her in their short meeting. Had Mr. Henley been threatening to turn him over to the authorities if he did not pay hush money? But there had to be more. Mr. Metcalfe had readily admitted his involvement with the Brotherhood to her. He'd said he *knew* things. Things Mr. Henley would kill for.

"Did he ever talk about that night, Christina? Did he ever tell you anything that might damage Mr. Henley?"

She nodded, and her unbound dark hair fell over her face, shielding her as she began to weep again. "I cannot tell you without damaging Stanley's reputation."

"Did he tell you what the key opened? He hurried away before he could—"

"He only told me to give it to you, and that you would know what it opened."

But she didn't. Unless this, too, was something she had forgotten that night. But she could only press Christina for the one thing that might save her life. "Please reconsider, Christina. If Mr. Henley killed Mr. Metcalfe over the knowledge you hold, and then suspects you might know, too, he might want to silence you, as well."

She gasped and pushed the hair away from her face to look at Gina. "Surely not!"

"I cannot be certain, but can we put anything past the man at this point? All I know for certain is that Mr. Henley must be stopped, by whatever means possible. Stanley would not want you dead, and your best protection is to tell the authorities, the Home Office and whoever else will listen. The more people who know the secret, the less reason Mr. Henley would have to kill for it."

"I will not be leaving the house for several months, Gina. Can I be safe in my own home?"

Gina wished she could reassure her. Wished none of this had ever happened. Wished, too, that she'd never enlisted Christina's help. She shrugged. "I do not know."

Christina sniffed. "It would feel like a betrayal if I told now." A fresh storm of weeping shook Christina's shoulders. She buried her face in her hands and Gina could not imagine the depth of Christina's sorrow until she thought of losing James. Oh, she was prepared to leave for Ireland and never see him again. But to know that he no longer breathed, no longer smiled? Intolerable, unbearable.

"If I could turn back time, I would rather die myself than be the cause of Mr. Metcalfe's death or your grief. And, though I would never ask it again, I cannot ever thank you enough for your help, and everything you've done. I will leave you now, but should you change your mind and decide to tell me Mr. Metcalfe's secret, send to me and I shall come at once."

Gina closed the door after herself, catching one last glimpse of Christina, her dark head still bowed over her hands.

A heavy mist descended, obscuring the light from the single lamppost at the end of the street. A dense fog would follow, and Gina shivered.

She'd begged off the affair she was slated to attend earlier, pleading a crushing headache. James had feigned disappointment, though she had read the relief in his deep violet eyes. And when the household had retired for the evening, she'd crept downstairs to "borrow" some clothing from the laundry tub. Now dressed in a gray woolen dress, brown boots a size too large and a frayed brown shawl over her head, she was virtually unrecognizable.

"Miss Gina?"

Or so she'd thought. "Is that you, Ned?"

The boy stepped out of the mist and pulled his cap off his tousled head. "Aye, miss. I thought it was you, but I couldn't be sure."

"I did not know how to dress. Will this be suitable?"

He grinned. "I 'spose so, miss. Wasn't takin' you anywhere fancy tonight. One o' the lads said 'e saw Mr. H go in the Cat's Paw. That's a gin house near Petticoat Lane." He stood back and squinted at her through the gloom. "They won't let me in there, miss. Say I gotta shave first. But y'look like you belong there, miss. Won't no one bother you if you keeps yer head down."

"What shall I do?"

"Listen, miss." He put his cap on and pulled the brim low over his forehead. "You orders somethin' to drink, and then you just disappears into the walls and listen, if y'know what

I mean. Maybe you'll see Mr. H, maybe not. Maybe you'll 'ear something about where 'e is."

Yes, she thought she could do that much. But what did one order in a gin house? She pondered that as Ned started off at a fast pace, leading her farther and farther from familiar surroundings. She wondered if she'd ever be able to find her own way home. "Will you wait for me, Ned?"

"Aye, miss. Outside."

She took comfort from that much, at least, as her environs became poorer and more dismal. They passed taverns and public houses where raucous conversations carried into the streets and drunks lay where they'd been tossed. The women she'd seen were surely disreputable, since all women with a mind to their reputations would be safely home after dark in this area.

"Where are we, Ned?"

"Whitechapel, miss. Just around the corner."

And, true to his word, he halted at a sign with a painted black cat raising one paw. Beneath it was a low door with a stone stoop to step over, and she wondered if that was to keep sewage out during a heavy rain. A dim light cast a yellow glow in a window just above the door. She was relieved the rising fog kept her from seeing more clearly. The stench was bad enough without having to see what caused it.

She took a sixpence from her boot. Would that be enough? Should she take off the boot and shake out a shilling? Sensing her hesitancy, Ned gave her a little push over the threshold.

Gina had never been in an establishment like this one. It was dirty, foul smelling and dark; she had to stop just inside the door to brace herself and take her bearings. A long counter against one wall served as the bar and had shelves behind it with bottles of various sizes and colors. Were they all gin? At least ten tables were scattered to each side of the door but only a few were occupied this late at night. Another door

opposite the one she'd entered was closed, and she wondered
if it led to the privy or apartments where the light had shone
just above the tavern door.

A man sitting at a table was staring at her and she quickly
went to the bar and placed the sixpence on the grimy surface.
The barkeeper, an unshaven man with few teeth and dirty
hands, shuffled toward her, looked down at her coin, took
a tin cup from the counter behind him and went to a barrel.
He pulled the tap, seemed to measure the amount with one
squinted eye and brought the cup to Gina.

She kept her head down and neither of them spoke.
As he walked away, she breathed with relief and took her
cup to a table near the door. She had passed the first test.
Now, according to Ned, all she had to do was make herself
inconspicuous.

After a moment, all interest in her ceased and the low tones
of conversation resumed. Once she became accustomed to
the drone of voices, she could distinguish a few words. Her
eyes adjusted to the meager light of the few candles and the
dirty oil lamp on the bar, and she noticed four men at a back
table. Though she could not make them out, or catch their
conversation, there was something hauntingly familiar in the
tone.

As she strained to hear, she lifted her cup to her mouth and
took a sip. She nearly choked. Struggling to catch her breath
and not spit the swill back into the cup, she forced the liquid
down her throat.

Gin? *This* was gin? Dreadful! How could anyone drink
it? She coughed and took another swallow to force the first
down. Her eyes watered and she wiped them with the back
of her sleeve.

When she looked up again, she was startled to see that
attention was again focused on her. Too late, she remembered
to keep her head down. The brown shawl she'd kept over her

head had fallen back when she coughed and she hurried to pull it back into place.

An argument erupted at the back table and Gina froze. She knew that voice now. And she could never forget the inflection of his voice when he swore. James Hunter. But what was he doing here? Looking for Mr. Henley?

She pulled the shawl even lower over her head, took another swallow of the gin and stood. She had to get out of there before she was recognized. Three steps and she was out the door, scarcely pausing to catch her breath. The fog had thickened and disoriented her, but she turned in the direction she thought they'd come and took several steps.

A hand seized her elbow and spun her around. "Good God! It *is* you! What the bloody hell do you think you're doing?"

Ned appeared out of the fog, his eyes wide and his mouth gaping. She waved him off quickly, knowing that, no matter how angry Jamie might be, he would not harm her. The boy disappeared into the fog before James noticed him.

To make matters worse, Charles was fast behind James, a look of pure astonishment on his face. "Miss Eugenia! How... What possessed you to..."

James turned her toward Whitechapel Street and took long strides in that direction, pushing her roughly ahead of him, as if he were afraid she'd bolt if he didn't keep her within sight every second. Rightly so.

"Charlie, run ahead and signal a coach. I'm taking Miss Eugenia home."

Charles disappeared into the fog without further questions.

"You had better have a remarkable explanation for this, Eugenia. Apart from your reputation, you have risked life and limb coming to this part of town at night. Night? Hell, any time of day."

"I...I..." But she couldn't answer. She was so breathless

from the pace he set that she could not say two words together.

"I cannot even imagine what your mother and Andrew will say when we tell them how out of hand you've become."

"No! You cannot!"

"Oh, can I not? I rather think I can, Eugenia. In fact, I consider it to be my moral obligation to you and my duty to your family."

"Moral obligation to me? And where, pray tell, was that mere days ago in Vauxhall Gardens?"

James shot her a dark look but pressed his lips together as they arrived on the wide High Street. Charlie had summoned a passing coach and the door was flung open, waiting for them. James wasted no time lifting her and placing her on the seat.

He turned back to his brother. "I will catch up to you at the Crown, Charlie." He turned to her again, climbed into the coach and called her address to the driver.

Alone in the dark interior, Gina could only stare at James, sitting across from her and regarding her with such fury that she couldn't think what to say. Was there no way to appease him?

He crossed his arms over his chest and stretched his long legs out in front of him. "Well, Eugenia?"

It occurred to her that he really had no rights where she was concerned, and decided to take that position with him. "I must say that I resent your high-handed treatment, sir."

He laughed, though she could detect no humor there. "High-handed? Well, take a good look, Eugenia. What you see is me acting with all the restraint I can muster. But if you'd like to see high-handed, I'd be only too happy to oblige."

She mirrored his action and crossed her own arms over her chest. "Furthermore, you will say nothing to your brother or my mother. Do you understand?"

"Me? Understand?" A look of astonishment passed over his face. "You cannot seriously think you will get away with this?"

"Oh, I shall. Have no doubt of that."

"You are mad to challenge me, Eugenia. I am not in my usual accommodating state of mind."

"Accommodating?" She sniffed. "All I have ever heard from you is 'no.' I cannot think of a single time you have accommodated me. From our mock of a courtship to... to..."

"I accommodated you when you confessed that you were going into society with the express purpose of asking questions and trying to ferret out Cyril Henley. I have kept my mouth shut and allowed your little subterfuge, and where has it got me? Here! Finding you in a Whitechapel gin house dressed like a...a..." He gestured at her woolen dress and shabby shawl.

"Servant?" she supplied.

"I was going to say a washerwoman, but if you bared a bit of breast—"

Her cheeks burned at that comparison and she glared at him. "I imagine that is a subject about which you know a great deal."

He was suddenly on the seat beside her, turning her face to his and bending close. "I have never purchased the services of a common whore, Eugenia."

Chapter Eleven

Eugenia drove him to such extremes that he could scarcely comprehend his own reactions. Had it been any other woman, he would have walked away. Hell, any other woman and he would have left her in that tavern to fend for herself. But Eugenia? He looked into her eyes and saw not fear or confusion, but anger and a heavy dose of desperation.

He released her chin and leaned back against the squabs. "What is it you are not telling me, Eugenia?"

Her sigh nearly made him relent. "I do not know what you are asking."

"Why? Why must you push yourself to such lengths? What drives you to such foolhardy endeavors? I think you are bent on self-destruction, and I do not know how to stop you."

She dropped her gaze to her hands, twisting the gray woolen fabric of her dress. "You cannot stop me, James. It would be better for us both if you would stop trying."

"You know we will catch Henley eventually. You know Cora's death was avenged that night when Daschel was killed in the catacombs beneath the chapel. And yet you press on with an almost crazed determination—against all good sense, against all reasonable care for your safety. There has to be more that drives you. What is it, Eugenia? Why can you not leave this to me?"

For the first time, he saw a flash of fear in Eugenia's eyes and he recalled the night at Vauxhall Gardens, when she'd hinted that it was already too late to save her. "Answers," she said so softly he barely heard her above the rattle of wheels and harness.

"To what?"

"That night. That night in the catacombs."

"You know the answers. You know who killed Cora, and who kidnapped you. If you are looking for an answer to why… well, there is no answer to that but for the darkness in some men's souls."

"I cannot go on without the answers. There is no future for me without them."

"Gina—"

"My entire life hinges on the answers, and there *is* no life without them."

A tiny seed of doubt began to take root. Had Eugenia told them everything that happened that night? Had they left any question unasked? Any truth untold? Or, God help her, had she lied? Had she been more involved with the Brotherhood than she'd admitted? Had she lied about what happened?

He gripped her shoulders and forced her to look into his eyes. "What have you withheld, Eugenia?"

Those glorious dark eyes welled with unspilled tears. "That I do not know."

"What, damn it?"

"What happened to me. I cannot remember most of it. Mr. Henley gave me opium, and my mind is a blur."

"But…what can you recall?"

"Nothing until the ritual, when I was lying upon that altar.

I remember Mr. Henley bending over me, and I thought he was going to…to…"

"He was. But I still—"

"And then you covered me and carried me from the altar. Someone asked me later if I was unharmed. Bella, I think. And I told her yes. But the truth is, I cannot remember. Only hurting. Aching in all my muscles. And my head pounding." The waiting tears began to trickle down her cheeks.

"You do not know if you were unharmed? But here you are, Eugenia, whole and well."

"Not that.…"

Jamie groaned as understanding dawned on him. "You think that…things…might have been done to you while you were unconscious."

She nodded and he realized she was holding on to her composure by a slim thread.

"Why didn't you tell us?"

The anger was back, refining her grief and uncertainty. "And have everyone look at me with pity? Have Mama shut me away in a spinster's room? Listen to whispers behind my back? I couldn't bear that."

"But what did you mean to do? Find Henley and simply ask him?"

"Yes! What other course do I have? Yes, I want him to tell me the truth—everything about those lost hours."

"Good God! And you think he'd actually tell you the truth? Don't be naive, Eugenia. He'd lie just to see the pain on your face. Hell, he'd lie on principle."

"What other choice do I have? Who else can answer that question? How can I ever build a future or a family without knowing if…if…"

He wanted to feel compassion for her, but all he felt was anger that she'd endangered herself for such an inconsequential thing. "What earthly difference does it make? I'd venture to say that a good portion of brides are not virgin on their wedding night."

Her eyes widened and she regarded him with astonishment. "*I* must know! Before I could marry, my husband has a right to know if I am whole."

He was still gripping her shoulders and he shook her roughly, as if that would rattle some sense into her muddled thinking. "Any man who loves you would take you as you are, without questions or guarantees. Any man who wouldn't is not worth your consideration."

"I cannot bear that I have lost that part of my life. I cannot tolerate the thought that I could go through life never knowing."

God help him, he could think of nothing to persuade her, nothing to comfort her, but to kiss her. To show her what his words could never say without disgusting her. He lowered his lips to hers, cherishing the salt of her tears mingling with the gin she'd had at the Cat's Paw—a potent brew, drawing up his suppressed longing, his denied needs.

Fear that he was taking advantage of her vulnerable state made him lift his head to mutter an apology, but she raised her arms to circle his neck and offered those rosy petals again.

"Yes," she whispered in a longing sigh. "Yes, Jamie."

It would have taken a stronger man than he to refuse that invitation. He deepened the kiss. And she did. Her heat, her taste, the sweetly innocent way she met his tongue, swept him into a tide of desire.

He moved his hand to her breast and she moaned deep in her throat. Even through the rough woolen dress, he could feel the taut bud of her breast against his palm. Now the moan was his.

This was madness. Insanity. He pulled away again. "Gina, you cannot mean—"

"Don't stop, Jamie. Not this time."

But the coach lurched as it drew up at the end of the street. Her eyes cleared as if she'd been sleeping and she seized the handle of the door. "Do not tell my family, Jamie. I beg you."

And she was gone, running up the steps and disappearing through the door. He sat there for a moment, waiting until he saw a light in an upper window. Pray she was safe for the night. Until he could decide what to do next.

Charlie was waiting for him at the Crown and Bear. He'd already claimed a back table and had a bottle of Devlin's private stock and two glasses. And God knew, Jamie needed a drink.

"Still no trace of the Gibbons brothers," he reported as Jamie sat down.

"Blast! Where can they have gotten to?"

"Just know where they're not. Not at the Cat's Paw, and not finagling free ale here," Charlie stated the obvious.

"I need to talk to them. I'd swear Henley killed Metcalfe and stole his costume to assault Miss O'Rourke, but there is always the possibility that he paid to have it done. Old Cox is dead and there's been an attempt on my life. I'd wager a fortune that there will be others. If anyone knows anything about it, I'd guess it would be Dick Gibbons."

"Aye," Charlie agreed. "If he's not behind it, he'll know who is. But I'm of a mind that we should simply put that vermin out of the way."

"Kill them?"

"Assassinate," Charlie corrected. "Though *exterminate* might be more fit for the Gibbons clan. Some men are in need of dying. They tried to kill you, and tonight after I put you and Bella in the coach, someone took a shot at me. Two someones, by the sound of the footsteps. It's a coward's method, and neither Gibbons would risk a direct attack on anyone remotely their size."

Jamie quickly looked Charlie over, reassuring himself of his brother's well being. "One shot?"

"Cowards. Had they stopped to reload, I'd have been on them."

There'd only been one shot the night he'd been attacked. Had he pursued the shooter, likely the brothers would have been waiting at the end of the blind alley armed to the teeth.

He suspected the idea to eliminate the Gibbons brothers had come from Marcus Wycliffe, but he knew his brother was not above such a thing. "The flaw in your plan to improve London by eliminating Dick and Artie is that we'd never get the truth from them then. But I must say I admire that you are not hindered by such lofty principles as proof. If you know in your gut that someone has tried to kill you, that is enough for you."

Charlie laughed. "Aye, well, we cannot all fit on that small patch of high moral ground you stand on, Jamie."

"Not so high, Charlie. I'd kill Henley if I could lay hands on him," he admitted.

Charlie sighed and sat back in his chair. "I am sick to death of that subject. Just for a moment, could we talk about more pleasant things? Miss O'Rourke, for instance?"

"She is safely home, if that is what you are asking."

"Only half of what I am asking. The other half is what the hell she was doing in a cesspit like the Cat's Paw."

"Looking for Henley, or for information about him."

"Good God," Charlie muttered under his breath. Then, "You put an end to that, did you not?"

"I thought I'd put an end to it a week ago. Since then, we'd reached a compromise. I'd keep an eye on her, and she'd confine her inquiries to the ton—mothers, sisters, friends of the bastard. Then I'd escort her home to be certain she was safely tucked up for the night.

"Now she had found herself a guide to London's underbelly. She thinks I did not see that boy waiting for her in the shadows, but I simply did not have time to deal with him tonight. But I will. Believe me, I will. Meantime, you can see how well our agreement worked?"

"Exceedingly." Grinning, Charlie leaned forward and placed his forearms on the table in an attitude of confidentiality. "Which confirms my suspicion."

Certain he'd regret it, he asked anyway. "What suspicion?"

"That Miss Eugenia is a match for you. Though you have most of the eligible heiresses of the ton eating from your hand, she resists your charms and you cannot abide that. I collect it is more than a matter of pride. More than a matter of protecting our brother's sister-in-law. You care for her, do you not?"

"Charlie, do not tweak me with this. I am not in a mood to indulge you."

"I would not mention it now but that she is part of our family. You would not dally with her, would you?"

Dally? No. He suspected it was rather more than that. "If you are asking if I am trying to seduce Eugenia, I am not."

"You've always kept your dalliances within the demimonde. Very discreet of you. Very safe. But I thought I saw something different happening with Miss Eugenia. Something a bit more dangerous."

"Dangerous? What the hell are you talking about, Charlie. How could she be a danger to me?"

"You've only been with women you could never love, Jamie. The demimonde, courtesans, mistresses. The moment some likely miss gets close, you back away. Our little Suzette is an excellent example. Did she ask too much? Surely she did not suggest marriage?"

He shook his head. "Suzette is too wise for that. But I sensed that she was growing rather fonder of me than she should. In her profession—and mine—close attachments are not a good idea."

"Your profession has nothing to do with it."

Jamie tossed down the rest of his drink and started to stand. His bed was calling. The last thing he needed on a night like this was a lecture from his younger brother.

"You need a good woman, Jamie."

"I've had a good woman. Several, in fact. Some were good. Some were *very* good. And some were…well, down-right—"

"Enough, then. But be warned—Eugenia is different than your usual interests. She is not adept at the little games that so amuse our set. Despite her foolhardiness tonight, she is too vulnerable to trifle with."

He settled back in his chair. There was nothing trifling about Eugenia, and he suspected Charlie was right—Jamie was acutely aware of her vulnerability. He felt differently about her than he had any other woman. Stronger. More… possessive? And he had more than a passing desire for her.

Charlie downed the remainder of his glass and lowered his voice as he continued. "I've watched you my whole life, Jamie. You've always kept yourself removed from close attachments and safe from disappointments and rejection. For whatever reason, you set your course for bachelorhood long ago. If you cannot offer her more, leave Miss Eugenia alone. She deserves better."

She did. He'd known that from the beginning, but he'd returned time and time again, craving her smile, the softness of her voice, the feel of her in his arms. He wished, now, that he'd left Charlie or Devlin to sweep her from that altar. Had he never known the feel of her in his arms, her sweet smell, her sighs, it wouldn't trouble him so much now.

A few more days. Surely he could endure a few more days.

"She should be safe enough from me. They will be leaving London quite soon anyway. Her mother has crates already packed. And, with a bit of luck, we shall find Henley and deal with him, hence there will be nothing left to throw us together."

Charlie nodded his understanding. "I think that is best for our families. An unfortunate affair would make gatherings quite awkward."

Jamie reached for the bottle. On his way home moments ago, he now felt like getting quietly, blissfully drunk.

Sitting between Hortense and Harriett, Gina trained her eyes on the stage where actors were posturing as they said their lines, but her mind whirled with the events of last night. If she were to be honest, she was relieved James had found her at that tawdry little gin house. She'd felt conspicuous and terrified. And she wouldn't have known what to do if someone had talked to her. Had Ned really thought she'd hear something about Mr. Henley there?

By their very presence at the same establishment, James and Charles Hunter had confirmed that they were on the same track, so she hadn't really been needed there. She shivered.

"Are you cold, Gina?" Harriett whispered, leaning closer.

"I just felt a little breeze on the back of my neck." As if the Devil had walked across her grave.

"Shh," Hortense warned them.

Standing behind them near the curtain of their box, James stirred and crossed his arms, as if impatient and ready to leave. He'd fetched the Thayer girls before he'd come for her, obviously not wishing to be alone with her. The twins were enjoying the attention of being squired about town by the elusive James Hunter, and Gina had kept the real reason to herself. It was much more flattering to think he craved their company than that he wanted to keep Gina out of trouble.

Ironically, the gravest danger to Gina was James himself. Her virtue would be forfeit with very little fuss if he but crooked his finger. Heat washed through her as she recalled the way she'd pleaded with him not to stop in the coach last night. And, just for a moment, she had thought that if she made love to James, it would wash away whatever Mr. Henley had done to her. As the moment had drawn out, she realized she'd been foolish to expose herself, her deepest fears, to him. And her only excuse was that, if he had made love to her, at least she would know, for better or worse, if she'd been defiled.

She'd do anything—*anything*—for the answer to that question. She'd ask questions, put herself in danger, pose as a lightskirt in a Whitechapel gin house, and more. And she suspected that the key to the answers to all her questions dangled at the end of her corset strings—if only she could find what it opened.

The music rose to a crescendo and Gina blinked. She'd been so lost in her own thoughts that she had missed the entire first act of the play. If pressed, she would not have been able to say what it was about. She clapped with the audience as the lights came up, guttering as the wicks were raised.

Charlie pushed the curtain aside and entered their box. "I say, did you notice that all eyes were upon this particular box? The excess of beauty here has charmed the audience. I would not be surprised if the actors ask you to leave so they may get their fair share of attention."

Hortense laughed and waved her fan furiously. Harriett

and Gina merely smiled at his ridiculous flattery while James lifted an eyebrow in amusement.

"What accounts for your interest in the theatre this evening, Charlie?" he asked.

Charlie grinned and shot a glance at the ladies.

Gina wondered what James had told him about her presence in the Cat's Paw last night. The truth, no doubt, but how much of it?

"Oranges!" came a cry from below.

She looked down and saw a girl with a basket of fruit, holding one perfect orange aloft for all to see.

"Mary!" Charlie tossed the girl a sixpence and laughed when she snatched it out of the air.

"She did not throw you the orange, Mr. Hunter," Harriett said.

He turned to them and explained. "Mary supports her mother and crippled brother. I always throw her a coin but never take the orange."

Harriett glanced at the pretty girl again, and back at Charlie. "That is very kind of you, Mr. Hunter. Not many are as charitable."

Charles looked embarrassed and shrugged. "'Tis little enough—a shilling here, a sixpence there."

Gina looked back at the girl in time to see her blow Charles a kiss. The incident spoke well for a man whose modesty prevented him from speaking well of himself. Mary turned away and began crying her goods again.

As Gina watched the girl weave a path through the audience, she noted a man approach her and say something in her ear. Mary appeared to shrink in size and began walking with the man toward the stage. Before they disappeared behind the curtain, he turned and looked directly at their box. Mr. Henley!

James had seen him, too. "Charlie, will you see the ladies home, please. I have sudden business to attend."

'E's one fer the ladies.... Ned's words rang in Gina's ears. Would Mr. Henley harm Mary in any way? Surely he would not dare with every charley and runner in London looking for him. The Brotherhood was disbanded. There were no more followers.

And yet her desperation for answers and the shortness of time overshadowed the lingering fear. So much so that she had once again dressed in the rough woolen dress and shawl, and had gone out to meet Ned. All she had now was the little key clutched in her hand and an idea nagging at the back of her mind.

Knowing, now, where she was and that she was not far from home, she'd dismissed Ned and stood in the shadows of a tree across the street from an abandoned estate on the outskirts of Mayfair. The gate stood open to an overgrown lawn and the house was partially obscured by trees that stirred in a chilling breeze. Behind the house, the spire of a small chapel rose above the trees—the place that had changed her life forever.

Gina shivered and drew her shawl closer. What secrets did this eerie estate hold? What had happened there that night, and all the nights before? Teasing dancing flicks of memory appeared and disappeared before her, leaving her with only vague impressions. Mr. Henley forcing bitter wine down her throat. Being carried somewhere and unable to fight. Hands plucking at her clothing. Then…then nothing.

The wind soughed through the trees, moaning like a lost child, and Gina sank deeper into the shadows, frozen in time—at that very moment in the catacombs beneath the chapel. Locked in an eternal cold. She wanted to feel again, to reclaim whatever remained of herself. And the only way she could do that was to find out, to finally know, what had happened to her during those lost hours.

She fingered the little key stashed in the slash pocket of her dress. Would it open a door here? Which door? And what would she find? Answers? More questions? Peace?

She reached into her mind, almost as if she could grasp and pluck out the memories that escaped her. And again the elusive memories teased her as if they were near, then flitted away, afraid to expose themselves to her scrutiny.

Her back straightened as she screwed her courage up to the sticking-place and her hand fisted around the key. She would not shirk, no matter how frightened she was. She took one determined step forward, then another.

A hand clamped over her mouth and an arm slipped around her to drag her backward, once more into the darkness.

Chapter Twelve

Gina twisted and fought like a dervish, trying to loosen herself from the unforgiving hold and clawing at the hand over her mouth. Dear Lord! Not again.

"Are you mad?" a familiar voice whispered.

She went limp with relief.

"Dare I release you?"

She nodded and breathed deep as he eased his hold on her. He still held her to steady her and she turned in the circle of his arms. "You nearly scared me to death," she whispered.

"No less a fright than you gave me," James said, a sardonic smile twisting the corners of his mouth.

"How did you find me?"

His mouth was mere inches from hers. "Coincidence."

"But—"

"It was a trap. Henley drew me away deliberately. He had cast Mary off by the time I got backstage. I gave chase, but he had already disappeared. He has set traps for me before, and I suspected he had done so again when a coach nearly ran me down. A clumsy attempt, to be sure, but one that put me on my guard. 'Twould appear half of London is looking to collect the bounty on my head. I will be lunging from runaway coaches, watching for falling objects and dodging bullets until this thing is over. All unnecessary since *you* will be the death of me."

Gina sighed. Though she'd listened to him carefully, her mind was overwhelmed with other things—the clean, spicy scent of his cologne, the way a faint dimple appeared in one cheek when he grinned, the warmth of his arms around her. She found she could only nod her understanding.

"I had a report earlier tonight that someone had seen a light in one of the upper windows here, so I came to investigate. I found nothing. But that still doesn't explain your presence here, Eugenia."

"A light?" She looked over her shoulder at the eerie deserted house.

"You're going nowhere but home, Miss O'Rourke."

"Directly after we search the house."

He looked astonished and angry at the same time. "I already have. You have sorely underestimated me. When I took you home after your ill-conceived foray into Whitechapel last night, I thought you would know enough to abandon such foolish tricks. If you do not, you leave me no recourse but to act as your missing conscience. I am taking you home, Eugenia, and we shall waken Drew and tell him what you are about."

Panic sent gooseflesh up her spine. "You would not dare!"

"Convince me not to, Eugenia. Give me a reason—just one—to hold my tongue. But be warned, it had better be good."

In her heart, she knew he was right. She knew she'd been foolhardy even though Mayfair was not Whitechapel, and that desperation had driven her to absurd lengths. She knew, too, that she'd put herself in danger akin to the sort that had landed her in trouble in the first place. She was ill at ease all the time, but she couldn't help herself.

Lacking a sane reason to convince him, she rose on her tiptoes and placed her lips against his. She felt him stiffen in shock, then soften to her insistence. His arms tightened around her as he deepened the kiss, invading her mouth with his tongue, testing her resolve. Did he think she'd relent? Beg off? Run home?

Oh, he'd sorely underestimated her.

Eugenia's sweet persistence took Jamie by surprise, though his body responded in the most primitive way. For the briefest of moments he'd been angry at her ploy, but then he'd understood her desperation. Understood it and knew he could never use it to take what he'd wanted for so long.

Ah, but what could a kiss or two hurt? Something to carry with him after she'd gone back to Ireland. Something to warm him in the long, cold days to come.

He lifted her slightly to fit her against him, to feel the hollow of her femininity. She moaned and clung tighter as he pressed her back against the tree that had sheltered them from vision. She tangled her fingers through his hair and held him close, as if she were afraid he'd withdraw. Oh, but not in this life.

She was breathing hard, her chest rising and falling rapidly. Giving her time to catch her breath, he lifted her a few inches more and trailed kisses down her throat to the little dip at the base. The scent of ambergris and moss rose to him as he ran his tongue over the vulnerable spot.

He could feel her trying to deepen the contact of their hips, but her skirts would not allow it. He began to hitch them higher, to wrap those graceful limbs around his waist, but he caught himself. He had not lost that last shred of his decency.

"No," she gasped. "Find a place. Now, Jamie. Now."

He could not mistake her intent. She wanted to finish this, to make love fully rather than their usual interrupted attempts. "You cannot know…"

"I want to, Jamie. I need to know."

He knew a public house very near. The proprietor would not ask questions this time of night. He draped the brown shawl over her head, took her hand and led her away from the deserted house and around a corner, but he balked. His sensibilities would not allow him to take Eugenia to a common public house. His flat was less than a mile away and he'd sent his valet on a fortnight holiday to have him out of the way should any attempts to murder him extend to his home. Now on the busier street, he flagged a coach, shouted his address and lifted Eugenia in, wondering if she would change her mind and if the moment of madness had passed.

He need not have worried. The coach was scarcely in motion before she was in his arms again, kissing him with a fervent desperation. He'd never sensed such honest and overwhelming passion before.

She fumbled with the buttons of his waistcoat, slipped her hands inside and awakened a rising anticipation in his too-responsive body. He needed her, craved her like no other. And he was well past embarrassment when the coach door opened and the driver gave him a wink.

"Shilling, sixpence, sir."

Jamie tossed him a few coins without looking and was met with a pleased, "Obliged, sir."

Shielding her from the driver's view, he escorted her up the steps to his rented flat, fumbled with the key and had her safely inside by the time the coach drew away.

Her shawl fell to the foyer floor as she reached up to him

again, her eyes already heavy-lidded in anticipation of another kiss. He complied, almost laughing as she pushed his jacket off his shoulders. He lifted her in his arms and carried her to his bedroom, knowing there was still a chance for her to change her mind. Pray for her sake that she did, because he could not.

The room was darkened but for the glow of banked coals in the fireplace. He placed her on her feet beside the bedpost and went to open a window to the summer night, and by the time he turned back, Eugenia was fumbling with the fasteners at the front of her gown. He watched her for a moment, feeling his libido riot with good sense.

She was not practiced in the art of undressing for a man, as his mistresses had been, but there was something very endearing in her innocent haste. Then she looked up from her task and her eyes met his. A blush spread across her cheeks even as her lips lifted at the corners in a shy smile.

He went to her and held her shoulders. "Are you certain, Eugenia?"

She nodded, a universe of promise in her eyes.

He slid his hands down to cover hers and take their place. One lace at a time he undid her gown, revealing fine silk beneath the rough homespun. Like Eugenia herself, the deeper he went, the finer the fabric. By the time her gown slid to the floor and he sighed at her lack of a corset, he was burning with his need to feel her beneath him, fitting herself to him, closing around him.

The sheer silk of her chemise and stockings taunted him, revealing, and yet not revealing her. He was uncertain how to continue without ripping the delicate fabric when she took matters into her own hands. Or, rather, took *him* into her own hands.

She quickly slipped the knot of his cravat, discarded the length of cloth and unbuttoned the neck of his shirt. She'd forgotten his waistcoat and had to push it off his arms. He smiled at her eagerness. She was new territory for him. He'd never made love to an innocent girl before, and he wanted this to be memorable for her. With that thought came another.

Leave Miss Eugenia alone. She deserves better.

Charlie's words sobered him. How could he do this to Eugenia? How could he take the incredible gift she offered and ask no more?

"No, Eugenia. I cannot do this. It was a mistake. I am so sorry for—"

She blinked and her eyes narrowed. "You *can*not? Or *will* not?" She pushed him in anger and, unprepared, he staggered backward, landing against the wall. "Is it because you have already seen me naked and did not like it?"

By all the saints! How could she ever think such a thing? She had haunted his nights ever since, but not with disgust—with longing and desire. "Eugenia, you will thank me when the passion clears. How could I take advantage—"

She threw herself against him, and bunched the fabric of his shirt in her fists as she shook him. "You cannot stop now, Jamie. You cannot. You owe this much to me."

The violence of her passion, the raw emotion in her voice, reached him and he understood what she wanted, what she needed. Though he suspected he'd regret it the rest of his life, he surrendered his conscience.

Lost. He was lost. All his lofty principles about leaving the ladies of the ton alone, of restricting his amorous activities to the demimonde, to women who had no power over him, went out that window on the late summer breeze.

"Easy, Eugenia," Jamie cooed.

Caught up in her own need, she pulled his shirttails over his head and he lifted his arms to help her. She swayed slightly at the sight of his bare chest. She'd never seen this much of a man exposed before. Her breath hitched and she realized she'd stopped breathing for a moment.

He steadied her and waited while she looked down at his remaining clothing. She skimmed her trembling fingers along the warm flesh above his breeches, seeking the button to the flap that covered him. Could she go so far as to… She slipped her fingers beneath the band but he stopped her and backed toward the bed to sit.

Toe to heel, he wedged his boots off, dragging his stockings with them, then lifted her in his arms and placed her on his lap. He traced the line of her hip beneath the fluid silk and sighed. "I am afraid I will rip your underpinnings, Gina."

He'd called her Gina. Oh, he could leave her underpinnings in shreds for all she cared.

With a little sigh, he pinched one corner of her chemise and eased it from under her to glide it up her sides and over her head. As she was exposed, she shivered and her nipples grew taut. She had thought it would be easier once she was undressed, as if the deed were almost done, but as Jamie dropped his gaze to her breasts she held her breath in fear. Oh, pray he did not think her inadequate. But his next move dispelled her worry.

He nuzzled her neck, stopping to worship her scar with his kisses, and half turned to ease her back against pillows that smelled of his cologne and his uniquely masculine musk. Something tingled deep inside her and she was suddenly impatient to have this done with. Despite the vague memories, despite the ever-present fear, to know, once and for all…

Leaving a trail of kisses in his wake, he lowered his head farther, drawing one firm areola into his mouth and teasing it with his tongue, nipping gently with his teeth. Oh! She had never felt anything half so delightful! She bent one knee to rest against him and he groaned deep in his throat.

He stood quickly, but before she could form a protest,

he had undone his breeches, dropped them to the floor and turned back to her. He was glorious. He was terrifying. Her heartbeat sped and she fought her rising anxiety.

Jamie was beside her again, kissing her with a fierceness that took her breath away and left no doubt that he wanted her. At least for this moment. For this small space of time.

She tangled her fingers through his hair, wishing she could hold him there forever. He was doing such wondrous things to her, such unspeakably pleasurable things, that she could not remain still. Again she raised her knee to glide along his bare hip, reveling in his heat and strength.

He groaned and moved lower, taking one breast into his mouth, and nibbled, gently drawing forth an answering heat in her middle. She felt as if she were straining for something as yet unknown, but she knew Jamie would reveal it to her in the fullness of time.

He slid his hand lower, to the juncture of her legs, and her raised knee made her vulnerable to his touch. He began a seductive rhythmic stroking at the top of her cleft that had her lifting her hips to meet him.

"Ah, that's it, Gina. Open for me. Let me in."

His praise warmed her and she was ready when he moved his hand just a bit lower and entered her with one long finger. She stiffened at that foreign invasion and caught her breath, then expelled it slowly as the rhythmic stroking began again.

Heavenly and naughty at the same time.... That could be said of more than Jamie's kisses.

"Like molten silk, Gina. So soft, so snug."

The pad of his thumb continued to stroke that sensitive little nub as he slipped one finger steadily in and out. Within moments she was arching to his hand, craving more, hungering to have him deeper inside her.

Unthinkingly, she reached for him, for that part of him that was uniquely male, wanting to know how he felt, and if she could give him the pleasure he was giving her. As her hand closed around his shaft, he groaned and jerked as if she'd hurt him, but she knew she hadn't by the deep sigh he gave her.

"Yes, Gina. Yes. Touch me."

She smiled, delighted that she'd pleasured him. As she rose to his hand, she tightened her hand around him, following the rhythm he'd set, finding it so insanely sensual that she shuddered.

Suddenly Jamie pulled away and moved down her body, stopping to explore her navel along the way, then dipping lower to where his hand had been. The first stroke of his tongue drew a shocked gasp from her, but then the sheer pleasure of it blanketed her in heat and had her incapable of thinking of anything but the next stroke of his tongue, and the next.

His hands bit into her hips to raise her slightly and give him freer access, but the building tension inside her made it impossible for her to remain still for long. She thought she would die with the insistent need. Little frissons of delight burst at her center and raced along her nerve endings.

"Jamie," she keened.

He rose between her thighs and the look on his face was raw and strained. "Steady, Gina. Do not fail me now."

Fail him? How could she ever fail him?

The staff she had so recently held had changed. Swollen to an even greater size, it looked red and angry, as if it would burst. Fear, primal and vivid, gnawed at the back of her mind but she fought it, knowing now that he would not hurt her.

Jamie lowered himself, hovering only slightly above her. The hard probe of his shaft at her entrance discomforted her and she had the first inkling of how different this would be than the welcome invasion of his strong fingers.

She looked up at him and he nodded, as if reading her

mind, then covered her mouth with his as he probed again, his tongue mimicking his shaft. She wanted to protest, tell him he would never fit, but she found her arms going around him, pulling him closer as she raised her knees and hips to meet him.

And then he was inside her, thick and strong, but shallow still. He withdrew just a bit, then thrust again, going deeper, ever deeper with each thrust. Pleasure mingled with pain, and back to pleasure again until he had buried himself inside her, rocking against her and awakening that sleeping bud to full blossom. The strokes of his shaft coupled with the deepened contact sent her into a spiral of pleasure and need. She wanted more, and more and more.

Her breathless moans shocked her and she marveled that they had come from her. But then, she'd never felt pleasure so powerful, so insistent, building to an explosive burst of rapture so intense that it racked her entire body.

"Yes," Jamie whispered, his breath hot in her ear. "God, yes. Come, Gina. Come with me."

Anywhere. Always. Forever.

Jamie stood at the window and watched the first tinge of violet stain the horizon. He would need to waken Gina soon if he was to have her home before the house was stirring, but not a moment sooner. Gina needed rest.

After they'd made love, she'd fallen asleep in his arms, her cheek and one hand resting on his chest and her leg crooked over his. He'd only been able to watch her, touch her—the curve of her cheek; her lips, dusky and swollen with his kisses; the violet shadows of sated fatigue beneath her eyes; the silken mass of gold and brown hair scattered across his pillow and the velvet warmth of her skin as he stroked her hip. She was the most glorious creature he'd ever known.

And when she'd stirred an hour later, he'd kissed her and

they'd made love again. Slower, sweeter, with all the wonder of first love and filled with all the power, all the ecstasy of their first time, but suffering none of the angst. More than anything, he wanted to believe that she had not been seduced by the moment, and that she desired him half as much as he desired her. But he was a man of the world, experienced in the art of seduction, and he knew that he'd caught her unaware and used her own passionate nature against her.

He turned and went back to his bed to study her, to burn the vision of her there on his memory. He did not deceive himself that she had fallen helplessly in love with him or that they could ever build a future given what he represented to her. No, he had served a purpose. Gina had wanted to know what making love was like, wanted that answer, and he'd been only too eager to give it to her, and flattered that she'd chosen him. But he should never have given in to her pleas. Should have been strong enough to give her up and preserve her virtue. He had failed her, but he would not do so again.

He reached out and touched her cheek, brushed a lock of silken hair out of her eyes. Leaning close, he kissed her forehead and whispered in her ear. "Arise, Eugenia. The night is done and the day awaits."

Chapter Thirteen

The afternoon was half gone by the time Gina was dressed and made her way downstairs in an agony of suspense. Had Jamie given her away when he'd brought her home before dawn? Or had he managed to escape unnoticed? She'd tried to make him leave her at the end of the street, but he insisted upon seeing her to the door with a promise to come later in the day, and there was no arguing with him.

She found her mother and sister in the parlor, conversing in perfectly normal tones. She breathed a sigh of relief. If Mama knew where she had been last night, and what she'd done, she would be in shrill high dudgeon.

Mama scarcely glanced up at her. "Good heavens, Eugenia! You look as if you have not slept in weeks! You really must stay in tonight and get some rest."

Bella came to her rescue. "Really, Mama, there will be time enough for rest when you have gone back to Belfast. Let Gina enjoy London while she can."

"Well! I do not need advice from you, Bella. Once you have children of your own, you will know how I feel."

Gina rolled her eyes and sighed. She was tired of her mother's endless nagging—never mind that she was right. Gina actually did need sleep rather badly. She'd been barely coherent last night when Jamie had gotten her home. Exhaustion and satiation had mixed in a powerful brew, muddling her mind so that all she could think was that she never wanted to leave Jamie's bed.

"I shall take a nap if that will reassure you, Mama."

Her mother contrived to look satisfied. "Nap? You are scarcely up, girl. The day is most gone. I do not think a nap will serve you now, Eugenia. I would prefer that you cancel your evening plans and stay in. Those Thayer girls are far too…too…"

"Too engaging? Interesting? Pleasant? Diverting?" Bella stood and went to the teapot to pour a cup for Gina. "Really, Mama. You complained when Gina had not yet made friends, and now you complain that she has. Give her a slack rein for the next few days, will you?"

Bella brought her the cup as she sat on the sofa and gave her a sharp warning look, as if she suspected that Gina had been sneaking out at night. "Thank you," she said in a soft tone, hoping Bella would realize it was for keeping silent and for supporting her as much as it was for the cup of tea.

Her sister gave her a quick nod that said she would be seeking Gina out later for some answers.

"Well," Mama sighed, leaning back against the cushions of her chair, "I really do not see why Gina should bother to go about in society. Three days hence, we shall be bound for Ireland. What point is there, really, in socializing now?"

Three days? Gina sat up straighter, her mind in turmoil. She could not possibly be ready to leave in three days' time. Mr. Henley, Jamie…

Bella answered to cover Gina's shock. "To make friends, Mama. To make connections that may serve her in the future."

How pleasant it will be to correspond with Hortense and Harriett to have all the *on dit*."

"And what good will that do her, I ask? Once we are back to Ireland, Eugenia is unlikely to leave again. What earthly use will she have for friends in England?"

"You should not map out Gina's life, Mama. Many things could happen. She had gentlemen callers in Belfast before we left, who will likely be awaiting her return. Should they have connections in London…"

"Pshaw! With both older and younger sisters married, Eugenia is quite upon the shelf. Who will have her now, even with the inducement of her not inconsiderable dowry?"

Gina cleared her throat and smiled. "Have you forgotten that I am in the room, Mama?"

"Oh, well…" Mama had the good grace to look a bit confused. "I was only stating the truth, my dear. You know I did not intend any insult."

Oddly, Gina believed her. "None taken, Mama." Her mother never intended insult, but she had no idea how high-handed she was. She had planned Gina's life to her own advantage and did not see any reason to consult Gina in regard to her preferences or to the details.

Mama stood and waved one hand airily. "Eugenia, I hope you will not be needing Nancy. I have some shopping to do and wish her to attend me."

To carry the parcels, no doubt. "I am quite at leisure today, Mama. Do go, and have a lovely time."

Bella expelled a long sigh when Mama departed, leaving them alone at last. "Gina, you are a saint if you can picture a life at Mama's beck and call."

"To tell the truth, Bella, I cannot picture it. Perhaps that is the only thing that keeps me calm."

Bella giggled and placed one hand over her stomach. "I

pray you will thump me over the head if I treat my children thus."

"I shall. That is a promise, Bella."

"As for you, Gina, I shall be glad to stand in for Mama. At least today." She stood and came to stand beside Gina's chair to give her a gentle thump on her head. "What were you thinking, Gina?"

"I do not know what you mean," she temporized.

"Do not come over all coy with me, Gina O'Rourke. You kept quiet when I was slipping out at night. I shall do no less for you. But you must see the danger in not telling anyone what you are about. Mary—the washwoman Mary, not the scullery Mary—reported that her spare gown was missing. Then Nancy brought it to me early this morning. She said she found it in your room when she was straightening up. What are you about?"

Heavens! She'd been so exhausted when she'd gotten home that she'd simply dropped the gown where she stood instead of hiding it in the clothes press. "Did she tell Mama?"

"She came to me, Gina, so she could avoid Mama's hysterics. I repeat, why did you need a washwoman's dress?"

"I wanted to go out anonymously. I took Mary's shawl, too, to cover my head. You know that no one notices servants, Gina. I thought I could go places inappropriate for a young woman, perhaps hear things I would not otherwise be privy to."

"No wonder you are exhausted. But you must stop, of course."

"Of course. Just as you did."

"I am not amused, Gina."

"Neither am I. Three days, Bella. That is all I have left before Mama whisks me back to Belfast. Three days to find those missing hours of my life."

Bella frowned and sat beside her. "I cannot imagine how

difficult that must be for you, Gina. You know I will help you in any way I can, but I cannot condone you prowling the London streets after midnight and putting yourself in danger. If I lost you…I could not imagine such a thing."

"You will not lose me, Bella. James has taken it upon himself to look out for me." Heat crept into her cheeks with the thought of just how well Jamie had looked out for her last night.

"Jamie is courting you, Gina. I have been hoping he would speak for you soon, and that you would marry and stay in London with Lilly and me."

"Oh, poor Bella. Had I known you were thinking in that direction, I would have told you sooner. Jamie is merely trying to keep me out of trouble. He is watching out for me. Ever since Mr. Henley accosted me in the Morris's garden—"

"What?"

"Mr. Henley came to me in disguise. He spoke to me, and he was dragging me into the shadows when Jamie came looking for me. And since then, he scarcely lets me out of his sight. I tried to discourage him, but he will not relent. Society might think we are courting, but his real purpose is to watch me. That is why I've been sneaking out. I cannot have him hovering all the time. People will not speak freely with him glowering like some looming gorilla."

Bella sighed and her shoulders drooped. "I was so certain…even Drew thought you were courting."

"No. The furthest thing from it." Though he'd done a fair imitation of it last night, after she'd begged him.

Bella squeezed her hand. "Very well, Gina. Since I know Jamie is looking after you, I shall hold my peace. *Three days,*" she repeated. "If there is anything I can do to help, you must tell me. Now run up and change. We are meeting the ladies and Mr. Renquist at *La Meilleure Robe* in half an hour."

* * *

The little dressing room was hushed when Gina came around from behind the dressing screen and stepped onto the platform in front of the mirror. She smoothed the curve of the fabric over her breasts and turned in a full circle.

Bella was the first to speak. "Stunning. Simply stunning, Madame. You have made our Gina look like a goddess."

Lady Sarah stood and touched the fabric. "Silk. Of course. The drape is magnificent, Madame."

Lady Annica smiled her approval. "I have little to add to *stunning* and *magnificent,* but perhaps *provocative* would do. You are going to drop jaws, Miss O'Rourke."

Madame Marie preened. "I cannot take all the credit, eh? Miss O'Rourke contributes to my creation in some small part, does she not?" The ladies laughed at Marie's joke as the modiste knelt to adjust a flounce.

"Pearls, I think," Grace Hawthorne contributed. "The luster will complement the color without detracting attention from the wearer."

"I think I shall have to commission a similar gown," Sarah mused, a teasing sparkle in her violet-blue eyes. "Though I would like it done in willow-green. It is Ethan's favorite color."

Madame Marie stood and adjusted the small puffed sleeves. "*Mais oui.* I shall 'ave to order fabric in every color at once. And you, Miss Gina, shall take this 'ome with you today."

A soft knock at the side door interrupted their laughter. "La! That François, 'e 'as the good timing, no? Now we shall see what a man thinks of our Gina. *Entrer,* François!"

True to Lady Annica's prediction, Mr. Renquist, holding a small carved wooden box, stopped short and his mouth dropped open when he saw Gina. Madame Marie went to him and gently lifted his chin with her forefinger. "Careful, *mon amour.* You will make me jealous."

He blinked and focused his attention on his wife. "No need, dearest. No one can hold a candle to you."

Marie laughed and headed for the door. "You see 'ow well I 'ave 'im trained?" She closed the door behind her.

Mr. Renquist nodded at the ladies and offered Gina his hand to step down from the platform and take a seat with the others. "I have several things to report, ladies. Shall we begin with the box?"

At their nods, he continued. "I have picked the lock and found several items." He opened the lid and gave it to Gina.

This, then, was the box she had asked him to purchase from Mr. Henley's former landlord. She rested the box on her lap and poked through the contents.

Mr. Renquist continued as she examined each item. "There is a cravat pin in the form of a dragon with small ruby eyes, a broken watch, a pocket knife, a list of household items and a small packet of unsigned letters."

"What sort of list?" Lady Annica asked.

Gina ran her finger down the list. "Candles, tinderbox, blanket, wine—"

"He was setting up new quarters, or a hiding place," Lady Sarah guessed.

Gina skipped over the cravat pin, unwilling to touch the wyvern from which the Brotherhood had taken their name, and lifted the packet of letters. She untied the ribbon that held them together and picked one random letter from the middle of the stack of ten.

It began without salutation and concluded without signature. Gina read it aloud for the rest of the group. "'I concur, dear Henley, that your position is untenable. I am working on a solution and beg that you be patient. I shall meet you Tuesday next at the usual place and time.' The writing looks feminine. But how can that be?"

Mr. Renquist nodded. "I thought the same thing, Miss

O'Rourke, and that would fit with another piece of information I've gleaned. One of the boys I employ from time to time reports that he spotted Henley with a woman. A woman of quality, according to him. That would confirm our suspicion that Henley has help from the ton."

"Blackmail?" Gina asked, thinking of Mr. Morris.

Mr. Renquist gave a philosophical shrug. "Or affection."

"Where were they seen?"

"At the Bucket and Well in Whitechapel. The place is a bit better than the usual Whitechapel taproom."

"Tuesday next," Bella mused. "Is the letter dated?"

"None of them are. Since the letters have been in the box for a week or more, I believe that meeting has come and gone. Nevertheless, since it appears to be their usual place and time, I shall be at the Bucket and Well this coming Tuesday. All day and night, if I must."

Tuesday next... Gina would be en route to Belfast. A quick sharp pain gripped her stomach. There had to be some way to conclude this matter by then. She covered her panic by unfolding a single sheet of paper and pretending to study it.

"Ah, yes. The ledger sheet. As you will see, Miss O'Rourke, that is a list of receipts and payments made to various individuals by initials, with the exception of the notations for 'Gibbons.' I would like to turn that particular item over to the Home Office, if you do not mind. Perhaps they will have the resources to match the initials and payment to certain individuals and events. I suspect this is a record of Mr. Henley's blackmail and murder attempts."

Gina nodded and scanned the list quickly, committing as much as possible to memory before she refolded it and handed it back to Mr. Renquist. "Should they be able to identify anyone from their initials, I would like those names. I conceive it could be quite useful to know who might have pertinent information, and who I should avoid."

"Of course, Miss O'Rourke. Forewarned is forearmed." He cleared his throat and finished his report. "The last item is a list of notorious criminals who have been known to kill for hire. I believe Henley has either hired them, or intends to hire them. It is possible he used these individuals to procure women for their…entertainments. What we lack is an explicit list of men he is blackmailing."

She handed him the list. "I have no use for this, Mr. Renquist. I would not know any of these people, nor would I wish to interview them. Perhaps the Home Office would find this useful, as well." She closed the lid on the little box, unwilling to give up anything more.

"Thank you, Miss O'Rourke, for not putting me in a difficult position. I am certain the Home Office will make good use of this information."

She glanced around at the group and sighed. "I do not know when, or if, I shall be seeing any of you again. My mother and I shall depart for Belfast three days hence. If the matter is not concluded by then, I hope I may prevail upon you to follow it to its end."

"But of course!" Lady Annica frowned thoughtfully and tapped one finger against her cheek. "Do not despair, dear Gina. We shall devote ourselves to a solution."

Jamie had gone early to the ball at Duchess House, leaving Charlie to escort Gina and the Thayers a bit later. He hoped Gina realized he was not deliberately avoiding her. He'd wanted to talk to Lord Marcus Wycliffe before he focused his attention on her.

Wycliffe always arrived early at such events, preferring to watch arrivals and thus know who was in attendance, a habit he acquired after an uninvited guest at a soiree had attempted to slip a knife between his ribs. Wycliffe never made the same mistake twice.

They stood alone with a glass of wine, watching the wide foyer as guests trickled in, most choosing to be fashionably late. Jamie did not meet his gaze as he made his request.

"I had the news today that Mrs. O'Rourke and her daughter are leaving London soon. Monday, if my information is correct."

"Really? Well, I cannot say I am sorry. The daughters have been somewhat of a distraction—the eldest murdered, Isabella cutting her way through the ton in her search for the killer, Lillian abducted by a scoundrel, and now Eugenia interfering in Home Office business and distracting you from your duties. Yes, I think it will be quite peaceful come Tuesday."

"In point of fact, I am here to tell you that there are some matters I need to settle with Miss O'Rourke before she returns to Ireland."

"Has she done something to compromise our investigation?"

Jamie sighed, ignoring the question for a different admission. "Actually, I fear I may have compromised Miss O'Rourke."

Wycliffe grinned. "*May* have? What did you do? Kiss her behind the hedgerow?"

Jamie bristled. He was not about to give details. "What I did or did not do is not the issue. What I do next is."

"I see. And what are you going to do next?"

"I intend to ask her to marry me."

Wycliffe choked on his wine and Jamie thumped him on the back. "What? You? Marry? Is this some perverted joke?"

"Not in the least. In fact, I believe it is the only solution. For both of us."

Wycliffe glanced around to be certain they could not be overheard. "I pray you are not swayed by excessive sympathy for her and her family. Or that you have not overreacted to some imagined impropriety. Truthfully, Jamie, I cannot see you doing anything to risk such dire consequences. Of all my acquaintances, I thought you least likely to commit any such offense. Or to marry, for that matter."

"You needn't worry overmuch. I fully expect that she will refuse me."

"You… Why?"

"She does not care for me."

Wycliffe cleared his throat and Jamie thought he heard a surreptitious rumble of laughter. "I've yet to meet the woman immune to your charms. What have you done to make her dislike you?"

"I carried her from the altar. I am a reminder of her deepest humiliation. Indeed, the worst day of her life."

Sobering, Wycliffe's expression turned grave. "If she will not marry you, why ask her?"

"I hope to persuade her. Apart from that, I fear for her. The communications we received from Francis Renquist today lead me to believe she would not be safe even in Ireland. If Henley wants her dead… You have sent men to bring in the blackguards on that list," Jamie said. "But there may be more whose names we do not have, and how can I protect her against that? I need her closer to hand."

"Can you control her?"

Could anyone? "I have as good a chance as her mother, and I'm more unlikely to relax my vigilance."

A large party arrived, turning the foyer into a cacophony of laughter and shouted greetings. On the wide steps outside, he could see Charlie arriving with his charges. Though he could only see the top of her head, his stomach lurched. He'd never been so nervous. He felt like a schoolboy in the throes of his first crush.

He should have called on her earlier in the day. Surely

leaving her alone to fret had not been a good move. She was, no doubt, furious with him once she regained her senses. How would he ever woo her back to trusting him?

Chapter Fourteen

Gina was in agony with suspense. When Charles had called for her instead of Jamie, he'd only said that Jamie would meet with them at Duchess House. Not so much as a personal word. Nor had he sent her a message or an explanation. In view of her behavior last night he would, no doubt, wish to distance himself from her as far as possible.

All she could do was to maintain as much dignity as possible. If he feared that she would weep, hurl accusations, make demands, or denounce him, he would be quite pleasantly surprised. She had only one question, and then he'd be free to go his own way. No matter that it would break her heart.

When they entered the foyer at Duchess House, she saw him in deep conversation with Lord Wycliffe. Charles called a greeting and she took a deep breath and cast him a bright, cheery smile. He blinked, then smiled in return. So he *had* been expecting trouble.

"Here comes my brother. I pray I will not be banished now that I've served my purpose," Charlie said.

"Never!" Hortense vowed. "So long as you dance."

"I shall dance until your toes tingle, dear Miss Thayer."

She giggled and fanned herself feverishly, and Gina suspected Hortense might have a secret tendress for Charlie. But Charles Hunter was an odd one—always open and charming though she sensed an underlying darkness.

Jamie bowed deeply to them. "My apologies, ladies. Alas, I had some pesky business to attend, but now that you are here, I shall devote myself to you entirely. Miss Harriett, will you consent to dance with me?"

Harriett glanced sideways at Gina, as if embarrassed that he had asked her to dance before asking Gina. "I should be delighted, Mr. Hunter."

Charlie frowned, watching Jamie as he led Harriett onto the dance floor. "Shall we find the punch bowl, ladies?"

They stopped to share pleasantries with acquaintances, and before they arrived at the punch bowl, Jamie and Harriett had rejoined them. When Jamie asked Hortense to dance, Gina suspected that he had a plan. Having done his duties to the twins, he could then leave without having to talk to her. Or, more worrisome, he would then have time to deal with her. That thought disconcerted her since it suggested that he had rather more to say to her than she'd like to hear.

And when, at last, he returned Harriett and extended his hand to her, she was not at all certain she wanted to dance. But she could not refuse without raising eyebrows, so she placed her hand in his and followed to the dance floor. As the waltz began, he pulled her into his arms and smiled.

"I trust you slept well?"

She trained her eyes on a point just over his right shoulder. "Tolerably."

He chortled. "You were sleeping well enough in my bed. Perhaps I should have left you there."

"Ten minutes more and the entire household would have known where I'd been."

"We came that close to discovery, eh?"

"Yes." But she wouldn't have cared.

"I need to talk to you, Gina. Everything has changed now, and we need to sort it out."

She nodded, a cold feeling settling in the pit of her stomach. Why did that sound so ominous? All she wanted was the answer to her question.

He glanced outside the terrace windows and muttered a curse. "Rain. We shall have to find a private room."

"Can it wait?"

"There is too much at stake."

He led her from the dance floor and toward the central passageway from the foyer. He opened each door and peeked in until he found one suitable then swept her into the darkened room. By the light from the streetlamp outside, it appeared to be a small parlor.

"Perhaps we should not—"

But his decisive closing of the door assured her Jamie meant to have this talk immediately. She perched on the edge of a small settee covered in deep blue brocade. At least they would have privacy.

He came to sit beside her and took her hand in his. "Gina, last night was…was…"

"A mistake," she finished. "I regret putting you in that position. I regret taking advantage—"

"Advantage? You?"

"I…I distinctly remember asking you to find someplace."

"So that I would not take you against a tree in public. Good God, Gina! I am amazed that you are even speaking to me."

Confused, she met his gaze for the first time since they'd entered the room and was struck dumb by the depth of passion there.

He squeezed her hand as he continued. "I think we both know we have been moving toward this for quite some time. You cannot deny the physical attraction between us. Given the strength of it, last night was inevitable."

"Inevitable," she agreed, "but regrettable."

"I do not regret it, Gina, though I am sorry to learn that you do. I have never known anything quite like it."

He seemed to expect some sort of reply, but she was so humiliated that she could not think what precisely. "It…it was lovely," she said for lack of better words.

"Lovely?" He arched one eyebrow at her as if she'd delivered an insult.

Heat swept over her as she recalled just how *lovely* it had been. "Ah, *quite* lovely?"

He stiffened. "I see. Well, I gather I shall have to do better in the future. Which, of course, brings me to the point of this conversation."

"Yes, please. What is the point?"

"Be my wife, Gina. Marry me as soon as it can be arranged."

"Marry? You cannot be serious."

Jamie seemed to lose patience with her reply. He stood and threw his hands up in surrender. "I have never been so serious, nor have I ever had such a difficult time convincing anyone of it. Marriage, Gina, is the logical culmination of our impetuousness last night. It is the most prudent way to solve the attendant problems."

She shook her head in disbelief. "Do you think I begged you so that I could trap you into marriage?"

He paced to the window and back. "Gina, I thought we'd both been swept away in the moment, judgment clouded by passion, as it were. But I begin to think I was the one swept away and that you had some other purpose."

"I doubt I could have stopped had I the chance. But when it began, when you first kissed me, I wondered…"

"Wondered what? If I had fallen in love with you? If I would make a fool of myself by proposing?"

Oh, she had muddled this whole affair beyond repair. He'd mentioned passion, and being swept away, but he'd never used the words she needed to hear. In the absence of that, the only thing she could give him was the truth. "I was desperate to know if I was a virgin. And I thought I could find out if I just—"

"Just let me make love to you? That's it? That's why you asked me to find somewhere private? To find out if you were virgin?"

He looked outraged, as if she'd done something unspeakable. In the face of his anger, she was afraid to speak. She only dared a nod.

He threw his hands in the air again and stalked to the window. "I cannot believe this. Did you ever stop to think that your little experiment would *cost* you your virtue if you were still intact?"

She nodded again, trying not to think how badly she'd wanted him, how she'd have made the same decision if she hadn't had that question, or how she'd thought she'd die if he stopped.

Or how deeply she loved him.

"Well, Miss O'Rourke, you are certainly no virgin now. You have been quite thoroughly introduced into the erotic arts. And you have demonstrated an aptitude for it, by the way." He went to the door as if he were finished with her, then turned around and fixed her with a glare so intense it made her squirm. "Was it worth it?"

She looked down at her feet. How could she answer that? That it had been worth everything she ever hoped to possess in this lifetime to have the memory of him for the rest of her life? That she was glad she would have that little piece of him to take back to Belfast with her? That, if she never married, never had children, she would at least know what it was like to have been loved by Jamie Hunter for the space of an hour?

But what was his answer? Had she been virgin? Or had Mr. Henley defiled her? Dare she ask again? She quietly cleared her throat and clasped her hands together in her lap to still their trembling. "Yes. It was worth it. Whatever your answer, it was worth it."

"Answer? You want *me* to tell you if you were a virgin? You do not know?"

Tears sprang to her eyes but she blinked them back quickly. Jamie would think her silly and would not want to see her weakness now. "If you would, please."

A myriad of emotions passed over his face so quickly that she could not read them all. But the final one, evident as he came toward her, was one of desire. He stopped before her and lifted her chin with his forefinger. "Gina, none of that matters. Can't you see that? Henley and the others—what they saw, what they did or didn't do—doesn't matter. You are who you are, not what someone may or may not have done to you. And you, my dear, are the most beautiful woman I've ever known."

"Jamie, that is not an answer."

"This is the only answer you need." He leaned forward and fit his lips to hers, cherishing them softly. She responded in the most primitive way, pulling him closer, astounded by the need that single kiss awoke in her. He came down on one knee to meet her on her level and deepen the kiss. She savored his intoxicating heat, losing herself to his passion and her own need.

He pressed her back against the cushioned seat even as he swept one hand down to free one of her breasts from the curve of her bodice and the filmy lawn of her chemise. When he dropped his head to take her into his mouth, she thought she would swoon with the sheer pleasure of it.

She tangled her fingers through his hair and pressed him harder against her, arching to him, desperate for the feel of him there. He did not pause in his ministration as he slipped one hand down to edge beneath her gown and sweep up her thigh.

Her breathing deepened as his bare hand found the soft flesh above her garter and beneath her chemise. His knowing hand found its destination—the small firmed bundle of nerves he had discovered only last night. She gasped and opened her legs to give him better access.

"Jamie…"

"I love the way you say my name when you are about to—"

"Oh!"

He chortled. "That's it, Gina. Just a little more and…"

She reached for him, wanting to give as much pleasure as she took, but he caught her hand and stayed her.

"Not here, Gina. Not now. Later."

Then he turned his attention back to her gratification, as if that was all that mattered to him now, and she accepted greedily, wanting even more as he slipped two fingers into her sheath, stroking, curving slightly to find a spot so exquisitely delightful that she nearly fainted with pleasure.

"Stay with me," he urged, as if he feared she would slip away from him.

"Please," she sighed, not even knowing what she pleaded for.

But Jamie understood what she did not, quickening his stroke and deepening the pressure until she uttered a soft scream of delight as the world narrowed to her center and then ruptured outward again in radiant heat and light.

"Yes," he praised. "Burn for me, Gina. Only for me."

Her breathing evened slowly and her mind cleared of the overwhelming passion. Oh, how could he do this to her? How could he know her body better than she knew it herself and give her such unspeakable pleasure? How could she let him go two days hence, and never know this joy again?

Jamie's own breathing slowed and he withdrew his hand, smoothing her skirts and nuzzling her ear. "You're like fire, my love. I've never known any woman to burn as bright."

Gina tried to make sense of his words, but all she could think was that he had not found the same release she had. "But you...you did not."

He smiled and kissed her cheek. "Were we truly private, my love, we would not be finished for hours. As it is, we've risked more than we should."

Heavens! They were at Duchess House. Behind an unlocked door! She stared at the door, fearing it would open any moment and expose their indiscretion. How had she so forgotten herself that she could allow Jamie such intimacies? How could she ever explain such a thing if discovered?

He laughed again, as if reading her mind. "I fear there is no such thing as good sense where passions are concerned. We shall have to be more careful. After we are—"

"We must return to the ballroom before they come looking for us." She patted her hair into place and smoothed her bodice, knowing there was nothing she could do about the blush that must surely be scarlet by the heat she felt.

"Ah, yes. We would not want them asking questions. At least until I have asked one of my own."

"Oh! Yes, questions. I completely forgot. I have not had your answer."

The warm reassuring look on his face faded as if he remembered their earlier argument. "After...*that?* Your answer is all you care about? That is all you want from me?"

"I…yes." Did he think she would ask more of him? She only wanted what he would willingly give.

He gave a joyless laugh. "'Twould serve you right to keep that information to myself."

"Jamie…."

He held up one hand, palm toward her in a gesture of denial. "No, Gina. Suddenly I am not in an indulgent mood. I'm likely to say nearly anything just to cut you as deeply as you've cut me."

"But—"

"You used me to your own purposes, Gina. Can you blame me if I take a bit of revenge against you?"

"You cannot withhold that information from me. I risked everything to know—"

"I risked more, Eugenia, but I cannot expect you to understand that." And the parlor door closed behind him.

Jamie stalked back to the ballroom, torn between anger and sympathy. The proposal had not gone even remotely as he'd planned. He'd hoped for a sweetly uttered acceptance, and had been poised to acquire a license to wed at once. He'd even been prepared for refusal and had devised an argument to counter it. But he could never have predicted Gina's admission that she'd only wanted to test whether she was virgin or not. What utter twaddle! She would not have him? Well and good. He would not trouble her further.

He spied Hortense and Harriett surrounded by beaux, and signaled Charlie to him. "Can you escort the ladies home tonight, Charlie? I find I have other pursuits."

His brother studied him, then laughed. "Our Miss Eugenia is responsible for this sudden dark mood, is she not?"

"Do not tweak me, Charlie. I am not in a mood for it." In fact, his body was still throbbing with unrequited lust and his head was filled with the memory of Gina, flushed and dewy from his lovemaking.

Charlie grinned, as if he guessed the reason for Jamie's ill temper. "Go on to your 'other pursuits' then, but leave Suzette alone. She has just warmed up to me, and I do not want her confused in her affections."

"Suzette is yours," he growled. "But mind that you do not neglect your duty where Eugenia is concerned. She is still in grave danger."

"Where did you leave her?"

He pointed down the corridor. "The small parlor."

Taking the front steps two at a time, he gained the street and hailed one of the hackneys that always waited outside large events such as the one at Duchess House tonight.

As the carriage turned onto Oxford Road, he caught a glimpse of a familiar figure, revealed through the clinging rain-soaked cape she wore. Missy Metcalfe? Should she not be home in mourning? "Ho, there, driver!" he called.

The carriage stopped and he hopped down with instructions to follow. He caught up to Missy just as she was rounding a corner.

She gasped as he took her elbow and turned her around. "Miss Metcalfe. Are you alone?"

Her eyes widened. "I am going home, Mr. Hunter. I beg you will not tell anyone you saw me."

"I shan't. I have a carriage. May I offer you a ride?"

She glanced over her shoulder toward the following carriage. "I do not think so, sir."

"You should not be out alone after dark, Miss Metcalfe. There are dangers for an unprotected woman."

A sardonic smile curved her full lips. "Would you be one of them, Mr. Hunter?"

He could scarcely miss that she was flirting with him. Or

that he found himself responding after Eugenia's stinging rebuff. "If encouraged."

"Then perhaps we should take that carriage."

Jamie signaled the hackney forward, handed Miss Metcalfe in and followed her, settling himself beside her.

She loosened the strings of the cape around her neck. "Would you mind terribly if we took a turn or two through Hyde Park, Mr. Hunter. I cannot go home too early as my parents might still be up, and they think I have already retired for the night."

"You pled a headache?" he guessed.

"Mourning," she replied with a little smirk.

Something about her answer set him on edge. He could not imagine his own sister behaving in such a manner if one of her brothers had been killed less than a week previously. According to the rules of mourning, Missy Metcalfe should not be seen in public for three months, and she should be clothed in dark or drab colors instead of the vivid persimmon she wore now.

"And are you not in mourning, Miss Metcalfe?"

"I am devastated, Mr. Hunter. Simply devastated."

Clearly an exaggeration if ever he'd heard one. Had there been no love lost between the siblings?

He leaned out the window and called to the driver. "Hyde Park, please, and keep driving until I tell you otherwise."

"Aye, sir." The driver laughed and Jamie knew he was thinking that he and Miss Metcalfe would be making the two-backed beast.

"Tell me, Miss Metcalfe, were you and your brother close?"

"As close as some," she demurred.

"Then I wonder at your being abroad so soon after his death."

"What good will grieving do Stanley now? If there was a time to help him, it has passed."

"Help him? Was he in trouble?"

She gave another little smirk as she nestled closer to him. "Enough trouble to get him killed."

She was a cold little piece. "Do you know who did it?"

"Now why would you ask such a question? If I knew, would I not have told the authorities?"

That would very much depend upon what Missy had to gain. "Unless you were frightened of the consequences," he suggested.

"I do not frighten easily, Mr. Hunter."

"I can see that, Miss Metcalfe. I confess to wondering what could have been so important as to bring you out to this particular place at this time."

She settled back against the cushions and gave him a sultry look. "Perhaps I was looking for excitement."

She'd been looking for something, or someone, of that he was sure. "At Duchess House?"

She shrugged, allowing her cape to slip open and reveal a very naughty décolletage. He was man enough to avail himself of the view, even if he was not inclined to take advantage of it. Her corset had pushed her breasts high enough that the rosy rims of her areolae were peaking above the lace ruching. An invitation?

"I thought I might recognize someone. Truly, I have been longing to see friends, and craving human contact." She heaved a sigh and the sleeve of her gown slipped down over her shoulder. She gave him a coy sideways glance from beneath her lowered lashes.

What a coquette! Human contact? Just how much contact did Missy Metcalfe crave? No stranger to flirtation, Jamie was nonetheless at a loss. He'd never been as expertly seduced by courtesans or demireps.

With great difficulty, he forced his mind back to his query. "Looking for anyone in particular, Miss Metcalfe?"

She shrugged again, allowing her sleeve to slip even lower and reveal a small beauty mark above one areola. Artifice? Or natural? "I thought I might find Mr. Booth. Did you see him there, sir?"

Adam Booth? He and Metcalfe had been friends. Wouldn't Booth be as surprised as Jamie to discover Missy about town alone? Or did Adam have more intimate knowledge of Missy's true nature?

He smiled down at the pretty girl, so unlike Gina in almost every way that the contrast was startling—and not particularly flattering to Missy. Ah, but Missy appeared to want him, and Gina did not. "I believe I saw him, but I did not have time to talk to him. Did you have business with him?"

"Business?" She gave another of those coy smiles that made him think she was enjoying a personal jest. "I suppose you might call it business. Though my motive was more that I am quite lonely."

She wiggled closer to him, rubbing her soft breasts against his side and placing her hand on his knee. Very brazen for a girl of Missy's class. He wondered how much further she'd go with even the tiniest encouragement. "Are you still lonely, Miss Metcalfe?"

She lifted her mouth to him as she slid the hand on his knee upward to cup his erection. Her voice was a purr as she answered. "Oh, I do not think so, Mr. Hunter. No, I think I am about to be quite thoroughly amused."

The patter of rain against the hackney roof muffled her soft moan.

Chapter Fifteen

The guests laughed at some witticism of Mr. Booth's and Gina smiled, trying to put the memory of her confrontation with Jamie from her mind. He'd been so angry he'd abandoned their group to Charlie and then disappeared. The mere thought of such a thing caused her to sigh.

"But I see our Miss O'Rourke is not much amused," Mr. Booth said with a sardonic smile. "I admit my wit is not a universal taste, but I am rarely met with such indifference."

Gina blinked as attention was shifted to her. "I am sorry, Mr. Booth. My mind was wandering."

"Indeed?" He pushed a shock of blond hair back from his forehead and regarded her somberly. "But I have been entertaining your group with the sole purpose of gaining your attention. It appears I will have to try harder. I hear a waltz, Miss O'Rourke. May I have this dance?"

With all eyes upon her, Gina could do little else but accept. She had been meaning to talk to Mr. Booth anyway. "Delighted," she said, taking his outstretched hand.

They had scarcely entered the dance when the music ended,

but instead of returning her to her friends, he kept her there awaiting the next dance. "Are you enjoying London, Miss O'Rourke?"

"As much as I've been able. My family has had no small amount of problems since arriving here."

"I have heard, Miss O'Rourke. You have my sympathies."

She believed him. His manner and speech were so warm that he was hard to doubt. "Thank you."

He hesitated before he spoke again, obviously choosing his words carefully. "Am I correct in thinking matters have eased for you, and that you and your sisters are well?"

For Bella and Lilly, matters were much improved. As for herself, she had certainly regained a healthy measure of courage and self-confidence. "Very well, thank you."

She fancied that he looked somehow relieved. But why would that be the case, unless he felt somehow responsible?

"I have heard whispers that you are leaving soon for Ireland. Is that so?"

She laughed. "I should not be surprised at the amount of information shared over teacups, yet I confess I am. Yes, it is true. My mother and I have berths aboard a ship departing on Monday."

"I am sorry to hear that, Miss O'Rourke. I should very much have enjoyed getting to know you better."

Warmth crept into her cheeks at his apparent sincerity. "No matter how much time we have to explore new possibilities, it is never enough, is it, sir?"

His smile was his answer. He looked around the ballroom and the expression on his face tightened, as if it had frozen in place.

Fear prickled the back of her neck and she turned in the direction of his stare. Dancers whirled past, obscuring her view. What could Mr. Booth have seen to cause such a reaction? "Are you all right, Mr. Booth?"

He blinked and came back to himself. "Quite. I collect the orchestra will be taking an intermission. Would you consent to stroll with me in the garden?"

A request, that if made moments ago she would have accepted, she now refused. "Thank you, but the paths must be wet from the rain. I'd prefer to stay inside."

"Oh. Yes, certainly. But I am loath to return you to your friends just yet."

As harmless as he seemed, she knew she dared not trust him, but she desperately wanted to question him. "Shall we find a quiet spot?"

He nodded and she followed him down the same corridor she and Jamie had taken barely an hour ago. Knowing the room would be vacant, she went directly to the small parlor and went inside, leaving Mr. Booth to follow and close the door.

She no longer had the luxury of time. Only bluntness would serve her now. She turned and tilted her head to one side. "We have met previously, have we not, Mr. Booth?"

He bowed his head. "We have, Miss O'Rourke, but I gather you do not recall the particulars."

"Enlighten me, sir."

"'Twas about two months ago. An estate on the outskirts of Mayfair."

"You were there that night?"

"To my shame."

"And mine," she whispered to herself. She sat and folded her hands in her lap to gain her composure before she dared look at him again. "I have always wondered what sort of man would attend such an affair. I would not have thought it of a man of your ilk, Mr. Booth."

"'Twas my first attendance at such an affair. I had been

led to believe it was voluntary by all the participants and for salacious purposes rather than the debacle it turned out to be. But then, I gather that was Daschel and Henley's method of recruiting postulants into their 'brotherhood.' I've heard from others that one attendance was enough to be drawn in, and that it was impossible to leave. Blackmail, you see. Dash was determined to convert us all to elemental base practices, while Henley merely wanted us to sink to his level. To control us."

Gina breathed deeply. As ugly as Mr. Booth's words were to hear, at least they had the ring of truth.

"I realized, after the chalice was passed and we all drank, and once I saw you, that you'd been drugged as the postulants had been. I am not mistaken in that, am I, Miss O'Rourke? You did not volunteer to be a virgin sacrifice?"

A gurgle of hysterical laughter erupted from somewhere deep inside her. Volunteer? "Never."

"Then I am glad to see you so well, and pleased that it ended the way it did, even though it had quite grim consequences for some of us."

In her own self absorption it had never occurred to her that others might have been affected. "What, prithee, were the consequence to you and your friends?"

"We've been blackmailed, Miss O'Rourke. Half our fortunes have lined Henley's pockets. We cannot denounce him without exposing our complicity. And we cannot expose our complicity without utter ruin to our families and loved ones."

A small tingle of sympathy worried the back of her mind. Impossible! Sympathy for her tormentors, albeit unwitting ones?

"And I furthermore collect that you have been seeking us out, one by one, and disposing of us?"

"Disposing? You mean...no! I want Henley caught and

punished, as much for my sister Cora as for myself. I want the authorities to lock him away forever, but I have not taken the law into my own hands."

"You did not kill Stanley Metcalfe?"

"No! I think he was trying to help me."

"You were the last person to be seen with him alive."

"Moments after he left me, I was assaulted by Mr. Henley."

"Christ! If Henley was there that night…"

"He killed Mr. Metcalfe. Perhaps to prevent him from giving me information."

Mr. Booth sank to the settee beside her. "He is a madman."

"Will you help me, Mr. Booth? Will you tell me where to find him so that I can inform the Home Office?"

"I do not know where he is hiding. He comes to us with his demands in public places, where we cannot attack him without drawing attention. He is a marked man, Miss O'Rourke. Leave his demise to others. It is far too dangerous for you."

"I cannot. I shall be taken back to Ireland soon, and I am desperate to have the matter concluded before then."

He took her hand and squeezed it. "Yes, then. I will help you. A day—two at most—and I will find information for you."

The door was thrown open and Charlie stood there, looking as outraged as a cuckolded husband. "Damn me, Miss O'Rourke! There you are! You gave me a bad turn. Come along now. 'Tis time I took you home."

"One moment she was dancing with Booth, and the next she'd disappeared completely. I swear, Jamie, that girl takes perverse pleasure in giving me apoplexy."

Jamie smiled and tipped his chair back on the hind legs. *Perverse pleasure* is precisely what he'd had with Missy

Metcalfe. Well, a form of it, at any rate. He hadn't taken her, even when she'd opened her legs in an invitation. Nor had he taken her up on those lush, full breasts so enticingly offered when she'd pushed her gown lower to reveal them in their full glory.

She'd been completely nonplussed that he'd refused her and had gone even further to tempt him, pinching and teasing those taut rosy buds herself until they'd tilted up to beg his mouth. Had it been Gina to do those things, he'd have found the scene insanely erotic. But Miss Metcalfe was so practiced, so contrived, that she'd been no more interesting to him than Suzette. And he suspected the rumors about her were kinder than the actual truth.

He suspected, in fact, that Missy might have been sent to distract him. He'd called her address to the driver and dropped her in front of her house a few minutes later, leaving her to adjust her own clothing.

Now, well past midnight and safely tucked away in a corner of the Crown and Bear, he merely sighed and nodded to Charlie's complaints. Gina was, undoubtedly, elusive. And perverse.

"She was with Adam Booth, by God. The two of them sitting there in the dark, her hand in his. I thought she was sweet on you, Jamie. I'd have sworn there was something powerful between you two."

Booth? Could she prefer Booth to him? The notion angered him. She'd given herself to him and, virgin or not, he damn well knew she hadn't given that up to anyone before last night. No, there had to be another explanation for their meeting.

"Calm yourself, Charlie. We had a rather nasty argument before I left the ball. Perhaps she was just trying to prick my pride." As he'd tried to prick hers with Missy Metcalfe?

"Must be a new experience for you, eh? A woman who does

not fall all over you? But I still think you should not amuse yourself with her. Keep your carousing to the demimonde."

Jamie merely ignored Charlie, it being far too late for such warnings now. Still, the thought of Gina's hand in Adam Booth's caused him a bad turn. He would have to have a word with the man.

"Ah, here they are," Charlie murmured. "Are you sure you want to do this?"

Jamie watched as Dick and Artie Gibbons sidled through the door, both scanning the room with a quick sweep of dull eyes. "They are utter strangers to truth and honor, Charlie. I really don't know why we bother. If we weren't so damned desperate…"

When Dick saw them he nudged his brother and they headed for Jamie's table. "Hear you was lookin' fer us t'other night at the Cat's Paw," Dick said.

"Aye, we were."

"Y'gots somethin' fer us?"

"We were hoping you'd have something for us."

"Like what?"

"Information. Have you found Henley's hiding place?"

Artie licked his lips, indicating he'd like a drink, and Dick eyed Charlie's glass. Jamie signaled Mick to bring two more glasses and a bottle of whiskey.

The brothers dragged chairs from a nearby table and sat, staring at Jamie as if they could unnerve him. Jamie leaned back in his chair again and crossed his arms over his chest.

Dick broke eye contact when Mick brought the bottle and glasses. Two quick shots later, he seemed ready to talk.

"Found it, but he'd gone." Dick rubbed the stubble that lined his dirty jaw. "Ain't found 'is new hole yet. Y' want more, yer gonna have t' pay fer it."

Jamie ignored the clear extortion and addressed the other

subject that had been on his mind. "Did you hear that Stanley Metcalfe was killed a few days back?"

Artie gave one of his wheezing laughs while Dick merely grinned. "Well, now. Ain't that interestin'."

"Do you know anything about that, Dick?"

"Maybe I got my suspicions."

"I've got mine, too. Want to compare?"

"You first."

"Henley, himself. Someone saw him at the masquerade."

Dick looked surprised. "So y' knows about that, eh?"

"Why do you suppose anyone would want him dead?" Charlie asked.

"Got in somebody's way, I'd say."

"How so?"

"Dunno. Askin' too many questions, 'd be my guess. Kinda like you an' yer brother."

Was that a none too subtle warning for him and Charlie? "Metcalfe aside, there have been an extraordinary number of attacks of late. For instance, someone took a shot at Charlie the night after Metcalfe's murder. I don't take kindly to that."

A shrug was Dick's only answer, but he looked down into his glass and would not meet Jamie's eyes nor look at Charlie. The hair stood up on the back of his neck. Every instinct he had pointed to the Gibbons brothers for that attempt. And here they were, sitting across the table drinking their whiskey. His fingers itched to tighten around Dick's throat and go for Artie after. Instead, he took a deep breath and gave Charlie a sharp warning look.

"Seems like London is getting dangerous for certain men of the ton."

"I don't give a ha'penny for nabobs," Dick said. "They c'n all go to hell, an' I wouldn't care."

"Who would you blackmail then, Dick? Where would you get your money?"

He gave a sideways grin. "We'd find a way. Right, Artie?"

Artie chuckled and bobbed his head.

Charlie narrowed his eyes. "Good idea, Dick. Because I'm thinking jobs might get pretty scarce for you. Hope you've put some money away for a rainy day."

"Never you mind what we gots," Dick snarled. Even Artie turned somber at the mention of money.

Jamie wondered again what these men did with their blood money and how much they'd be paid for killing Charlie and him. One thing had become evident—the Gibbons brothers were not their allies. Either Henley had something on the or he was paying more, and nothing Jamie could say would sway them.

Suddenly, Jamie was done with them. The price to his soul for dealing with such scum was too great and nothing but treachery could come from it. He pushed his chair back and stood, and Charlie followed suit.

"I'm out, lads. No more games. No more bribes. You'd do best to stay out of my sight."

A look of such anger passed over Dick's face that Jamie suspected he was planning revenge. "You sure you wants to make enemies o' us?" he asked.

"Never surer of anything in my life."

Dick and Artie stood together and measured themselves against Jamie and Charlie. The decision made, they backed toward the door and faded into the night.

From the bar, Mick Haddon grinned and raised a glass to them.

By the time Charlie arrived at the Argyle Rooms with his charges the next night, Jamie was waiting anxiously. After what Charlie had told him last night about Eugenia and Adam Booth being closeted together in a darkened room, he'd been ready to call the man out. Never mind that he was one of Charlie's best friends.

He stood in conversation with their host, Lord Geoffrey Morgan, and watched as a footman lifted Gina's cloak from her shoulders. When she turned toward the room, he broke off in the middle of his sentence. Gina wore a gown of French blue fashioned with a bodice that dipped to a low point between her breasts, revealing only the lush curves to each side. Oh, but it hinted at so much more. A white mother-of-pearl cameo fastened to a matching blue ribbon circled her throat. The gown was tenfold more seductive than Missy Metcalfe's bold gown of last night.

Behind him, he heard a man whisper to his companion. "Good Lord! Who is that breathtaking creature in blue? And what would I have to do to gain an introduction?"

"I believe that is Miss Eugenia O'Rourke. She is the sister of Andrew Hunter's bride, and the chit who was betrothed to the Marquess of Olney but ran off with Devlin Farrell."

"Wild blood, then? All the better. Here's Morgan. Shall we maneuver that introduction?"

As the men moved from behind to face them, Jamie was ready. He'd be damned if he'd allow another man to taste what he'd tasted. Gina was his.

That thought astonished him. *His.* Gina was *his.* Damned if he didn't love her. Why had he never realized that before? Oh, the mere thought of her, the memory of her, had haunted him since they'd met. He'd wanted her for as long as he had known her. He'd been saddened by the realization that she could never love him because he was a memory of everything loathsome to her, but he'd never stopped to realize that he *loved* her. Yesterday he had *proposed* to her. But he'd never recognized his own feelings for what they were. Love had happened to him at last, and it was undiluted Hell.

"'Lo, Morgan," one of the men said.

Geoff Morgan nodded. "Hoppes," he acknowledged. "Worick."

"Excellent diversion," Hoppes said by way of pleasant-ries. "Worick and I were wondering if you could introduce us to that comely creature who just arrived with the Thayer twins."

"Afraid he couldn't," Jamie answered for Geoff.

Geoff covered his surprise and regarded Jamie with an appraising eye. "Uh, yes. My good friend Hunter, here, has laid claim."

Hoppes and Worick regarded Jamie with a jaundiced eye. "Declared yourself, have you?" Worick asked.

He nodded.

"Haven't heard any announcements," Hoppe added.

Jamie gave them a cold smile. "You will."

"If she should change her mind, tell her I am waiting."

Change her mind? She hadn't the least notion yet that she would say yes. But she would. He'd do whatever he had to do to make that happen. "She won't."

Both men gave a quick bow to Geoff and backed away.

"Congratulations?" Geoff ventured.

"She hasn't said yes."

"Will she?"

Jamie shrugged. "I may have some persuading to do."

"Just made up your mind, eh? From the interest she is garnering, I'd make my intentions clear very soon, Jamie."

Excellent idea. "Thanks for the advice," he said, handing his wineglass to Geoff and heading for Gina's group.

Charlie saw him coming, glanced between him and Gina, and took a single step back to make room for Jamie at Gina's side. She was engrossed in conversation with Harriett Thayer and she hadn't seen him.

"Miss Eugenia," he greeted her with a bow.

She turned to him and his heart stood still for a moment, then resumed beating in a rapid measure. She was dazzling and conjured memories of their night together. Her lips curved in a smile, then dropped into a straight line as she evidently recalled their last conversation. He'd been boorish and bad-tempered, but she'd tweaked his pride rather badly. He'd apologize and find some way to make it up to her.

He extended his hand in a silent invitation, then held his breath at her hesitation as she stared at a point over his shoulder.

"Miss O'Rourke! How fortuitous. I have been looking for you. Might I beg this dance?"

"I was… Of course, Mr. Booth."

Chapter Sixteen

Gina glanced over her shoulder at Jamie. He was staring after her with such a thunderous look that she suspected she would answer for it later. But she could not depend upon finding a moment with Mr. Booth later.

"Did I interrupt something, Miss O'Rourke?"

"Not precisely, sir. I collect Mr. Hunter was about to ask me for a dance, but I wanted to talk to you."

He grinned, clearly pleased to have been chosen over Jamie. "I am gratified. As it happens, I have been able to uncover a bit of information for you. 'Twill be difficult to discuss this over a dance. Shall we take a turn about the room, instead?"

She took his arm as he led her to the perimeter of the dance floor. Her excitement built when he laid one hand over hers as they walked slowly. "I wish there were someplace we could be private, Miss O'Rourke. This is not the sort of thing one would wish to be overheard."

"I have not been here before, Mr. Booth. I do not know if there are any private venues."

"There are some private rooms, but I believe that would cause a bit of a scandal, would it not?"

She laughed. If Mr. Booth knew just how accustomed she was to scandal, there would be no denying him. She gestured to the niches with upholstered benches along the far wall, which provided quiet, private opportunities for conversation.

He led her to one near the back of the room, and therefore away from the light of the chandeliers and the sound of the orchestra. He waited for her to be seated, then sat quite close to her and tilted his head toward her. "There, quite cozy, are we not?"

She smiled and folded her hands in her lap. Mr. Booth was flirting and she did not want to give him an opportunity to touch her in a familiar manner. "Quite," she agreed.

He took a deep breath and fastened his attention on the toes of his shoes. "After we talked last night, I spent a great deal of time wrestling with my conscience. Though I had no complicity in what was done to you, Miss O'Rourke, I still bear a measure of responsibility and guilt for my presence there, and that is why I have agreed to help you.

"I was not the only one to be drawn into the promise of entertainment of a salacious sort. Metcalfe was another. I can see now that Henley and Daschel were slowly accustoming us to experiencing ever increasing debasements. He took us on an excursion to Bedlam, then to those tableaus with nak—unclothed females in provocative poses. At each turn, he increased the titillation, likely believing that we would join him in his 'brotherhood.' Please believe me when I say that I had no knowledge of his true purpose that night."

Gina sighed deeply, wondering just how many men present that night would make Mr. Booth's claim. And were they true? Or merely an excuse? She glanced at him from the corner of her eye and thought he appeared sincere. She had learned nothing if not that appearances could be deceiving. But he hadn't asked for forgiveness, so she remained silent.

"And because I feel a need to atone, I have begun asking questions. There are very few of us left—those who were there that night. It ruined a good many lives, you know."

A polite way of saying Mr. Henley was blackmailing them? Yes, he'd already told her this. "How much have you paid, Mr. Booth?"

He gave her a quick appreciative glance. "To date? At least a quarter of my fortune, Miss O'Rourke. And I have heard by the grapevine that I am not the only one. Henley has made quite a fortune on this, and I've begun to wonder if it wasn't the whole purpose from the beginning. He and Daschel were both living beyond their means. What better plan to improve their fortunes than to draw the ton's wealthiest men into a scandal, and then bleed them to keep quiet?"

"You will not make me see you and the others as victims, sir. You could have refused Mr. Henley at each step."

"I am painfully aware of that. He played on our basest instincts and won, to our everlasting shame. Henley must be put down like the rabid dog he is."

"Quite an advantage to you and the others if he were. I cannot help seeing your motives as being rather self-serving."

For the first time, Mr. Booth looked angry. "What would you have me and the others do, Miss O'Rourke? Pay with our entire fortunes and allow Henley to go scot-free? Why, I have come to think Henley continues the blackmail to enrich himself in preparation for an escape."

She fell silent. Perhaps enlisting Mr. Booth's aid had been a mistake. Could she ever join forces with anyone who'd been there that night? Could she ever trust him?

"I doubt it will make much difference in the end," Mr. Booth continued in a lowered voice. "Henley is determined to ruin us all. And he has more than money as a motive for some of us."

"Because you can testify against him?"

"I do not believe he is much worried over that. How could we testify without exposing and implicating ourselves?"

Gina had thought that same thing. Self-interest was a powerful emotion. She could not expect anyone to step forward if they would suffer in any way for doing so.

"Nevertheless, Miss O'Rourke, I have been able to determine a few things. First, I believe that Henley killed Metcalfe."

She was certain of it, but one question remained. "Why? If he was extorting money from Mr. Metcalfe, would killing him not run counter to his purpose?"

"I believe there was some sort of personal grudge. And in such cases, it tends to be a woman."

How could it be possible that Mr. Henley would have tender feelings for any woman and still do the things he'd done? And yet, Mr. Renquist had reported that Mr. Henley had met with a woman, and Gina had seen the proof of that in the letters.

"I believe there may be a chance to trap him through her, but I have not been able to find out who she is. I am still looking. I hope I shall have a name soon."

"I shall pray for it, Mr. Booth. The poor thing needs to be warned what sort of man he is."

Mr. Booth nodded in agreement. "I shall keep looking, Miss O'Rourke, but I do not see him frequently. Only when he wants money."

"When was the last time you saw him, sir?"

"The night of the Morris masquerade. He was collecting from me, but he was obsessing over something he said he'd misplaced in his last move."

Gina turned to him. "When was that?"

"Very recently, I believe. He said he'd gone back to his

previous rooms but that the landlord told him everything he hadn't taken had been disposed of."

Could this *something* be the box Mr. Renquist had purchased for her? But she couldn't recall anything of particular value except for the dragon cravat pin. Had she missed some clue in the items? Mr. Renquist had turned the list and letters over to the Home Office, but she still had the box.

"Miss O'Rourke?"

She came back to the conversation with a start. "Yes?"

"There is one more thing."

She met his gaze and waited.

"The last time I spoke with Stanley Metcalfe, he was very nervous. He mentioned that he knew something, or had learned something, that Henley would kill for. Whether he meant that figuratively or literally, I cannot say."

Yes, Mr. Metcalfe had been quite nervous when they'd met at the masquerade, and moments later he was dead. She sighed. There had been altogether too many deaths.

"Do you wish me to continue asking questions?"

"Please, Mr. Booth. Anything might help. Most especially, if you could find out where he lodges…but be careful."

He nodded as he stood, and offered her his hand. "I should take you back to your friends, Miss O'Rourke. We have been gone longer than a dance or two."

Heavens! She had lost track of time.

But she needed a moment to think about the things Mr. Booth had told her. She shook her head. "Go on without me, sir. I need a moment to collect my thoughts. And thank you so much for your help."

He bowed and backed away from her, a puzzling expression on his face.

Her head spun. What had he said? That he suspected Mr. Henley had killed Mr. Metcalfe over a woman? But what women might Mr. Henley and Mr. Metcalfe have had in common? Christina Race? Surely not! Christina had been hopelessly in love with Mr. Metcalfe. Then, Miss Metcalfe? Ridiculous. Unless…Mr. Henley had somehow wronged the girl, as he'd wronged Gina.

Suddenly she wanted to go home and examine the contents of Mr. Henley's wooden box. Was there some damning clue in the tiny cravat pin with its ruby eyes? Something that would betray where he could be found?

Jamie studied Gina from across the dance floor. She had shaken her head and Booth had left her there alone, retreating with an air of extreme nervousness. Now she looked down and a dark ringlet fell over her shoulder. She brushed it back and continued deep in thought. What could cause her utter distraction? An indecent proposal?

He shifted his attention to the retreating Booth. He should go after the bounder and beat him within an inch of his life. If he had hurt Gina in any way, had caused her the least distress, he would pay for it.

But Gina stood and began walking toward him and he put Booth from his mind. They had matters to discuss. Things to settle between them. She came directly for him and he was gratified that she did not attempt to avoid him further.

"I think we need to talk, Mr. Hunter."

He raised an eyebrow. "Ah, I am—Mr. Hunter? So you are still angry with me?"

Her lush lips twitched. "A bit. You were not quite a gentleman last night."

"You were not quite a lady," he reminded her.

"But you left me unfulfilled."

"Really? Hmm. I do not recall it quite that way. I believe I was the one to leave unfulfilled."

She flushed but bravely met his gaze. "I am referring to the fact that you did not answer my question."

God. How could he give her an answer that would satisfy her? The truth was so…blasted unsatisfactory. Lie? But that was not in his nature. She tilted her head to one side, and still he did not answer.

She took a deep breath and exhaled slowly. "Very well. I shall wait for you to get over your pique. Meantime, there are other matters we must discuss. I have information regarding Mr. Henley, and—"

He took her arm and turned her about. "And we should not discuss this where we could be overheard."

He guided her down a corridor to a salon, ushered her through the door and gestured for her to sit on a small settee, leaving the door ajar for the sake of propriety, and to preclude any repeat of last night in the sitting room at Duchess House.

When he turned back to her, she appeared so proper that he almost sighed. "Now, Miss O'Rourke, I would like to hear any news you might have of Mr. Henley or any of his cronies."

"Last night I enlisted Mr. Booth to assist my inquiries, and he has brought me news."

"How in the world did you persuade him to take that risk?"

"I asked him if we had met, and he seemed embarrassed. He was beneath the chapel that night, and confessed that he was ashamed to have been even a small part of that. I used his guilt to gain his consent."

Ah, then he could let Booth live. Fortunate for them both since a duel at dawn could draw all manner of unwelcome attention.

Gina smiled at him, evidently proud of her machinations. "Tonight he brought me news. According to Mr. Booth, Mr. Henley has been blackmailing a good many people. I believe he may be putting money aside for an escape. A rather grand one, from the sums I gather he's been collecting."

Jamie nodded as he paced with his hands behind his back. He knew all this from Mr. Morris, but he did not want to stop Gina when she'd finally trusted him enough to bring him such news.

"I have also come to believe that Mr. Henley is involved somehow with a woman. Perhaps one who meets with him frequently."

This was new information. "Do you know who she is?"

"I fear not. Though surely there cannot be too many who would be willing to trust him."

"If they knew his true nature," he appended. "Society at large does not know of the events that night, or before. Everyone has been quite close-mouthed. Husbands would not want their wives to know, nor would unmarried bucks want such news spoiling their chances to land an heiress."

"There is more. Mr. Booth suspects the woman is from the ton. He thinks that Mr. Henley killed Mr. Metcalfe over her. Nothing else makes sense, since killing Mr. Metcalfe would dry up the funds he was extorting. Do you know of anyone Mr. Henley might have been close to before he was exposed?"

He tried to think of the women he'd seen with Henley. Since he'd been friends with Metcalfe, he'd been seen in the company of Missy, and also Miss Race. Apart from that… Wait! That was why he had recognized Miss Race—he'd seen her in the company of both Metcalfe and Henley on a few occasions: the theatre, soirees and a few more questionable events. Could she—surely not. An unknown woman, then. Someone who traveled in their circles, but had not been previously connected with Henley. Yes, it made sense. A personal grievance was the missing motive for Henley to kill a friend—especially one who was paying him for his silence. He would inform Wycliffe at once of this new avenue to investigate.

He thought aloud. "We could find Henley through this woman."

She looked uncertain, as if she wanted to say more, then she shrugged and the moment was gone. "I am glad I could help. I would do more, you know. Whatever is necessary."

He admired her bravery and determination. "I wish you would do less, Gina. I do not like you putting yourself in harm's way."

"You will be getting your wish very soon now. Mother and I are leaving in two days. Meantime, I intend to do everything I can to bring an end to this."

"Two days..." Jamie's gut twisted. Two days, and Gina would be gone from his life. Two days, and life would return to its dull sameness.

He reached out to touch her cheek when the unmistakable report of a pistol being fired reached them. The sound had come from the street and he crossed the little room to look out the window.

Almost directly beneath them, a body lay facedown on the cobblestone. By the manner of the man's dress, he had been in attendance at one of the events at the Argyle Rooms that night. As he watched, people began to gather around the body. Jamie recognized Geoff Morgan and Charlie among them.

"Charlie?" he called.

His brother, kneeling by his friend, looked up, an expression of grave concern on his face. "Booth," he mouthed.

Beside him, Gina struggled to catch her breath. "No..."

"Find the twins and stay with them until I come for you," he told her.

"But—"

He dashed down the corridor to the servant's steps, the quickest path to the street below. He did not realize Gina had followed him until he was beside his brother.

"What the hell happened?"

Charles looked furious. "We were just talking."

He turned Booth over to reveal a bloodstain oozing over the crisp white linen of his shirt and a look of utter surprise on his face, frozen at the moment of his death. Charlie closed the man's eyes.

There was a soft moan, a hand gripping his sleeve. He turned to find Gina's attention riveted on the dead man. "Because of me. He was killed because he was helping me."

She was near hysteria. He needed to give her something to focus on, and he needed her to be safely inside, away from this debacle.

"Go inside, Gina. Find the Thayers, and stay with them."

She took a step back, then another, her attention never leaving Booth's body. Worried that she was in shock, he reached out to her, intending to take her to her friends to have them calm her while he and Charlie got to the bottom of this tragedy.

Another loud report reverberated in the narrow street and Jamie spun Gina behind him, shielding her from harm. In the confusion, the gathered men shouted and began to scramble away from Booth's body. But Charlie, face up, lay motionless on the cobbles, a terrifying crimson stain spreading across his left shoulder.

Geoff Morgan and a few others sprinted in the direction the shot had come from.

Jamie gave Gina a quick shake to startle her from her shock. "Run, Gina. Find a doctor, and send him to us. *Hurry.*"

He knelt by his brother, relieved to hear Gina's retreating footsteps as she ran to do as he asked. He unfastened his cravat and pressed it to Charlie's wound, trying to stem the flow of blood.

"Charlie? Charlie, wake up. Stay with us, man. Come on. Open your eyes, Charlie. Fight, damn it!"

His brother's eyes fluttered open. "Christ…where'd that come from?"

"Shut up. Save your breath. Gina's gone for a doctor."

Charlie gave a faint nod. "Don't think it's too bad. Barely hurts."

"You're in shock, you idiot."

Charlie's chuckle turned into a gasp for breath. "I'm fine. Go after…killer."

"I'm staying with you until help arrives. Did you see who it was?"

"Think…Gibbons."

"Did you see them?"

"Smelled them."

"Who were they after? You or Booth?"

"Both. Second shot came…from a second pistol. Not… enough time to reload."

That was good enough for Jamie. He'd get word to Wycliffe immediately. And his brothers.

Morgan and the others who had chased after the shooter returned and Morgan shook his head, his lips pressed into a grim line. "Gone," was his only comment.

The Gibbons brothers knew every alley and hiding place in the city. It would not be difficult for them to simply disappear. But now Jamie knew their favorite places, and knew the brothers were not wily enough to realize that every Hunter, every runner and every agent of the Home Office would be after them.

A moment later Gina was back, a doctor who had been in attendance in her wake. Jamie stood as the doctor began to cut Charlie's jacket away from the wound to assess the extent of the damage. There was so much blood. Could Charlie survive?

Gina came to stand beside him. "He will recover, Jamie. God would not be that cruel."

He slipped his arm around her, pulling her close, wanting to believe her and grateful for the comfort she offered. Comfort she'd been denied when her sister had been murdered and she'd been placed on an altar.

He kissed the top of her head as a crowd gathered behind them, not caring who might see or gossip. "Gina," he whispered for her ears only, "I need you to go home and be safe or I will not be able to do what I must."

She nodded and backed away to rejoin the Thayer twins, who were now entrusted to Morgan's charge. He'd see them safely home.

Chapter Seventeen

When Lord Morgan had delivered Gina home and come in to give Andrew the news about Charles, the ruckus had woken everyone but Mama, who always took laudanum to sleep—a habit she'd acquired after Cora's death. Moments later, Lord Morgan and Andrew had left together, but not before Andrew loaded a pistol and pushed it in the waistband of his trousers. She had no doubt they were off to rouse Lord Lockwood, the eldest Hunter brother. Oh, how she wished she were a man and could be doing something instead of waiting!

She took advantage of her mother's habit and filched an extra vial from her mother's night table and poured a measure for herself—anything to dull the horror and allow her to sleep. She could think of nothing but the events of the past hour. Mr. Booth dead. Charles Hunter at death's door. What could possibly happen next?

She sat in the overstuffed chair before the fireplace in her room, staring into the banked embers and thinking that the bitter taste of the laudanum was vaguely familiar. With an uncomfortable jolt, she realized that this was what the

Brotherhood had drugged her with. Even now the effects were seeping through her, making her drowsy.

The small mantel clock struck three times, stirring her from her reverie. Nancy had gone to bed long ago, so she sighed deeply and stood to remove her dress. The French-blue gown was simple, since it fastened in the front, but her stays took longer to loosen.

And there, at the end of one lace, was the little key for which she still hadn't found a lock. A key that Mr. Metcalfe had given her. Mr. Metcalfe—another man who was now dead because he had tried to help her. How would she ever gain absolution for being responsible for so much pain and devastation?

She untied the key and lay it on her writing desk. If she did not find the lock before she left for Ireland, she would give the key to Jamie. Perhaps he would find the lock one day.

Her dressing gown lay across her bed and she slipped it on and tied the sash and blew out her candle. The embers in the fireplace cast eerie shadows on the wall behind her. Something in the flicker made her shiver, and she thought she saw a movement in the deeper shadows near the window. Was it the effects of the laudanum?

Ridiculous. She was imagining things. The events of the evening had disturbed her. But there it was again. Ah, her own reflection in the cheval mirror in the corner. She gazed at herself, wondering where the carefree Eugenia O'Rourke of Belfast had gone. Forever changed. Because of Cora. Because of Jamie.

The reflected gleam of her eyes caught her attention and she went closer to the mirror, as if she would find the answer to her questions in her own eyes. But it was not her in the mirror. It was the girl she'd been *that* night. Helpless, she watched as the scene played out in her mirror.

She lay on a cot or pallet of some sort that had been placed on a bare stone floor. She tried to open her eyes, but couldn't. She was not witless, but helpless. Deep, quiet voices floated around her, speaking words she couldn't recall. But there were names she recognized. Hunter. Daschel. Henley.

She forced her eyes open, a monumental task. Shadowy figures in deeply hooded robes moved about her, stripping away her clothing, touching her, anointing her with sickly sweet oil and laughing. Then there came a softer voice. A woman's voice. She leaned close, her face still in shadow, and cooed something in Gina's ear, something that had terrified her then but she couldn't remember now. Others came to touch her but, oddly, she couldn't feel them. Her senses were deadened. It seemed as if these things were happening to someone else—dreadful things that made her close her eyes again and forget.

Gina blinked and the vision in the mirror shifted. Now she was wearing a transparent gown of pleated lawn, fastened low between her breasts and dropping to the tips of her bare toes. Her dark hair, crowned by a diadem, was loose and fell to the middle of her back. One of the robed men produced a carved box and turned it upside down. He took a small packet from the drawer and poured the contents into a cup, which was brought to her and pressed to her lips. A heavy wooden door swung open and she heard a distant chanting. Her head was tilted upward by a robed man and she was forced to drink a bitter brew as distant church bells chimed. Lethargy. Torpor. She could not think, could not move, merely stand in a witless state.

It's time, someone whispered in her ear as men on each side of her took her arms and led her forward. The shadows shifted, and she was lying supine on a stone altar as a dagger descended toward her throat....

Gina gasped, sucking in deep breaths of night air as her hand went to her scar. She was trembling, barely able to stand.

Oh, she'd prayed to remember, and now she had. Memory or dream? Did it matter? She knew those things she'd seen in the mirror were real. Somewhere between her anointing and being dressed in the Egyptian gown, her mind was still blank, but the rest was finally clear.

She held to her bedpost to keep from sinking to her knees. All those horrid memories, and she still didn't have the answer to her question. But Jamie knew. She could only assume the worst, and that he had been trying to spare her pride by remaining silent. But he wouldn't lie to her. Jamie never lied.

She had been ruined, and nothing could change that. Nothing could ever make her clean again, or worthy of Jamie's love. And he knew it, too.

And Henley would have to pay.

Henley. Oh, the box! Henley's little box—the box in her vision! She went to her writing desk and took the carved box from a drawer. She tried to push her key into the lock Mr. Renquist had forced, but it didn't fit. She turned it over and felt along the carvings for something to trigger the little drawer into opening. She found it in the curve of a flower. The slightest pressure tripped a spring to pop the drawer back. There, in a drawer shallow enough to avoid detection, was a folded piece of paper and a small paper packet that held yellowish brown flakes.

She sniffed and recoiled, knowing only too well from the bitter odor what the packet contained: opium. But the paper? She unfolded the sheet and found a list of names. Were these the men Mr. Booth had told her about? The men Mr. Henley was blackmailing? She ran her finger down the list and stopped at—

James Hunter
Charles Hunter
Andrew Hunter

Adam Booth
Stanley Metcalfe
Marcus Wycliffe
Eugenia O'Rourke

And other names she did not know. Could Mr. Henley be blackmailing Jamie and his brothers? Impossible. Why, she was on that list, and it was no secret they'd all been at the chapel that night. They'd rescued her and Bella. No need to pay hush money. But two of the men on that list were dead, another wounded, and God only knew how many more of the names she did not know were dead.

She squared her shoulders, determining to give the list to Jamie as soon as she saw him. He would know what to do with it. But she would keep the opium and the key. She might still have use for them. *Two more days. Two more nights.* She would make the most of them.

Dawn was breaking before Charlie stirred and groaned. Jamie shot out of his chair and leaned over his brother. "Charlie, are you awake?"

"Aye." He sighed, still not opening his eyes. "Am I going to live?"

Jamie jerked the bell pull to alert the staff at Lockwood's London mansion to summon his other brothers. "Of course, you dolt. The doctor said the ball did not do much damage. As long as you do not infect the wound, you'll be weak awhile but otherwise right as rain."

Charlie opened his eyes at last and tried to push himself up until Jamie propped him and pushed pillows behind his back. "Then why does it hurt so deuced much?"

"Because you are father's secret daughter."

Charlie chucked. "Womanish, am I? That's what I like about you, Jamie. Y'don't waste time with sympathy."

Jamie smiled. Coddling Charlie would be the surest way

to alarm him. "Sympathy would be lost on you anyway. And the doctor said you'll be up and about in a day or two."

Lockwood burst into the guest room, Drew and Devlin Farrell fast on his heels. "Charlie?"

"Good God, all my brothers in the same room! It must be worse than I thought."

Drew went to pull the draperies back from the window, exposing a violet-pink dawn above adjacent rooftops. "Sarah will be given the news as soon as she rises, so I expect she will be here soon."

"We'd best get down to business before she starts hovering—fluffing pillows and spooning porridge," Lockwood said. He took a chair near the foot of Charlie's bed. "Tell us what happened."

Charlie frowned and lay back against his pillows. "Damned if I know. Booth was in deep conversation with Miss O'Rourke for a time, then greeted a few people and departed. I thought it was time he and I had a chat, so I followed him out to the street. That is when he was shot."

"Did he say anything before he died?"

"He was shot in the gut—couldn't catch his breath before he expired. There was no time to search him before Jamie and the others arrived. Then…" Charlie shrugged and winced when the action caused him pain.

Drew squeezed Charlie's other shoulder. "An inch or two lower, and it would have pierced your heart, Charlie. You were very lucky."

"Yeah. Lucky."

"You mentioned the Gibbons brothers," Jamie reminded him.

"Didn't know they were such crack shots," Charlie said. "I always thought if they came after me, it would be with a knife. I did not see them—anyone, in fact—but the shot came from the alley. Perhaps I smelled garbage, but I thought it was them."

"Little difference between the two," Lockwood assessed.

"If Morgan hadn't chased after them, they'd likely have picked Jamie off."

"What made them so bold? Most often they are like rats, doing their business in secret."

"Jamie threw down the gauntlet when they wouldn't cooperate and he refused to pay them for nothing," Charlie said.

Devlin rolled his eyes. "A bit rash, eh, Jamie?"

"In retrospect."

"But I think it just as likely that Charlie is acquiring quite a fearsome reputation in the rookeries." Devlin sighed deeply and shook his head. "I warned you it would gain you respect, Charlie, but it also makes you a target."

"So Wycliffe was right about there being a contract out on a Hunter. Just the wrong Hunter."

"Or all of us," Drew concluded. "He'd have reason enough."

"The question is, what shall we do about it?"

Jamie assessed the gathering. Lockwood was looking every inch the family patriarch, Drew appeared rather deadly, Charlie had an angry look about him and Devlin was, as always, unreadable. And Jamie? Well, he was suddenly considering Wycliffe's veiled suggestion that the Gibbons brothers were a danger to society a bit more seriously.

Lockwood sighed deeply and stood. "I shall have to think on this, perhaps discuss it with Marcus." He went to the door and paused. "Oh, and I hear that Mrs. O'Rourke and her daughter are leaving day after tomorrow."

Drew slid a sideways glance at Jamie. "I must say that I will not miss her much," he confessed. "But I will be sad to see Eugenia go."

"And you, Jamie?" Lockwood asked.

Jamie crossed the room and went to stand by the window. "I had hoped Mrs. O'Rourke would change her mind, but I collect that is not to be."

"And Miss Eugenia?"

"Yes, damn it. I will be sorry to say goodbye."

"Have you considered…?"

Jamie gave Charlie a nasty look. Just how much had he told their eldest brother? "I have considered everything, Lockwood. It is hopeless."

"Everything?"

He gave Lockwood a curt nod.

"Then I am very sorry for you, Jamie. Such opportunities rarely come twice in a lifetime. But since she will be going home, I suppose the least we can do is see that justice is served."

Sunday at noon was not a usual time to pay calls, but Gina had hoped the family would be gone to church, and that she might have a private word with Christina. And now, studying the hollows beneath her friend's dark eyes, she was glad she'd come. Christina did not look well.

"Have you been out at all?" Gina asked. "Just a short stroll through your garden might be the very tonic you need."

Christina looked at Gina with an air of hopelessness. "Father told me this morning that Mr. Booth was killed last night."

She nodded. "That is why I've come."

"To tell me about Mr. Booth? But I already know."

"To ask your help again, Christina. I feel as if there is more that you know. Perhaps something you have not thought about, or something you forgot. Something that will help us put an end to all this."

"Us? But what could we do, Gina?"

She took Christina's hand and led her toward the door to

the garden, unwilling to risk being overheard by the servants. "Mr. Henley should be stopped by whatever means necessary. And you, Christina dear, are my safeguard. I shall tell you everything, and you will report to the authorities in case something…untoward should happen to me."

Christina blinked in the bright sunlight and clutched Gina's sleeve. "Do not tell me anything, Gina. Too much knowledge is a dangerous thing."

"Then tell me Mr. Metcalfe's secret."

She shook her head and covered her heart with one hand. "There is really nothing I can tell you."

She was hiding something that could have damaged her fiancé! Gina knew that instinctively, just as she'd always known when her own sisters were hiding something. Did it regard Mr. Henley's paramour? "Can you think of a woman Mr. Henley might have been close to? Someone he kept company with? One of your friends, perhaps, or a widow who could go about unchaperoned?"

Christina's eyes widened and Gina knew she'd come close to her secret. "Stanley and I used to keep company with Mr. Booth and Missy, but that was more so that Stanley could keep an eye on her. He always said she was wild. Sometimes Mr. Henley would accompany us but he would not bring a woman. That is why I was surprised when he brought you to that tableau."

"He was cozening me, Christina. Trying to make me trust him so that I would go with him when the time was right."

Christina sat heavily on a bench in the middle of the garden and turned her face up to the sun. "And you did…"

"But there must have been others. Someone he favored at balls and soirees?"

"Just me and Missy. And once, Mrs. Huffington."

Gina recalled hearing that name before but she could not put it with a face. "I do not believe I have met her."

"She is the ward of Lady Caroline Betman. The orphaned child of a dear friend, I think. Widowed twice though quite young."

Would that fit with what Mr. Booth had told her? But what would Mr. Henley want with a poor relation? He was a money-grubbing extortionist, intent upon amassing a fortune from other men's coffers. Could he have been cozening Mrs. Huffington for the same purpose as he'd cozened Gina? Or was there more? A young woman widowed twice? Could there be something, well, murderous about her? Something that complemented Mr. Henley's nature?

Suddenly Christina blinked, took her hand and squeezed tightly. "Gina, you must go home immediately. I have had the most extraordinary feeling…oh, what if you are the next to be killed?" She stood and hurried back toward the garden door. "We should not be outside."

Gina followed, curious at Christina's sudden change of mood. The moment they were inside and the door was closed, Christina turned to her, earnestness written clearly on her face. "You must listen carefully to me, Gina. About Mr. Henley. He used to watch Missy as if he wanted to seduce her. I always thought that odd—after all, he was Stanley's friend."

"I rather thought Mr. Henley wanted to seduce most every girl he met," Gina said.

Christina led the way straight through the sitting room toward the front door, leading Gina with a hand on her arm. "It occurs to me now that he may have been planning to put Mr. Booth out of the way so he could have Missy even back then. I shall send her a letter at once, but you must also warn her at the first opportunity. Come to me tomorrow. I need to think. It is all so confusing."

Gina nodded as she was fairly thrown out the door and into Nancy's waiting arms. How very astonishing!

"Did you make her angry, miss?" Nancy asked as they entered the foot traffic on the street.

Gina paused to look back at the door. A curtain moved in an upper window, as if someone had been watching her. "I must have."

They walked slowly, since Gina had no desire to return to the house where her mother would be in a frenzy of packing and making arrangements for their departure. She knew she and Nancy would have to pack the trunk that had been delivered to her room that morning, and she was surprised by her own reluctance. A month ago, she'd have given anything to be going home. But today?

Today she only wanted to enjoy the afternoon, which had turned crisp as a precursor to autumn. She wanted to think of seeing James at the family dinner Lord Lockwood was hosting to mark their departure, and the musicale after. She wanted to think of anything, in fact, but her imminent departure.

Nancy tugged at her sleeve. "Oh, miss! There's Tom, the milkman. Might I have a word with him? Who can say if I will be seeing him again?"

The lament was so akin to Gina's emotions that she could only smile and nod. An empty park bench beneath a tree offered her refuge, and she sat where she could watch her maid talk and flirt with the strapping young milkman.

She had just lulled into a pleasant lassitude when a hand on her shoulder and a voice from behind her interrupted her thoughts.

"No. Do not turn around, Miss O'Rourke. I have a knife at your back. I would hate to use it so soon. No scenes, eh?"

Everything inside her screamed with terror. Mr. Henley! She would recognize his voice anywhere now. She took several deep breaths to steady her nerves before she could speak. "What do you want?"

"I hear you may be leaving in a day or two, m'dear. Is that so?"

She nodded.

"Ah. Well, I had been putting our meeting off until a bit later, but now I think I shall have to move it up."

"You would not kill me here. I would scream. Half the park would see you and give chase."

"You underestimate me. I do not intend to kill you *here,* chit, unless you force my hand. If I wanted you dead, you would be dead. I've had more opportunities than you know. No, I only wanted to inform you that you will never be safe from me. I will have my revenge—sooner or later, here or in Belfast. I will come for you. You owe me, and I will damn well collect."

Cold anger drove her fear away. She would not be his victim yet again. She braced herself, catapulted from the bench, and spun around to face him. His look of utter amazement at her boldness was reward enough for the risk she'd taken. "Your days are numbered, Mr. Henley. You cannot elude James Hunter for long. He grows even more weary of your threats than I. Do your worst or slink back into the hole you came from."

His eyes darted right and left as if measuring his chances of killing her and escaping. "*Your* days are numbered, Miss O'Rourke. Yours and everyone who ever helped you."

She watched him run toward the street before she sank back to the bench, her knees turning to water. The moment she caught her breath, she would ask Mr. Renquist for a pocket pistol. Mr. Henley could not come for her if she went for him first.

Chapter Eighteen

Jamie watched Gina, in conversation with Sarah and the Thayer twins, across the music room at Lockwood's manor. She wore a greenish concoction that put him in the mind of spring and everything fresh and new. Her frequent glances in his direction had not gone unnoticed by Drew, who nudged him with a question.

"Are you really going to let her go back to Ireland? Have you asked her to marry you?"

He'd started to. And then she'd told him she'd only made love to him to discover if she'd been virgin or not, and *he'd* felt like a deceived maiden. Even as the hurt resurfaced, he knew he'd been an idiot, let his wounded pride get in the way. Gina would never have slept with him if she hadn't felt something.

"No," he admitted.

"Time is running out. 'Twould be a bit unfair to ask her at the docks, eh?"

"I do not know if she loves me, Drew."

His brother laughed. "Then you're deaf and blind. Charlie

old me weeks ago. I could see it the moment Mrs. O'Rourke announced her plans. In fact, everyone seems to know but you."

Gina chose that moment to look toward him and a faint smile lifted the corners of her mouth. He returned the smile and was rewarded with a soft blush. She loved him? Only two weeks ago, she had told him that he was a reminder of all that had happened to her, and that she was uncomfortable in his presence. When had that changed?

He had taken a step toward her when Drew stopped him. "You haven't said how you feel, Jamie. Do not speak for her if you cannot match her feelings."

"If she loves me half as much as I love her, I'll be content."

Gina appeared nervous when he arrived at her side and gave a small bow. "Miss O'Rourke, might I have a word with you?"

She looked askance at his sister and, at her nod, she accepted his hand. He could have sworn he detected a little tremble there. After all they'd been through, how could she possibly be afraid of him?

"I wished to speak with you, too. There are some things I must give you."

He led her to the terrace and stepped out to the balustrade, his curiosity piqued. "What things?"

"I have uncovered something new. There is a woman associated with Mr. Henley. I do not yet know how, but she is someone who has been helping him. Perhaps hiding him."

"How do you know that?"

"I…I saw a packet of letters. One of them said that the woman was working on a solution to his problem, and that he should be patient. Oh, and that she intended to meet him again at the usual place on Tuesday."

Jamie had seen that very letter just yesterday in Wycliffe's office. It, along with several others, had been left anonymously on his desk. At this very moment, a number of agents and runners were trying to track those letters back to their writer. "*You* found them?"

"There is more."

Jamie sighed, not missing that she hadn't answered his question. What was she up to?

She plucked a small folded paper from the center of her décolletage and presented it to him. He accepted the paper, still disconcertingly warm from her skin, unfolded it and read the lines. "A list of names?" And a very curious list, indeed. "Where did you get this, Gina?"

She looked at him straight on and squared her shoulders, the endearing gesture that warned him not to ask too many questions. "I believe that is Mr. Henley's handwriting."

Jamie would have to compare the list to other documents in order to verify her conclusion, but he did not doubt her. He read the names again. Booth, Metcalfe and half a dozen others were dead. Frisk had fallen down a flight of stairs. Destin had been run over by a coach when crossing a street. Warren had been thrown from his horse onto the cobbles and cracked his head. Accidents? That many coincidences were unlikely in view of this list. Charlie had been shot last night and, but for the grace of God, would also be dead. And then there were the attempts on his own life.

"A murder list," he concluded.

She shivered. "That is what I feared. Charles…"

"Upstairs being coddled by every maid Lockwood employs. He intends to break free tomorrow." And then he registered her name on the list. Eugenia O'Rourke. Henley wanted Gina dead. He took her arm and turned back to the house. "We need to get you safely home and under guard."

She shrugged his hand away. "I am not going anywhere

Jamie. One day is all I have left. Tomorrow will be my last day in London."

"You have no choice. Once I tell Wycliffe—"

"You won't tell Lord Wycliffe. Nor will you tell your brothers. Not unless you and everyone else on the list is locked away, too. Even then, I doubt it would stop Mr. Henley. He found me in the Morris garden, he found me at the theatre and he found me in the park this afternoon. He told me I was not safe, even when I return to Belfast, and that if he wanted me dead already, I would be. He promised he would come for me when he was ready. He will find me anywhere I go. I cannot hide, Jamie. So I may as well fight."

Such cold fury gripped Jamie's heart that he could happily have snapped Henley's neck like a twig. Gina's bravery was admirable and her logic was irrefutable, but both were far too dangerous.

"If it wasn't me? If it were Hortense or Harriett, would you be so unreasonable? Or would you allow them to avenge themselves?"

Damn. She was right. Hadn't he and Wycliffe allowed Bella to flirt with disaster in order to get to the bottom of the Brotherhood? And wasn't Gina every bit as determined as Bella had been? But this was Gina. *His* Gina. How could he refuse her anything she asked? "Do not leave my side, Gina. Is that understood?"

She brightened and touched his cheek. "Thank you, Jamie. You will not regret this."

"I already do."

She turned to the terrace doors, prepared to go in now that their conversation was over, but he hadn't concluded his business yet. He slipped his arm around her and pulled her against his chest. She looked surprised and not a little curious. He lifted her chin with his forefinger and kissed her plush lips with as much tenderness as he felt in his heart. And when it was done, he uttered the words he'd never thought to say to any woman.

"I love you, Gina O'Rourke. Marry me."

Her eyes widened and her mouth opened. "I…I…"

"You cannot be surprised how I feel about you, Gina. It is plain enough that all my brothers and half the ton knows."

"But you never indicated…never said…love. Why, you've never even answered my question."

"What question is that, my love?"

"Am I…was I…virgin?"

That damned question! Why wouldn't she let it go? "Take it on faith, Gina."

"Faith? But why?"

Because he did not have the answer she needed to hear, and he could not lie. There had been no telltale stain on his sheets, but that alone did not answer her question. Many women did not go to their marriage beds intact, and time, circumstance, accidents and nature could account for the lack of evidence. But, more importantly, he feared that if she believed Henley had used her while she was unconscious, she would destroy her life over it. And his.

"It doesn't matter," he said. "Leave it alone, Gina."

She looked at him with such incredulity that he wondered what he'd said wrong. She opened her mouth, then closed it to a tight line, as if talking to him would be a waste of time, then spun around and went back into the music room, leaving him there without an answer to *his* question.

Oh! That infuriating man! Why wouldn't he just say it? He would not have balked at telling her that she'd been virgin. But he hadn't, so why wouldn't he simply tell her she'd been raped—which most certainly had to be the answer. She glanced over her shoulder to see him staring after her, a look of utter astonishment on his face.

And that remarkable proposal! How she wanted to say yes! She'd marry him in an instant if she only knew that she was worthy. How could she ever answer his question unless he answered hers?

Had she not been looking over her shoulder, she would not have bumped into a beautiful girl dressed all in pale yellow—not a good color for her since her pale yellow hair faded against the backdrop. Still, nothing could have dulled her lively green eyes.

"Eugenia O'Rourke, is it not?"

"How…how did you know?"

"Why, you are all the talk of the ton."

People were gossiping about her? "What are they saying?"

"That you are the woman who has brought James Hunter to heel. If that is so, Miss O'Rourke, well done! I gather that is quite an accomplishment."

Jamie had followed her back through the doors and had gone to stand by his brothers, watching her with a brooding look.

The girl followed her gaze and raised her eyebrows. "My! That is a very dark look Mr. Hunter is giving you, Miss O'Rourke. Did you quarrel?"

She laughed. "Do you think that society will still imagine I have brought him to heel?"

"Love and hate are but two sides to the same coin." She dimpled. "I am Mrs. Huffington. Georgiana Huffington. I fear I am a virtual stranger to London and have met almost no one. I only arrived early in June."

Georgiana Huffington? Divine intervention? That was the name Christina had associated with Mr. Henley, and an opportunity not to be missed. "What a coincidence, Mrs. Huffington. We have friends in common."

"Have we? Well, I've been told London is actually a small

town dressed in city clothes. Who, might I ask, do we have in common?"

"Mr. Cyril Henley."

Mrs. Huffington's smile dropped and her face drained of color. "I...I have met the man, but I would not call him a friend."

Gina gave her a reassuring pat on her shoulder. "Have you seen him recently?"

"I saw him at a garden tea not a week ago, but we did not speak. When he saw me, he went in the other direction. I think he was not there long."

Had Mr. Henley fled because of Mrs. Huffington? "If you do not mind me asking, how did you meet?"

"A mutual friend. I met Miss Melissa Metcalfe through Harriett Thayer, and it was Miss Metcalfe who introduced me to her brother, Mr. Booth and Mr. Henley."

They had walked near the fireplace and Gina was relieved to note that they were quite alone. She had detected a note of reluctance in Mrs. Huffington's voice and did not want to risk being overheard. "Am I correct in thinking you are not pleased with the association?"

"Miss O'Rourke, I scarcely know you. I conceive we are having an unusual conversation for two women who are so recently acquainted. I am not accustomed to speaking so frankly to casual acquaintances."

"And you do not wish to speak ill of anyone, I am certain. I hope you will not think me presumptuous, but my family has had some dealings with Mr. Henley, and I would like to solicit your honest opinion."

"You would do better to ask someone more closely acquainted with him. We have only met on two occasions."

"I gather that was enough to form an opinion?"

Mrs. Huffington looked down at her feet. "Yes."

"An unsatisfactory opinion?" she guessed.

"I think, under the circumstances, I will have to trust you. If I can spare you what I suffered, I feel it is my obligation. But what I have to say is for your ears only, Miss O'Rourke, or I shall say nothing at all." Mrs. Huffington looked around, almost as if she expected to find Mr. Henley lurking nearby. Servants were placing chairs about the room in preparation for the performance and not paying the least attention to them.

Gina nodded, her heartbeat racing. If she could trust Mrs. Huffington, she could enlist her aid in locating Mr. Henley.

"I met Miss Metcalfe at a crush in early July," Mrs. Huffington began. "I recall that precisely, because I was fresh out of mourning and we had just come to town. Miss Metcalfe and her brother were part of a large group of merry-makers. They invited me to join them in an excursion to Vauxhall Gardens. Lady Caroline, my aunt, said she could see no impediment after the group was vouched for by Lord Daschel, whom she knew quite well."

Gina scarcely blinked at the mention of that loathsome name. Lord Daschel had been a founder of the Brotherhood, and responsible for seducing Cora into meeting him the night they killed her.

"We took a barge across the Thames, laughing and jesting the whole way. It was then that I met a Mr. Booth and Mr. Henley. I thought I had truly 'arrived,' if you know what I mean—terribly flattered to be a part of such a haute gathering."

A smile came to Gina's lips. She knew the feeling quite well. She, too, had wanted to belong.

Mrs. Huffington removed a lace-edged handkerchief from the little reticule dangling at her wrist and dabbed delicately at the corners of her eyes. "In the beginning, it was great fun. We danced and watched the fireworks, and then Mr. Henley brought us libation, toasting often and encouraging us to drink deeply."

Just as he'd done with Gina when they'd left the theatre and gone to another part of town for the tableaus. She recalled growing quite tipsy rather quickly, and had begged off subsequent glasses of wine. Even so, she'd been quite ill the next day.

"I began to feel fuddled," Mrs. Huffington continued. "Then Mr. Henley took my hand and asked me to walk with him. I thought there could be no harm in that and that perhaps it would clear my head. The walks were well lit and there were people all about. But we were no more than out of sight of the rest when he led me down quite another path. I learned later they call those paths 'dark walks' or 'lover's walks' because they are not lit.

"I did not grow alarmed until Mr. Henley stopped and began to press me for favors." She twisted her handkerchief as she recalled the events of that night. "Perhaps it was because I am a widow that he thought I would be receptive to such a ploy, but I demanded he stop at once. He did not. The more I struggled, the more…inflamed he became. I think…I really think, he enjoyed my terror."

Gina covered the woman's hand with her own. "You needn't continue, Mrs. Huffington. I perceive the drift of your story."

"There is more, but I have not spoken of it since that night. I have not even told Lady Caroline. I was afraid she would not trust my judgment after that."

"My experience was much the same. But we went to a tableau at a mansion somewhere in Kensington." Though she had been much more naive than Mrs. Huffington. She had gone back that second, nearly fatal, night.

Mrs. Huffington shuddered. "It was dreadful. I actually feared I would not escape with my virtue. But when he'd nearly ravished me, he stopped and said he wanted to 'save' me. Do you truly think he was remorseful and wanted to save my virtue?"

She thought it much more likely that he wanted to save Mrs. Huffington to be a victim for the ritual, for all that, as a widow, she could not be a virgin. "Did he call on you afterward? Or invite you to join his group another time?"

"Yes, but I declined to go. I have not spoken to any of them since."

"Did you know that Mr. Booth and Mr. Metcalfe are both dead?"

Her green eyes widened in astonishment. "Gracious! Were they in an accident? How perfectly dreadful. I shall have to call upon Christina tomorrow."

Gina shook her head. "No accident, I fear. I desperately need your help, Mrs. Huffington. We need to find Mr. Henley before anyone else dies."

Mrs. Huffington took two steps backward and narrowed her eyes. "I am sorry, Miss O'Rourke, but I cannot help you."

The guests began to take seats facing the pianoforte and Gina knew she would not have time to cajole Mrs. Huffington's assistance. Plain speaking would have to suffice. "Lives may hang in the balance, Mrs. Huffington."

But the lovely woman merely shook her head and backed away. "I wish you luck, Miss O'Rourke."

After the last note had been played, Jamie's attention was divided between his conversation with his brothers and watching Gina. Despite their earlier agreement, he was certain she was up to something. He had meant to leave her alone until it was time to take her and the Thayer twins home, but now he thought he would have to nip any plot Gina might be nurturing in the bud.

Marcus Wycliffe and Devlin joined their little group and Jamie only half listened to the conversation when one word caught his attention.

"Gibbons? Sorry, what did you say?"

"Artie Gibbons is dead," Wycliffe repeated.

"How?"

"Bullet," Devlin said. "I wonder if he had any last words."

Jamie nearly choked on his wine. Lilly had gone a long way in civilizing Devlin, but he was glad to see that Devlin still maintained his wry humor.

"And Dick?"

"As you might imagine," Wycliffe said.

"I might imagine nearly anything where Dick Gibbons is concerned. Either devastated and grief stricken or furious."

"Devastation would require some actual humanity."

Then it would be hell to pay for anyone Dick suspected of the deed.

"After the botched attempt on Charlie, I suspect Dick will be going after every Hunter and anyone attached to them."

"Only if Artie had something to do with the attempt on Charlie."

Devlin snorted. "If? Do cockroaches scurry from the light? Aye. Whether Artie held the gun or just stood by Dick as he pulled the trigger, the attack on Charlie was engineered by a Gibbons. Dick will make that connection."

Jamie glanced at Gina, who had wandered closer to the group, and he wondered how much she'd heard. Enough to widen her eyes, it seemed.

"I warned them that they did not want to cross a Hunter, but you know how they are…were," Devlin continued. "So blasted sure they could do whatever they pleased without consequence. They got away with everything else they've ever done, so I believe we owe our thanks to whoever pulled that trigger."

They all raised their glasses in a silent toast to one another and Jamie wondered which one of them had actually "pulled that trigger." Lockwood and Wycliffe were more than capable of it, Drew had not come to Charlie's side until this morning, and Devlin might have even considered it his duty. Hell, Jamie would have done it himself if he hadn't been keeping watch by Charlie's bedside.

He drank to Devlin's toast and then reminded them, "Alas, the job is only half done."

"Dick will be harder to kill." Drew nodded. "He'll be looking for it."

They grew thoughtful for a moment and then Wycliffe changed the subject. "I hear there is to be a tableau at Marchant's tonight."

"I know some find them entertaining, but I find them deucedly dull," Devlin said.

Lockwood placed his empty glass on a tray borne by a passing footman. "That would depend upon the subject being reenacted. A Waterloo battle scene might be amusing."

"I believe tonight's subject is great works of art."

Devlin yawned and glanced toward his wife, across the room in conversation with guests. "I think I shall find something infinitely more amusing to entertain me."

Drew laughed. "I will pass, Wycliffe, but perhaps Jamie could join you."

Jamie had his own plans, and they didn't include watching members of the ton dress up in costumes to replicate works of art on a stage. He had an idea of where he might find Henley's mystery woman. "I have to pass. Perhaps another time?"

Wycliffe chortled. "Well, if I cannot lure anyone into sharing my misery, I believe I will drop by my office to see if there is any news, then go home and make an early night of it."

Chapter Nineteen

The night had turned cold by the time Gina arrived home, escorted by Andrew and Bella instead of Jamie, who had made his apologies and then promised to come see her tomorrow afternoon. Or had he merely been trying to avoid her? Regretting his proposal?

She had waited an hour before donning her cloak and sneaking out the garden door to meet Ned. She'd overheard Lord Wycliffe's announcement of a tableau at Marchant's. A few discreet questions had revealed that this was Lord Marchant's palatial home in Mayfair, and therefore not the same location as the erotic tableau where she'd met Christina Race. But, if Mr. Henley favored tableaus, perhaps he would be there. And if he was, she would summon the authorities at once.

Ned was waiting for her, barely perceptible in the shadows of a tree partway down the street. He emerged and came to her side. "Where to t'night, Miss Gina?"

"Do you know where Lord Marchant's house is?"

"Aye, miss. Follow me, eh?"

As they rounded the corner, a dark form stepped in their way. "Oh, I do not think so," he said.

She and Ned both squeaked in fright before they realized it was Jamie standing there, apparently waiting for her.

"Oh!" she gasped. "You frightened us to death!"

He looked them up and down. "A slight exaggeration. But do not think to divert me from the point, Eugenia, which is that you were not to investigate anything unless you were at my side."

"And yet you were going out without me."

Jamie pressed his lips together and pointed at Ned. "Hie back to your crib, boy. Miss O'Rourke will not need you further tonight, or any other night, for that matter."

After a nod from Gina, Ned took off at a lope, but she knew he'd be there tomorrow night, too, if she needed him. The moment Ned was out of sight, she turned and faced Jamie.

"Where are we going, then?"

"You're going home. I suspected you were up to something, so I came by here before going about my business. Home, Gina, where you will be safe and sound."

She shook her head. "Together."

He took her arm and turned her back home. "Where I am going, no decently raised woman would go."

Decently raised? Insufferable. "Tell me."

"I am going to a gaming hell. Thackery's, to be precise. It is not the sort of place decent women go."

"Since you will not answer my question, I do not know if I am decent or not. So shall we go without further delay?"

"Gina—"

"I can guess your arguments. My reputation. My good name. My safety. But those things mean nothing if I am already ruined. And nothing in view of the fact that I am leaving England after tomorrow. Who will remember me a fortnight hence? Who will care where I went or with whom?"

"No."

"Why are you going, Jamie? For gambling? For a woman? Or on my business?"

"Henley is not just your business. He taints everything he touches, and he must be stopped."

"Then do not worry over me. I am already tainted, am I not?" Oh, those words were bitter, but they finally hung in the air between them—his to refute or not.

He looked helpless, and she knew he could not counter her argument. Instead, he pulled the hood of her cloak over her head and draped it to shield her face. "The fewer people who recognize you, Gina, the better."

His coach was waiting around the corner and he called an address to the driver and handed her in, settling himself beside her. "When we get there, Gina, try to say as little as possible. Do not speak to anyone I have not introduced you to, and keep your head down. Perhaps we will get out of this without damage."

"What is our purpose there?"

"I am hoping we can discover who Henley's mystery woman is."

"At a gambling hell?"

"This one is a bit more democratic than the others. Courtesans, the demimonde and better cyprians frequent Thackery's and mingle with the guests. More business than gambling is done above stairs. More to the point, when he was free to go about in society, Thackery's was Henley's favorite establishment. Any woman who kept his company would be familiar with the place."

Cyprians? Did he mean prostitutes? "Is it squalid?"

Jamie laughed. "Very fashionable, actually, and clean. The food and drink are a bit more than passable. Only the customers are squalid."

Gooseflesh rose on Gina's arms. They would find the woman there, she was sure of it now. "And if we find her?"

"If so, I intend to persuade her to tell us where to find him. At the very least, once we learn her identity, we can set a watch on her and she will eventually lead us to him."

Eventually. Gina did not have *eventually*. She only had tomorrow. She looked up at him and slipped her hand into his to give it a little squeeze. "You…you will write to me and let me know when he is captured, will you not?"

He gave her an infinitely sad smile. "Immediately."

She nodded her understanding and was silent for the remainder of the ride, though Jamie did not release her hand and she gathered strength from that. She wanted to feel his determination, his warmth, as long as possible.

When the coach pulled up to an indiscriminate building near St. James Street, he got out, lifted her down and adjusted her hood. "Remember, keep your head down. With luck, we shall get our answer soon and not be here long."

Inside, she allowed a footman to take her cloak, realizing she'd be conspicuous and draw more attention with it on. Jamie smiled at her, evidently approving her choice.

He led her into a large central room, a gambling salon with many tables throughout. There were cards, wheels and dice, and men clustered about to watch the play. Raucous laughter, quiet curses and the even tones of the croupiers punctuated the low tones of a three piece orchestra playing quietly in one corner.

A set of wide stairs led upward to a mezzanine that surrounded the room where men and brightly dressed women strolled, looking down on the players below. A massive chandelier that glittered with a thousand crystals hung from a gilded ceiling. Gina was ashamed to say that she was fascinated with the place. It was unlike anywhere she'd ever been—part palace, part carnival.

Jamie purchased a stack of counters and gave her a few. "If they think you are about to play, they will not bother you or make you go upstairs."

"What is upstairs?"

"A ladies' salon and a few private rooms, for those who have had too much to drink, and others who…are seeking other diversions."

She glanced upward again, looking more closely at the ladies. Some were beautiful and dressed expensively, others were a bit more worn looking, and not quite as well turned out. Cyprians. Women who sold their favors. Women she'd never thought to mingle with, but who were now more like her than not.

She glanced down at her own gown, nearly scandalous by the standards of the ton, but prim in this place. She had the sudden urge to tug her bodice a bit lower just to fit in.

"'Lo there, Hunter. This your new mistress?"

She turned to look at the man who had just addressed Jamie. He was flushed and obviously in his cups. Jamie seemed annoyed, but he forced a smile and tucked Gina a bit tighter against his side. "She is, and I'll thank you to keep your hands off her, Cavendish."

"Just in from the country, I vow. Haven't seen her before. Leave it to you to find the freshest meat, eh?"

She almost laughed when Jamie's jaw tightened.

"What's your name, poppet?"

She opened her mouth but Jamie interceded. "Mary."

"Mary? I vow 'twould be Merry if you came with me, girl. And I vow I'd make merry, as well." The man laughed with hardy enjoyment of his own joke.

Jamie didn't bother with a reply and led her toward the staircase instead. "Stay within sight of me should we get separated, Gina. I am going to talk to some of the regulars to see if Henley has been around at all, then ask who they last saw him with."

How clever. "I shall converse with some of the ladies, too," Gina said.

"Ladies?" He laughed as they began to climb. "I think you had better stay close to me, *poppet*."

And before she could catch her breath, she was in a smaller salon than the one downstairs, with softer lighting and mirrors and murals the length and width of the room. Pastoral scenes or…or…oh! Horned satyrs and naked women cavorted across the countryside and appeared to be copulating in every possible manner! Chubby-cheeked Pan-like creatures spilled wine over couples, and Gina wondered at the symbolism of such a thing until she saw one figure licking the libation off another. Her cheeks burned and she knew she was giving her naïveté away.

Jamie pressed a wineglass into her hand. "Breathe, Gina, and take a drink. It will steady your nerves."

Bringing Gina to Thackery's was a monumental mistake, but he hadn't been able to figure any way around it. He did not fool himself that he could have taken her home and she would have stayed there. Keeping his eye on her would be considerably better than letting her wander about London unprotected. He could only hope that she would go unrecognized, although, as she'd been quick to point out, she would be gone in another day.

At his side, Gina took a long drink of her wine and then smiled up at him. "I believe I am better now. Thank you."

Ah, she'd suppressed that little lilt in her voice he loved so much and that betrayed her origins. Not that it would fool anyone, but any edge she could get would make her feel better. He wanted her confident, but not too confident.

He could not help but note that she was drawing attention

from males and females alike—being sized up by her competition and being measured for pleasure by the buyers. He'd best make it clear immediately that she was spoken for, at least for this evening.

He lifted her chin with his forefinger and bent close, making his intent obvious. "Make this look good, Gina, or you will be fending off eager supplicants the rest of the evening."

She raised on her tiptoes and fit her mouth to his. Not a tender offering but a deep and passionate kiss. No man would ever mistake her intentions, and no woman, either. In fact he, who knew it to be false, was having a difficult time reminding himself that the kiss was for the benefit of the salon, and not for him.

When she slowly withdrew, he whispered, "Well done, poppet."

She chuckled at his jest and straightened his cravat just as an attentive mistress would have done. Lord! How could he leave her side long enough to ask his questions?

"Well met, Hunter. Why don't you introduce me to your new lady love?"

He turned to find Henry Lector grinning ear to ear. "I am not ready to share, Henry."

"Now, is that fair? Have you signed contracts? Is she a one-man woman?"

Gina blinked and he was afraid she'd give herself away, but when she merely tilted her head to one side and said, "One at a time, anyway," he nearly guffawed.

Lector nodded and moved away, not entirely discouraged but willing to wait his turn. But there'd never be a turn. Jamie would see to that.

One thing was clear, Gina was a distraction to his purpose. Any conversation he would have with her by his side was bound to disintegrate to a flirtation if not an outright proposition. With reluctance, he released her hand.

"Will you be all right if I talk to some of these men alone, Gina? It should only take a few minutes."

"I will sit quietly in that corner." She nodded to a far corner where a bench sat in an alcove devised for tête-à-têtes.

"I shan't be long."

He watched Gina until she had taken a seat and began studying the murals with obvious interest. With a niggling feeling that he would regret leaving her alone, he joined a group of Thackery's regulars, positioning himself so that he could keep an eye on her.

Edward Tully was the first to greet him. "Well met, Hunter. We were just talking about Charlie. Is it true?"

He nodded. "Just a scratch. He should be up and around by tomorrow."

"Catch the bloke?" Albert Howland asked.

"One of them."

"How many were there?"

"Two, we suspect. But I did not come to Thackery's to discuss my brother. I've been looking for an old friend."

Tully regarded him with a jaundiced eye. "Who would that be?"

"Cyril Henley."

Eyebrows went up at that. "Friends, eh? I'd never have figured you two would have much in common," Howland said.

"We have some friends in common. People I'd like to locate, if possible."

Tully drank from his glass before he spoke. "Haven't seen him in a couple of months."

"I did. Now, let me see. Where was that?" Howland frowned and stared at the ceiling as if he expected the answer to appear there. "Was it here, or at the Morris masquerade?

Yes, the night Stan Metcalfe was killed. He did not stay long, though. Said he had some place to be."

"Busy man," Tully said noncommittally.

Jamie was reasonably certain Tully knew more than he was saying. "Quite. Has he not been around here with his mistress?"

"Ah, yes! That's it. He was here a few nights ago. After the Morris masquerade. He and Misty. That's what he calls her. Play on words, what?"

"How so?"

"Mystery. Misty. She always wears a domino, don't y'know. We've speculated endlessly about her true identity. We gather she's from the ton, or why the domino?"

"But you haven't recognized her?"

Howland laughed. "We scarcely look above her neck since she wears her gowns so low. But I'd recognize those breasts anywhere."

Tully chortled. "Sweetest little mole just at the top of her left nipple. We've taken bets, but no one has proven yet whether that mole is the result of nature or artifice. My money is on nature."

"And mine is on artifice. There is not much natural about that saucy wench. All I can say for certain is that she is by nature a blonde." Howland drank deeply and winked.

Blonde? Hell, he knew half a dozen blondes who'd known Henley. That was not much help. But Misty? Damn! There was something pricking the back of his mind. The description, vague though it was, sounded familiar.

Subtle questioning of a few more men confirmed Tully and Howland's information. Misty, whoever she was, was a favorite of the men. She asked nothing of them but their attention and was generous with the views she provided to one and all, and generous in more ways to a few; she had been known to go to a room with other men if Henley was not available.

He could not imagine Gina behaving in such a manner. He turned to check on her and groaned. He'd almost rather have found her talking to a man than his former mistress.

"So you are our Jamie's newest obsession, eh?"

Gina turned from her study of the mural and smiled at the beautiful Frenchwoman. She wasn't certain what to say. *Our* Jamie's newest obsession? Did he patronize all the women of Thackery's?

"We could 'ardly miss that kiss, mademoiselle. That is unlike 'im—to show public affection. 'E must think you are very special, eh?"

The thought warmed her. She shrugged. "Perhaps."

"Your name, mademoiselle?"

"Mary. And yours?"

"Suzette. Ah, do not worry over me. I am Charlie's now."

Good heavens! Did the Hunter brothers share their…cyprians? "I am not certain if I am Jamie's or not."

"'E 'as not made up 'is mind? Well, do not fret, little Mary. Even if it is only for tonight, 'e is most generous." Her delicate hand went to her throat and she flicked a diamond and sapphire necklace there. "'E gave me this at our parting."

Uncertain what to say, she ventured, "I am sorry."

Suzette laughed, a musical trilling sound. "No need, Mary. It is the nature of our profession, yes? A man grows bored, a man moves on. I would 'ave missed 'im more if 'is brother was not as good."

"Charlie gives you good gifts, too?"

The girl laughed again. "La! You are most amusing, Mary. But I 'ave come to ask if Jamie 'as mentioned Charlie. I wish to go see 'im, but I think Lockwood would not admit me to 'is 'ouse."

"Oh, of course. Charlie is quite well, I believe. I recall that

Jamie mentioned he would be up and around tomorrow. He is weak, but otherwise well."

"So well informed? Well, I am glad to 'ear it. If Charlie is weak, I shall be 'appy to do all the work." She laughed again. "Quite 'appy, *n'est-ce pas?* Though 'is skill is greater than my own. A skill as great as our Jamie, eh?"

Gina was certain she had missed something. She was about to ask for an explanation when Jamie arrived before them.

"Suzette," he greeted her. "I see you have met Mary."

"She is so precious, Jamie. I am impressed. I would not 'ave thought you would be amused by such…innocence."

Ah, it was an insult! She eyed Suzette and stood, taking Jamie's offered hand. "Oh, but I was not worried over you at all, Suzette. In fact, Jamie has never even mentioned you."

Suzette's eyes narrowed.

Jamie gave just the slightest bow as he turned her away.

"Really," she said under her breath. "You might have warned me I'd be running into your cyprians."

He laughed. "Suzette is my former mistress. I do not frequent cyprians."

"And you've passed her on to your brother. Is it a family thing?"

This time he guffawed. "'Tis only polite. Suzette has… skills."

"Odd. She said the same of you."

They had reached the top of the stairs and taken no more than two steps downward when Jamie halted at the sound of greetings from below. "Bloody hell!"

He spun her around and topped the stairs, then turned her down a corridor past the salon.

"What—"

"It's Gilbert Sayles and his friends. Lady Annica's cousin? You danced with him at your first ball. He was smitten, Gina. He will recognize you."

He threw a door open at the end of the corridor and she hurried in, dreading the thought that she might shame Lady Annica by her presence here.

Even the solid click of the door closing and locking could not pull her away from the vision in front of her. A single candle burned by a lavish bed, but the light of the single flame was reflected in what seemed to be a thousand mirrors. The walls were lined with them, and even the ceiling over the bed bore one. The draperies and bed hangings were either purple or deep violet—she could not tell which in the flickering shadows. But one thing was certain. This was a room made for illicit assignations.

"Sorry," Jamie said. "We will have to wait him out."

A carafe and glasses waited on one bedside table. Jamie poured himself a little and tasted it. "Brandy," he said.

She nodded. "Just a bit."

As she watched him pour measures into two glasses and bring one to her, she noted how interesting it was to see him from both sides. The mirrors were truly amazing. Had she ever noticed the tight curve of his buttocks before? The lean strength of his legs? The broad set of his shoulders? Had she been blind?

She took the glass from him and lifted it in a silent toast. "Will you have to pay for the room now that we've availed ourselves of the amenities?"

He grinned. "Should I have let you run headlong into Gilbert?"

She shook her head, thinking of her own tarnished condition amid cyprians and mistresses. "I think I am where I am supposed to be." She was certainly where she *wanted* to be. Here. With Jamie. For whatever time they had left together.

His expression turned serious. "Gina…"

Tonight. That was all she had. Tonight. And then there

would be no more Jamie. No more tenderness and soft sighs. No more honesty.

But there was still tonight.

Chapter Twenty

The raw emotion in Gina's eyes took his breath away. She wanted him. Could he take her tonight and let her go tomorrow? Could he leave now, never to make love to her again? No, he couldn't. A paradox. A riddle with no answer. He could only stand there, waiting. Wanting. Praying.

She took a step toward him and he started breathing again. When she entered his arms and he closed them about her, he felt whole. As if he held all that mattered in the world. And when she lifted her lips to his, he took them as they'd been offered—completely, sincerely, with a raw truth that humbled him.

He fumbled with her clothing as they kissed, undoing her gown quickly, but slowed by the corset laces. He did not take the time to unfasten them entirely, just loosen them enough to push the offending corset and chemise down over her hips, leaving her in only her white stockings and slippers. He carried her to the bed and threw the coverlet back, wanting to see her against the crisp linens, but she dragged him with her, her fingers working the knots of his cravat. He tossed her slippers over his shoulder but decided to leave the silk stockings as an erotic reminder of the sensuous nature of their encounter. His jacket, his waistcoat, his shirt, boots, breeches and drawers were quickly shed, and he lay on the bed beside her.

Her hair had come undone, tangling around her shoulders like a dark mantle. Her cheeks were flushed with the heat of her passion, and he loved her as much for that as anything. That she wanted him so desperately in this way was immensely satisfying. That she would give herself over to his handling was a sacred trust.

Tonight he would love her as she deserved.

He kissed her deeply, sighing when she invited him in with her tongue and her soft little moans. Oh, God, the sounds she made when he did something new—found a tender spot or deepened a caress—inflamed him, and he used them as a guide to her pleasure. He took his time, cherishing every moment.

When she could scarcely breathe, he left her mouth to kiss his way down to her breasts and cherish them both by turns. Her ripe, berrylike nipples were sweet on his tongue, teasing him, promising him delights to come, and he took them greedily.

He could read her heightened state of arousal in her rapid breathing and the restless way she arched to him. She would need release soon or he would lose her to the darkness of the other side of passion—pure lust without the refinement of love. His own need was mounting with alarming intensity, but he could not slake it at her expense. He pushed it back with all the determination he had, knowing the reward would be everything he wanted.

The woman-scent of her refused denial and he trailed his tongue lower, lower, still lower, until he found that other berry that pulsed against his tongue and told him that she was his for as long as he could hold her on the razor edge of release—not

completely there, but on the brink. He knew how much pressure she would need, and the precise moment to apply it, bu
kept her keening for that release, denying it to intensify i
when he granted it. She was like wildfire, burning hot and
fast. For him. Only for him.

"Please…please…please…" she chanted.

And still he waited, savoring the sweet-salty taste of her
the scent that aroused something bone-deep in him, a primitive need.

She curled upward, her fingernails biting into his shoulders
to drag him over her, to force him into her, but he pushed her
back. Soon. A moment more. Just one moment more…

And there it was—the gasp and catch in her breathing
that told him she was seconds from swooning. He flicked his
tongue and pressed firmly as she arched, her head thrown
back as the first shock wave crested. He rose above her and
thrust deeply, entering her at the precise moment her climax
began, and she screamed with the pure ecstasy of it. She
was new to this depth of eroticism, but she had mastered i
quickly.

She was snug and tight, her inner muscles rippling and
tightening around his shaft in a slow, deep roll that drew a
growl of primordial pleasure. But he was not quite done. He
carried her along to another climax when her body gripped
him as he thrust again and again, deeper and faster until his
own release mingled with hers. The world spun out of control,
blocking reason and thought. All that existed was pleasure,
pure and primal.

Translucent tears trickled from the corners of her eyes as
the storm passed and he came back to the moment. And to
her. She was glorious, the most arousing thing he'd ever seen,
and he loved her as he'd never thought he'd love anyone or
anything.

She reached up to touch his face and trace the line of his

jaw as he hovered over her. "Ah, Jamie. I have no words to express…"

There was passion written in her every touch and sigh, speaking what she could not. Still rooted within her, he grew hard again at the vision of her beneath him. When she felt his quickening, she smiled and stretched her arms above her head, opening herself to him and giving him the gift of her trust.

The gift humbled him and he vowed to cherish it. He returned her smile even as he accepted her invitation, moving again, building her arousal with a patience born of self-denial. Oh, she had much to learn about the depth of a man's passion, and he was committed to teaching her.

Gina looked around at the ruins of her room. Open trunks, a wooden crate, boxes and tissue were scattered everywhere. She scarcely knew where to begin, and Nancy was too busy helping Mama to spare a moment for her.

And, oh, she did not want to be leaving so soon. She had too many reasons to stay in London now. And one reason greater than all the rest. James Hunter. Her knees grew weak just thinking of the things he'd done last night. Things she'd never imagined in her wickedest, wildest dreams. Things that left her trembling and sated and exhausted today. And, yes, things she wanted to do again and again. But only with Jamie, and therein lay the problem.

After today, she would not have Jamie in her life. He wanted her, but not enough to answer her question. And with that uncertainty always hanging in the air between them, she knew she could not build a life with him.

But they still had tonight, and she would not squander that. If he would not take her to his flat, she would go back to Thackery's with him and race for the dock in the morning.

"And this is what you get for waiting so long to pack, miss," Nancy told her as she stood at Gina's bedroom door.

She looked at the mound of gowns laying across her bed. "I cannot pack the French-blue gown, Nancy. It is my favorite, and I think I will wear it again tonight. Heaven only knows when I will find a chance to wear it in Belfast."

"And that's another thing, Miss. You ought not to be going out tonight. Mrs. O'Rourke arranged for a coach to be here before dawn to take us to the dock. Why, you'll barely be home and changed by the time we'll have to leave."

There would be sufficient time for her to sleep on the ship, but tonight would be her last chance to see Jamie. Her last chance to tell Hortense and Harriett how much they meant to her, and to thank the ladies of the Wednesday League for their help, and for carrying on once she was gone. Yes, tonight would be her final farewell to what might have been. And to Jamie.

She shook her head. "Ought or not, I am going. There are people I need to see and say goodbye to, and there is no purpose to me pacing in my bedroom."

Nancy shrugged. "I would think you would want to say your goodbyes to your sisters, miss."

"They will be at Lady Sarah's crush tonight. The guest list is quite large, so please do not wait up for me, Nancy. I may be dancing 'til dawn." Oh, what an accomplished liar she was turning out to be.

Nancy harrumphed. "Your mother says she wants you home before midnight."

"Midnight? But I cannot possibly be home so soon."

"The boat leaves at dawn, miss. You'd be boarding in your ball gown."

Her stomach knotted as she pictured herself standing on a deck waving goodbye to her sisters and Jamie. Pictured leaving everything and everyone she loved behind.

"Then…then a ball gown it shall have to be," she said.

"I am sorry, miss, but you know your mother will be having apoplexy if you are not home by midnight. Because of what happened to Miss Cora, I would not put it past her to alert the night watch if you are not." Nancy closed the door behind her with a note of finality.

Midnight! Too soon! Why did Mama have to choose today to care when she came in? There would be no time to tryst with Jamie. No time to say a proper farewell or to hoard memories for the lonely days ahead.

She stubbed her toe on the little carved box peeking out from under her bed and stared. How had she forgotten? Henley. She knelt and opened the lid. There, just as she'd left them, the key, the packet of opium and the pocket pistol she'd borrowed from Mr. Renquist lay secreted.

Here, at least, was something she *could* do. Her last chance to find Mr. Henley.

Gina, dressed in the seductive French-blue gown, stood in conversation with her friends, smiling and laughing as if nothing else mattered. As if *he* did not matter. They hadn't been able to find a moment alone since he'd called for her earlier this evening and found Hortense and Harriet waiting with her. Had she engineered that?

Perhaps she'd been right not to trust him alone with her. Even standing across a room, his body responded to the memory of her beneath him, twisting with passion, tangled in the sheets, gripping him and holding him inside her, calling his name. He could not conceive that this night would be the end of it all. He needed her like he needed air to breathe. She was more potent than whiskey and coursed through his veins like thick, raw honey.

"Good God, Hunter!" Marcus Wycliffe said. "That hot

look could melt glaciers. Have a care if you do not want the entire ton to know what you are thinking."

"Blast the ton," he muttered.

"Is it true? She's leaving in the morning?"

"Less than twelve hours." He glanced at the tall case clock in one corner as it struck ten. "By my reckoning, eight."

"And you've not spoken for her?"

"Oh, I've spoken. She will not have me."

Wycliffe made a sound that was suspiciously like a laugh. "What of your formidable powers of persuasion?"

"She wants an answer…a truth…I cannot give her."

"Ah, yes. And the truth is everything to you, is it not?"

Everything? More than Gina? More than love? Or were Gina and love the only truth that mattered? "It has always been my bulwark," he admitted.

"I hope it will comfort you when she is gone," Wycliffe said.

He was growing tired of hearing that. Did they think he did not dread it—his brothers and Wycliffe? "Is that what you came to talk about, Wycliffe? Or was there something else?"

"Ah, yes. Dick Gibbons."

"Have you brought him in?"

"He's gone to ground. No one has seen him since Artie was killed. No funeral arrangements, nothing. I cannot decide if he simply does not care or if his brother's body and a decent burial means nothing to him. Only animals walk away from their dead, but I doubt Dick is any better than that."

"So now what?"

"I want you on the case. If anyone can find him, you can."

"Ask Devlin. He's got eyes everywhere."

"Jamie, since you're so fond of the truth, do you know who got to Artie?"

He grinned. Wycliffe suspected Devlin. "What makes you think I know?"

"A bit too coincidental, don't you think, that Charlie was shot and not twenty-four hours later, a Gibbons turns up dead."

"It could have been any of us," Jamie admitted. "But you chose Devlin because he has the ruthlessness for a cold kill. If I knew, I wouldn't lie about it, but I wouldn't tell you, either. Whoever killed Artie Gibbons did London a favor."

Wycliffe crossed his arms across his chest. Jamie knew the man was pragmatic enough to realize that what Jamie said was right. But he would also be concerned about any of his operatives who might have overreached the law by taking matters into their own hands.

"It wasn't you, Jamie. You stayed by Charlie's bedside all night. Where were Lockwood and Drew?"

"I must assume they were having brandy in Lockwood's library, assuming that I was at Charlie's bedside."

Wycliffe gave him a long look and then nodded. The matter was closed and he changed the subject. "Give me the name of Mrs. O'Rourke's ship and I'll find a reason to hold it in harbor. Will a week be enough to change Miss Eugenia's mind?"

"Thank you, Marcus, but no. I've already used my best argument. If I couldn't sway her with that, I can't imagine what else I could do." Jamie sighed and slapped him on the back.

Perhaps one last try? He approached her group and greeted the ladies, then requested a dance. Gina placed her hand in his as he led her toward the dance floor. "You are well, I trust?" he asked.

The color in her face heightened. "Tolerable."

He laughed. "Only tolerable? If I recall, you were doing quite well last night."

She smiled shyly. "Actually, I have a small ache…"

Of course she did. He'd been an idiot not to realize she would. Considering the extent of their activity, a small ache was likely an understatement. "I'm sorry. Unaccustomed muscles. 'Twill pass, and quickly, I think. Is it of consequence enough that you would prefer not to dance?"

"A stroll in your sister's gardens might suit me better."

Suit him better, as well. He would prefer to have her to himself. He led her out the terrace doors and she shivered in the night air. He began to shrug out of his jacket but she waved it away, so he slipped his arm around her instead and she nestled against his side. "Will you meet me later, Gina?"

Her pause was so long that he knew it would be a refusal. "Mother expects me home by midnight. We leave at dawn."

He stopped by a fading rosebush. "Can I not persuade you to stay?"

"The cost would be too great."

That question. That damned question that had ruined more than Gina's pride. She would have to give it up, or he would have to destroy her with an inconvenient truth. And neither of them could compromise without denying who they were. He turned her in his arms and leaned down to place a kiss on her lips, still swollen from last night.

"Faith," he whispered against those dewy petals. "Can you not find a little faith?"

"No more than you can lie."

Why did she have to be so blasted stubborn? Would she really throw everything good away for the sake of a single forgotten moment? Was her pride—or whatever it was that drove her—more important than her future? Than him?

He tamped down hard on his rising anger and tried to reason with her. "And if you should find yourself back in Belfast with a growing belly?"

By her look of surprise, he gathered she had not thought of such an eventuality. "I... Surely not."

As for him, he had no intention of fathering a bastard. "You would not be the first woman to be surprised by such an event, Gina. A hasty marriage two or three months from now would have society counting the arrival of our first-born on their fingers. Is that what you want?"

"No, but…I did not mean for any of this to happen. What we did—" She stopped to sigh and start again. "My mother has already lost one daughter forever, and two to marriage. All she wants is to go home. I cannot delay her further."

"If your mind is made up, Eugenia, I will not beg. But, should I find out in the future that you have given birth and not given me the chance to make it right, there will be hell to pay." He took her elbow and led her back to the ballroom. He had to control his anger before he said something he would regret, but with her name on Henley's list, he could not leave her where she was vulnerable. Once inside, he gave her a formal bow and left her.

Chapter Twenty-One

Gina wavered between grief and anger. How could she leave Jamie? How could she stay if he would not answer her? His stubborn refusal to say the words that would end her agony of uncertainty infuriated her because, without that answer, she was surely leaving on that ship in the morning. And now she could only watch him join his brothers across the room and feel the emptiness of her life.

And his threat! *Should I find out in the future that you have given birth and not given me the chance to make it right, there will be hell to pay.* Hell to pay? Absurd. But then she realized her hand had gone to cover her belly without her realizing it. Oh, she could not think about that now.

The weight of the pistol in the pockets beneath her gown and the key tied to her corset strings reminded her what she had to do. Tonight was her last chance to find justice for Cora. And for herself.

"You are looking quite thunderous, Miss O'Rourke."

She turned to find Georgiana Huffington standing beside

her and forced a smile. "Really? I was only thinking of all I have yet to do before I can leave tomorrow."

"I wish we had met sooner, Miss O'Rourke. I think we might have been friends. As it is, we shall have to be content with friends in common. I called upon Christina Race today. I wished to condole with her over the loss of her fiancé. Mourning is something I have had a fair amount of experience with."

"Did you find her well?"

"Melancholy, but fit enough. She gave me a message for you." The woman handed her a folded paper.

Her curiosity was piqued. "Will you excuse me a moment, Mrs. Huffington?" She did not wait for a reply before she unfolded the page and scanned the lines, barely pausing to note that it had not been sealed.

My dear Eugenia,

     After considerable introspection, I have come to believe that Stanley would not have wanted me to keep his secret in view of what has transpired over the last several days. For better or worse, you should know, though what you will make of it, I cannot say.

     The night of his death, Stanley confessed to me that he had participated in Mr. Henley's rituals. His guilt over that troubled him more than he could express. He wanted to make amends, but did not know how without bringing his family shame. Perhaps the following will help you find the answers you seek and make whatever amends are possible.

     Stanley was terribly concerned regarding his sister, Missy. Despite her flirtation with Mr. Booth, Stanley believed she had formed an "unhealthy" friendship with Mr. Henley. It was, in fact, Stanley's belief that she and Mr. Henley had become lovers, and that Mr. Henley was wielding undue influence over her. If she is, indeed, close to Mr. Henley, perhaps she will be able to answer your questions.

I am, as always, your staunch friend,
Miss Christina Race

Gina's head spun. Missy Metcalfe? She did not particularly like the girl, but could Missy have fallen for Mr. Henley's superficial charm? Been so deeply under his spell that she had lost all restraint and good judgment?

Mrs. Huffington placed her hand on Gina's arm. "Are you well, Miss O'Rourke? You've gone quite pale."

"Yes. Yes, I am fine. I must thank you for bringing this to me so promptly. I may yet be able to use it."

The woman blushed. "I confess I read it. My curious nature is my greatest failing. I do not know what any of it means, but I fear it could mean danger for you."

Gina shrugged. There was only one way to find that out. She gathered reassurance from the weight of the pistol in her pocket. "I must speak to Miss Metcalfe at once. Do you know where she lives?"

Mrs. Huffington's green eyes widened. "Is that wise, Miss O'Rourke? Surely, in view of Christina's letter—"

"I really have no choice, Mrs. Huffington. She may be the only one who can help me find the answer to a question."

The woman seemed to consider this for a moment, and then made a decision. "I saw Missy here earlier. Shockingly, I have seen her at other fetes since her brother's death. I do not know what she is after, but she makes me very nervous, indeed."

"Here? Where?"

"In the gardens. As if she were waiting for someone."

Gina glanced at the terrace doors. Did her answer lie on

the other side? She had taken several steps in that direction when Mrs. Huffington halted her with a hand on her arm.

"Oh, please, Miss O'Rourke, I do not think this is wise."

Most likely not, but how long could it take to wheedle an answer from Missy Metcalfe? "If I have not come back inside within half an hour, please inform Mr. James Hunter of what I've done."

Mrs. Huffington watched her leave, a worried look on her face. As Gina turned to close the terrace doors behind her, the girl was already turning to Jamie. Pray she did not tell him soon enough to frighten Miss Metcalfe off before she'd gotten the information she needed.

Quite alone on the terrace, she went the few steps down into the garden, shivering in the cold and wondering if Missy might have watched her and James kiss earlier. She strolled conspicuously down the center path to a fountain, then sat on the edge, contemplating the various paths that converged there.

The rustle of skirts alerted her and she looked around to the path behind her and schooled her face to unconcern. Yes. It was Missy, cloaked in mourning black. "Good evening, Miss Metcalfe."

"As I live and breathe, Miss O'Rourke. What are you doing alone in the garden?"

"Thinking of you, actually. I was just given a letter from Miss Race, explaining that you might be able to help me."

The light from a nearby lantern fell on Missy's face as she sat beside Gina. She was undeniably beautiful, but there was something secretive in her smile. "I shall be pleased to help you in any way you require, Miss O'Rourke."

"Excellent. Then can you tell me where I might be able to find Mr. Henley?"

"La! How should I know that?"

"Miss Race said you knew him quite well."

"Did she? Then I am amazed she has not asked me. Why, just this afternoon when we had tea, she told me she had a message for you and asked if I would deliver it."

Gina could not hide her surprise at this. Two messages from Christina? "Do you have it with you?"

"She would not trust it to be written, but bade me deliver it in person. That is the reason I am here. I pray I am not too late."

"Too late for what?"

"Why, to warn you against Mrs. Huffington."

How very curious! "Does she mean me some harm?"

Missy stood and took Gina's hand, drawing her to her feet. "Christina did not know for certain, but she felt you should not trust her. She said that Mrs. Huffington is...well, *involved* with Mr. Henley, and that you have been looking for him. She seemed to be concerned that you might believe lies the woman might tell. Has she talked to you, Miss O'Rourke? Told you anything that you might find difficult to believe?"

Mrs. Huffington? Involved with Mr. Henley? Could it be possible? She proceeded cautiously. "We exchanged pleasantries. No more."

Missy sighed. "Thank heavens she has not filled your head with falsehoods."

"What could she possibly say? And why would she want to mislead me?"

"Who knows, Miss O'Rourke. 'Tis rumored she had something to do with her husbands' demises. And the woman is an incorrigible liar. Perhaps she is trying to protect Mr. Henley. But what Christina told you is true—I may know how to find Mr. Henley."

Gina's heart beat so rapidly that she feared it might beat out of her chest. She squeezed Missy's hand. "Now? Could you tell me where he is now?"

"Perhaps we could find him if we leave immediately."

"I shall just fetch my cloak and—"

"No time. We must hurry if we are to catch him. 'Tis now or never, Miss O'Rourke."

"But where is he?"

"There are several places he might be."

Was Missy the liar? Or Georgiana Huffington? Or could Christina, herself, have misled her in both directions?

"Are you coming, Miss O'Rourke?"

'Tis now or never, Miss O'Rourke....

"How long ago?"

"I... Half an hour. She said to wait half an hour before telling you."

Jamie cursed and raked his fingers through his hair. He wanted to shake Mrs. Huffington, but she couldn't have known the danger Gina was in. "Did she say where they might have gone?"

"No. I brought a letter to her from Miss Race. She read it, and when I mentioned Missy Metcalfe was in the garden, she went there immediately. I was to tell you only if she hadn't come back within half an hour. Before I came to you, I looked outside, Mr. Hunter, and neither of them were in the garden."

"Thank you, Mrs. Huffington. If you will excuse me." He bowed and went to the foyer, signaling Wycliffe along the way. The footman brought their coats and Jamie waited until they had entered the street before he spoke.

"Miss O'Rourke has gone missing."

Wycliffe's eyebrows shot up to his hairline. "You jest."

Jamie did not deign to answer what was surely a rhetorical question. "The question is where she has got to."

"Ideas?"

"A few. First, we shall call on Miss Race."

"Christina Race? What has she to do with all this?"

"Likely nothing beyond her connection to Stanley Metcalfe. But Mrs. Huffington said she'd given Gina a note from Miss Race, and Gina had gone off to the garden almost immediately. Something is afoot, Marcus. She was angry with me, but I don't think she'd have gone with Missy unless she thought she had matters well in hand. I'm hoping Miss Race will know where they might have gone."

"Give me time to summon the watch."

"To hell with the watch. Get Devlin and my brothers. Catch up with me at Miss Race's."

She'd known before they arrived where they were going. There it was, rising out of the fog. The Ballinger estate, the spire of its eerie chapel rising like a stake from the heart of the grounds. The very place she'd been going to come tonight with her little key after everyone had retired.

Would she find, at last, the door it opened? Missy guided her through the iron gate and to a path that curved around the house and led to the chapel.

The pistol in the pocket that lay against Gina's thigh comforted her. "Do you think he's here?"

"If he is not here now, he will come soon. He… Christina said this is his favorite place."

She shivered with more than the cold. Christina, indeed! Henley loved this place because it was the scene of all his debaucheries. The scene of her disgrace. Her hand went to her throat as she paused at the chapel door.

"Come, Gina. It will be warmer inside," Missy cajoled.

She stepped into a small vestibule, waiting for a memory or a feeling of familiarity, but nothing came. She must have been unconscious or heavily drugged when she'd been brought here.

Missy lit a candle, opened another door and nodded for

Gina to precede her into the vestry. Black cowls hung on pegs and were scattered on the floor, and an overturned bench gave testament to the chaos of that long-ago night.

A bone-deep chill seeped through her. Anxious to dispel the aura of evil, she passed through the vestry to the nave. A barren altar lay ahead of her, and in front of that, a red rug thrown back from an open trapdoor.

Her stomach clenched. Though she had no memory of it, she knew she had been carried down those wooden steps into the inky darkness below. She slipped her hand into the slit in her seam to accommodate the pocket and gripped the handle of the pistol, taking comfort from the fact that, this time, she was prepared to defend herself.

Missy passed her and opened a door behind the altar—the sacristy, where vestments and sacred vessels were kept. She retrieved a pewter chalice and a bottle of sacramental wine. "I am parched, Gina. Mr. Henley is obviously not here yet. Shall we have a sip of communion wine?" She giggled as she poured the wine into the chalice.

Gina looked down into the chamber beneath the trap door. "Are you certain he is not here? He could be down there."

"Nonsense. Had he heard us, he would have come up. We shall have time for a drink before we go below to wait for him."

"How will he know to look for us there?"

"He… I have heard he lives down there." She busied herself placing the chalice on the altar and pouring a generous measure of wine into it.

The list Mr. Renquist had found! *Candles, tinderbox, blanket, wine.* They'd suspected Mr. Henley was setting up new quarters, and so he had. Ah, but Missy had known it, too. And now Gina knew what she had to do.

* * *

Miss Race entered her sitting room, a look of astonishment on her pretty face and her parents behind her. "Mr. Hunter, Lord Wycliffe. What… How can I help you?"

Jamie wondered how much her parents knew about the events that had led them there. He had no wish to cause trouble for her, but he needed information quickly. No time to cozen or cajole. "Miss O'Rourke is missing, Miss Race. Do you have any idea where she might be?"

Her dark eyes widened and her hand went to her heart. "No! Oh, I pray he has not got her."

"Who, Miss Race?" Wycliffe asked.

"Mr. Henley, of course. She was looking for him, but I have prayed that she would not find him. It can mean nothing but trouble for her if she does. Stanley said…"

Jamie remembered the list of names in Henley's writing and finished for her. "He said Miss O'Rourke was in grave danger, did he not?"

Miss Race nodded. "Stanley said Mr. Henley considered her 'unfinished business.'"

"Do you have any idea where he might have gone? Where she might have followed him?"

"I fear not. She called upon me yesterday, and I thought she was going back to Ireland. When Georgiana called today, she did not mention her. Well, but I asked Georgie to give Miss O'Rourke a message for me."

Jamie tamed his sense of urgency. "What did it say?"

Miss Race blushed and glanced over her shoulder at her mother and father, then squared her shoulders in a way so like Gina that his heart twisted. "I told her that Stanley and I believed that Missy had become Mr. Henley's secret lover, and that perhaps Missy would have the answers Gina so desperately needed."

So desperately that she'd risk her life. He'd been a bloody

fool to think he could spare her that pain. If only he'd had the sense to answer her question, perhaps she'd be safe in his arms this very minute. But then he realized that answer alone would never have been enough. She'd wanted justice for her sister, as well.

He sighed deeply. "Is that all, Miss Race?"

"Yes."

"Thank you," Wycliffe said as they turned to go. "Sorry for the interruption of your evening."

Miss Race followed them to the door, and placed her hand on Jamie's sleeve. She lowered her voice to a whisper. "Missy came to call today, too. She asked ever so many questions about Gina—where she was going to be tonight, when she was leaving for Ireland, that sort of thing. I did not think much about it then, but…I wonder if she had something to do with Gina's disappearance."

Hell yes. "If she did, Miss Race, do you have any idea where she might have taken Gina?"

"No. But I keep thinking of what Stanley said about unfinished business. What do you suppose Mr. Henley wants with her?"

Unfinished business? And then it all fell into place. Where else would Henley conduct his lethal business? He leaned down and gave Miss Race a quick kiss on the cheek. "Thank you, Miss Race."

Missy swirled the wine in the chalice. "I think it is a bit stale," she said as she offered the untasted cup.

Gina closed her fingers around the folded packet in her pocket as she lifted the cup to her lips with her other hand. She pretended to drink and then jumped, as if something had startled her. "What was that?"

Missy frowned. "What?"

"I thought I heard something. In the vestry."

A tiny uplift at the corners of Missy's mouth betrayed her. "I shall see if anyone is here. Meanwhile, drink up, Gina."

How foolish did Missy think she was? The minute she started for the vestry, Gina poured the contents of the chalice down the trapdoor and quickly dumped the packet of coarse powder into it. When Missy turned back, she lifted the chalice again and tipped it up as if finishing the last drop, then managed a look of chagrin.

"Oh, sorry. I drank it all. My thirst was greater than I thought, and you were right—the wine has turned. Quite fusty and bitter, but still drinkable." She went to the altar and poured more wine into the chalice before handing it to Missy.

Missy hesitated as she looked down into the cup. "There is likely more wine below."

"It is not that bad. Surely you will not make me drink alone."

Missy shrugged and took a deep drink, making a face when she was done. "Ugh. Quite nasty. That should teach Henley to leave bottles lying about."

Gina breathed easier. She wondered how long it would take for the drug to have an effect.

"Shall we go down?" Missy asked, taking the candlestick and joining her by the trapdoor.

Praying she wouldn't slip on the spilt wine, Gina began to descend the uneven stone steps. She could smell the spilt wine, but couldn't see it. Then other odors assailed her—dust, damp and faint traces of pungent incense—teasing the back of her mind, awakening the dim impression of foreign sensations.

At the bottom of the stairs, she found herself in a narrow antechamber with a small closed door to her right. The first uneasy stirrings of actual memories began to wrap their tendrils around her. Ahead lay an arched opening, and she had a vague memory of a crypt beyond.

Behind her, Missy stumbled, caught herself by leaning against the stone wall and giggled. "Clumsy me. The wine must have gone straight to my head."

Gina hoped something had, though she guessed it would be the contents of that packet. "Here, let me help you," she said, taking the candlestick from Missy before she could drop it and plunge the antechamber into darkness.

"You? Help me?" Another giggle.

"Sit, Missy, before you fall."

"What're you say…say…saying?"

"If my experience bears out, Missy, you are about to have a nice long nap."

Missy's blue eyes widened with disbelief. "You…you… tricked me."

"Yes, I did. Now sit down before you fall and crack your head."

Missy sat with a soft thump. "He'll kill you…for this."

Or for any number of things, she supposed. For exposing him. For escaping him. For hunting him down. It didn't matter why, because it didn't change the facts. And he wasn't going to kill her. Quite the opposite.

Missy's heavy sigh told her the girl had surrendered to the drug. She wondered how long she had before Mr. Henley would appear. She would have to work fast.

She tried the latch to the side door. Locked. Of course it was. She reached inside her décolletage and plucked her corset string, pulling upward until the key appeared. She fit it to the lock and turned. The door swung open with a faint creak.

She could not seem to make herself take that first step over the threshold, so she held the candle high to illuminate the room. It was the room in her dreams—though small, the dark stone walls seemed to swallow the light. A cot stood in the center of the room and there was an empty sconce that would have held a torch. A cup lay overturned on the floor, and crumpled in one corner was the pink gown Gina had worn to meet Mr. Henley that night.

It was true, then. All of those vague impressions, those demivisions were true. She'd been drugged and stripped here, and dressed in that filmy thing that had been removed at the altar.

And more. The hands touching her, anointing her with some sort of oil. She remembered Mr. Henley's face, leering down at her, leaning over her and saying something that still eluded her. And…and Missy, shrouded in one of the dark cowls, her eyes glittering with excitement.

And, still, the answer to her question eluded her.

Any remaining scruples she'd had about drugging Missy disappeared in the midst of those memories. She closed the door but did not lock it. There was nothing there to frighten her anymore. She paused to check on Missy's breathing before squaring her shoulders and passing under the arched opening to the crypt.

The evil in that chamber struck her like an open hand. Gooseflesh rose on her arms and raised the fine hairs on the back of her neck. She touched her candle to an unlit torch in a sconce by the entry and the room danced to life in the flickering light. Each stark detail had been etched on her mind, just waiting for the right stimulus to bring it back in its full horror.

A row of vaults bearing past generations of Ballingers was set into the stone walls, and she wondered what they might have thought of the way their final resting place had been desecrated. A brazier was tipped over and long-dead coals lay scattered on the floor. Everywhere, the scent of cloying incense had permeated the stones and now bled out measured doses into the air.

Gina gagged, the odor pulling her deeper into her memories. She spun around, finding the stone altar, a pagan symbol rising behind it. She thought of Cora, splayed on that altar, her blood staining the stone beneath her. Was it still there? Cora's blood? Her blood?

Fascination drew her to that slab, and she found dark stains upon it. Bile rose in her throat and she grew dizzy. The scar on her neck throbbed as if the dagger had only now pierced her. Her hands flat on the altar, she braced herself until the waves of nausea passed and a deadly calm overtook her.

She regained her balance as she heard a sound behind her. She turned to find Cyril Henley, dressed in the black cloak he'd worn each time she'd seen him, not ten feet away. He'd come down one of the tunnels that fed into the crypt. She backed against the altar, wanting something solid at her back.

"Mr. Henley," she acknowledged in a voice so calm she smiled.

Chapter Twenty-Two

"Miss O'Rourke. How convenient to find you here."

"Convenient? Did Missy not tell you she would lure me to you?"

He grinned. "So you know about Missy, eh? Where is she?"

"The antechamber."

A brief look of concern passed over his face. "What did you do to her?"

"I gave her the contents of the packet in the little wooden box you left behind."

He circled her to the right, keeping distance between them as he edged toward the arched door and the antechamber to take a peek into the darkness where Missy lay. "All of it?"

She shrugged, matching his manner of unconcern. "I believe she drank it all."

"You stupid cow! You could have killed her."

"I really wouldn't know. I just assumed it was the same dose you gave me in July. How much was in *that* packet?"

"She'll be insensible until this time tomorrow."

"Ah, well, then. A pity she will miss all the excitement." She slipped her hand into her pocket and felt the butt of the pistol.

"Do you think you'll escape this time, Miss O'Rourke?"

"I'm fairly certain of it." She removed her hand from her pocket and pointed the pistol at Mr. Henley's heart.

He laughed. "You don't have the nerve for it. If you did, I'd be dead now."

How odd that she felt so calm—as if everything for the past two and a half months had led her to this place and time. "You would be dead if I didn't want something from you."

"I have nothing of yours, chit."

"You have answers. I have questions."

He laughed, a manic sound that made her certain he was quite mad. "I thought you knew everything."

"I want to know if you are the one who killed Cora."

His grin spread. "Ah. Cora O'Rourke. Sweet thing, she was. Looked a bit like you."

She would not be distracted. "Did you?"

"Hmm. There were several of us who held the knife. 'Twas Daschel who carved her up, but yes, I might have been the one to deliver the coup de grâce."

Her finger twitched. Oh, how she wanted to pull that trigger. But not yet. Not quite yet. "You are a pig, Mr. Henley. Not human at all."

He shrugged. "I've worked at it, little Gina. I may call you that?"

"No." She braced her arm with her other hand as the pistol began to waver. "What of Mr. Metcalfe? Mr. Booth? Charles Hunter and the others?"

"Metcalfe was a personal delight—tried to talk his way out of it. Someone else took care of Mr. Booth for me. That idiot Artie Gibbons botched the job on Hunter and his brother. Still, there's no escape for them. I've posted bounties on them all. Sooner or later, one of the Whitechapel scum will succeed."

"Were I to guess, Mr. Henley, I'd say the threat will cease to exist when you do. Without the reward, there will be no incentive."

"Canny little bitch, aren't you? But that is supposing I cease to exist instead of you."

"One more question, Mr. Henley, and I may let you live if you answer honestly. Did you rape me in the antechamber before the ritual?"

He blinked, then a salacious smile spread over his hateful face. "You don't remember, Gina? How very amusing."

"I frankly do not care what amuses you. Just answer me, Mr. Henley."

"I am crushed you could forget our time together. Well, I wouldn't call it rape, exactly. You did not put up much of a fight. You just lay there and let it happen. I rode you hard, you know."

Her jaw clenched and her hand began to tremble again when she lowered her aim to Mr. Henley's crotch.

"Aye, when the others left, I had my way with you. What did it matter if you were virgin on the altar or not? I was to have first breach anyway."

But his jovial, almost taunting manner had changed ever so subtly to carry an undercurrent of anger. And he would not be angry if he were telling the truth. Dear God! He was lying! He hadn't defiled her! *That* was the unfinished business he had with her and the reason he had not simply killed her when he'd had the chance! He still wanted to rape her. She laughed at him.

His smile drew back to a sneer. "You weren't laughing then, Gina. You bled like a stuck pig."

She was almost weak with relief. "Poor Mr. Henley. Second

best to Daschel, and a complete failure on your own. Why, you do not even lie well."

They glanced toward the arch at the clatter of boots on the stone stairway. Jamie? Or Henley's friends? He glanced at her and back at the door and she knew he was measuring his chances of escape. Her hand wavered as she tightened her finger on the trigger. "Do not move, Mr. Henley."

"Gina!"

Jamie's voice carried from the antechamber. They must have found Missy and feared the worst for her.

"Whore!" Mr. Henley cursed and lunged at her.

He caught her off guard, landing across her middle, driving her to the ground and rolling to put her on top to use her as a shield, the pistol locked between them. If she pulled the trigger now, she was as likely to shoot herself as Mr. Henley, who was now trying to wrest the pistol from her hand.

"Release her," she heard Jamie demand in a cold voice somewhere near the entry to the crypt.

"Easy, Henley," another voice soothed—Lord Lockwood, she thought.

"Back away," Henley said, his voice muffled beneath her.

"You won't get away this time, Henley," Andrew told him. "Give up."

Should she pull the trigger? There was an even chance of the ball hitting Mr. Henley. She took a deep breath, gripped the pistol still crushed between them with her whole strength and rolled to expose Mr. Henley's back. She could not pull the trigger for fear of killing herself, but neither could she allow him to use the pistol against Jamie or the others.

He jerked his hand in an effort to wrest the pistol from her, then twisted as she rolled sideways. Her wrist gave way from the stress, leaving Mr. Henley with possession of the pistol.

He laughed and swung the barrel up to her heart, forgetting everyone else in his hatred of her.

Time slowed as she watched his finger curl around the trigger. She squeezed her eyes shut, not wanting to see his triumph. A single shot reverberated in the crypt and, miraculously, she did not feel a thing. She heard the sound of a pistol dropping to the floor and suddenly she was being dragged upward.

"Gina?"

She opened her eyes. Jamie was holding her, studying her, his gaze traveling the length of her. "Are you hurt?"

Weak with relief, she sagged against him. "I am fine, Jamie. He did not hurt me."

She could feel the tension leave his body as he held her tighter. "Thank God. Thank God…."

He turned with her in his arms and she saw Lockwood and Andrew bending over Henley's still body. It was over. Finally over. She was shivering violently and realized she must be suffering shock. And all she could think was that, "You can put me down now, Jamie. I have to be home by midnight."

He only laughed and held her closer.

Epilogue

September 25, 1821

The summons to Andrew's library before dawn did not come as a surprise. Charlie had brought her home last night, leaving the others to clean up the mess she'd made. And, after Mama's vapors, she had written a letter of gratitude to the Wednesday League. She never could have gotten through the last weeks without their support and understanding. They had understood and helped her reclaim her pride and her life. Without them, she would still be cringing in corners. Then she'd managed to get a few fitful hours of sleep and had just begun dressing for the voyage. Now she was prepared for almost anything as she passed the stacks of crates and trunks in the foyer and knocked on the library door.

At a soft call, she entered.

It did not appear as if any of the brothers had been to bed. Charlie, his arm still in a sling, and Andrew, looked relaxed while Jamie and Lockwood appeared as if they'd just returned from some errand or other. There was an empty chair in front of Andrew's desk and he motioned her toward it.

She perched on the edge of the seat and took a deep bracing breath. She could not tell from their faces if the news was good or bad. She risked a glance at Jamie and was reassured by a little smile lingering on his lips.

Andrew poured her a cup of tea from the silver pot on his desk. "Breakfast should be ready soon, Eugenia, but we wanted to talk to you before the others come down."

She nodded and accepted the teacup and saucer.

"Cyril Henley, as you know, is dead. There will be a short obituary in the *Times* tomorrow. Nothing will be said of his activities or the nature of his demise."

She smiled, pleased that there would be no gossip. She could not bear the thought of her family being caught in controversy and speculation again.

Andrew cleared his throat and continued. "We took Miss Metcalfe home and explained her condition to her parents. To say they were shocked and mortified is an understatement. They are making immediate arrangements to remove to a small village in Tuscany to complete their mourning. Mr. Metcalfe will return after a few months, but Miss Metcalfe will remain. Lord Wycliffe made it clear that her only hope of escaping prosecution is to remain abroad.

"As for your name on Henley's murder list, Devlin has put out the word that Henley is dead and there will be no reward for any further attempts on anyone's life—yours most especially, Eugenia."

She glanced quickly at Charlie and Jamie.

Andrew caught her look. "There are a number of cutthroats who are now out of work, and one in particular we are still in search of, but I feel it safe to say that *you* are no longer in danger."

She took a sip of her tea and realized that everyone was

looking at her. "I, ah, thank you all. I am dreadfully sorry for any trouble or inconvenience I have caused—"

"Inconvenience?" Jamie repeated with a little quirk to his mouth. "You have hunted Henley to ground when the Home Office could not. To the contrary, we owe you a debt of gratitude."

She smiled. "If only I could handle Mama half so well."

"Your mother is handled," Jamie told her. "It seems your ship has been delayed. Whatever decision she makes, you will have sufficient time to make yours."

"Mine? Is there some decision I have to make?" They seemed to have taken care of everything.

Andrew stood and nudged Charlie while Lockwood opened the library door. "Jamie has asked for a private word with you. Do you mind?"

Heat washed through her. Mind? She shook her head as Jamie came toward her and took her hand to lift her to her feet. The library door closed softly, and they were alone.

He pulled her into his arms and tilted her chin up to him. "Eugenia O'Rourke, I love you to utter distraction. Will you marry me?"

Yes, her heart cried, but she could not help teasing him one last time. "And?"

"The question." He nodded and took a deep breath. "Yes, my love. You were virgin."

She laughed. "Oh, Jamie. I adore you. I cannot tell you what it means to me that you love me enough to try to lie."

He looked indignant. "Confound it, woman! It is the truth," he protested.

"Even when you attempt a lie, you tell the truth. Because it is true, Jamie. Mr. Henley gave it away before you arrived last night."

He lowered his lips to her, dropping small kisses on her cheeks, her lips, her throat as he spoke. "That never mattered to me. In every important way, you were. I am the first man you've lain with, the first man you've given yourself to, the first man you've loved. And if luck is with me, I will be the only man you ever need."

"Yes," she answered his question and confirmed his wish. He was the only man she would ever need. She'd wanted a simple answer. Uncomplicated and true. He'd given her the only one that mattered. The truest one of all.

* * * * *

COMING NEXT MONTH FROM
HARLEQUIN®
HISTORICAL

Available October 26, 2010

- **REGENCY CHRISTMAS PROPOSALS**
  by **Gayle Wilson, Amanda McCabe, Carole Mortimer**
  (Regency)

- **UNLACING THE INNOCENT MISS**
  by **Margaret McPhee**
  (Regency)
  Book 6 in the *Silk & Scandal* miniseries

- **LADY RENEGADE**
  by **Carol Finch**
  (Western)

- **THE EARL'S MISTLETOE BRIDE**
  by **Joanna Maitland**
  (Regency)

REQUEST YOUR
FREE BOOKS!

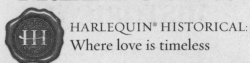

HARLEQUIN® HISTORICAL:
Where love is timeless

2 FREE NOVELS PLUS 2 **FREE GIFTS!**

YES! Please send me 2 FREE Harlequin® Historical novels and my 2 FREE gifts (gifts are worth about $10). After receiving them, if I don't wish to receive any more books, I can return the shipping statement marked "cancel." If I don't cancel, I will receive 6 brand-new novels every month and be billed just $4.94 per book in the U.S. or $5.49 per book in Canada. That's a saving of 20% off the cover price! It's quite a bargain! Shipping and handling is just 50¢ per book.* I understand that accepting the 2 free books and gifts places me under no obligation to buy anything. I can always return a shipment and cancel at any time. Even if I never buy another book from Harlequin, the two free books and gifts are mine to keep forever.

246/349 HDN E5L4

Name _____ (PLEASE PRINT) _____

Address _____ Apt. # _____

City _____ State/Prov. _____ Zip/Postal Code _____

Signature (if under 18, a parent or guardian must sign) _____

Mail to the **Harlequin Reader Service:**
IN U.S.A.: P.O. Box 1867, Buffalo, NY 14240-1867
IN CANADA: P.O. Box 609, Fort Erie, Ontario L2A 5X3
Not valid for current subscribers to Harlequin Historical books.

Want to try two free books from another line?
Call 1-800-873-8635 or visit www.morefreebooks.com.

* Terms and prices subject to change without notice. Prices do not include applicable taxes. N.Y. residents add applicable sales tax. Canadian residents will be charged applicable provincial taxes and GST. Offer not valid in Quebec. This offer is limited to one order per household. All orders subject to approval. Credit or debit balances in a customer's account(s) may be offset by any other outstanding balance owed by or to the customer. Please allow 4 to 6 weeks for delivery. Offer available while quantities last.

Your Privacy: Harlequin Books is committed to protecting your privacy. Our Privacy Policy is available online at www.eHarlequin.com or upon request from the Reader Service. From time to time we make our lists of customers available to reputable third parties who may have a product or service of interest to you. If you would prefer we not share your name and address, please check here. ☐

Help us get it right—We strive for accurate, respectful and relevant communications. To clarify or modify your communication preferences, visit us at www.ReaderService.com/consumerchoice.

HH10R

HARLEQUIN®

A *Romance*

FOR EVERY MOOD™

Spotlight on
Inspirational

Wholesome romances
that touch the heart and soul.

See the next page
to enjoy a sneak peek from
the Love Inspired® Suspense
inspirational series.

*See below for a sneak peek from
our inspirational line, Love Inspired® Suspense*

*Enjoy this heart-stopping excerpt from
RUNNING BLIND
by top author Shirlee McCoy,
available November 2010!*

**The mission trip to Mexico was supposed to be an
adventure. But the thrill turns sour when Jenna Dougherty
and her roommate Magdalena are kidnapped.**

"It's okay. I'm here to help." The voice was as deep as the
darkness, but Jenna Dougherty didn't believe the lie. She
could do nothing but lie still as hands slid down her arms,
felt the rope around her wrists.

"I'm going to use a knife to cut you free, Jenna. Hold
still."

The cold blade of a knife pressed close to her head before
her gag fell away.

"I—" she started, but her mouth was dry, and she could
do nothing but suck in air.

"Shhh. Whatever needs to be said can be said when
we're out of here." Nick spoke quietly, his hand gentle on
her cheek. There and gone as he sliced through the ropes on
her wrists and ankles.

He pulled her upright. "Come on. We may be on
borrowed time."

"I can't leave my friend," Jenna rasped out.

"There's no one here. Just us."

"She has to be here." Jenna took a step away.

"There's no one here. Let's go before that changes."

"It's dark. Maybe if we find a light…"

"What did you say?"

"We need to turn on the light. I can't leave until I know that—"

"What can you see, Jenna?"

"Nothing."

"No shadows? No light?"

"No."

"It's broad daylight. There's light spilling in from the window I climbed in through. You can't see it?"

She went cold at his words.

"I can't see anything."

"You've got a nasty bruise on your forehead. Maybe that has something to do with it." His fingers traced the tender flesh on her forehead.

"It doesn't matter *how* it happened. I'm blind!"

Can Nick help Jenna find her friend or will chasing this trail have Jenna running blindly again into danger?

Find out in RUNNING BLIND, available in November 2010 only from Love Inspired Suspense.

SHLISEXP1110